Maybe he was right....

Maybe Callie couldn't spin all the separate ends of her family ties together into a long, strong yarn that could be woven into a whole. But she had to try.

Zach lifted his hand and touched her lips, just a brush of his fingertip, but it felt as if her skin had been seared by fire. "I know you have to try. I wouldn't expect anything less of you. You want what's best for everyone, but sometimes that just doesn't happen, Callie. And that's not your fault. Sometimes you can't make it all come out right."

Tears blurred her vision. She blinked them away. She didn't like being this vulnerable. She didn't like having her innermost hopes and dreams exposed—particularly to a man as perceptive as Zach Gibson.

And she knew what was going to happen next. He was going to kiss her....

Dear Reader,

Marian and I are thrilled to be contributing our story, *Family Practice,* to the Harlequin Heartwarming line. For many years we've wanted to be able to write a book that concentrated on the emotional aspects of falling in love and staying in love and less on the physical side of the equation. Thanks to Marsha Zinberg and her wonderful editorial staff, we've been able to do just that.

Callie Layman is a newly minted M.D. She returns to her small northern Michigan hometown—with real misgivings—to care for its colorful inhabitants and to try to blend the disparate elements of her own complicated family situation, including precocious and antagonistic eleven-year-old stepsiblings, a pregnant stepmother and rebuilding the bond between herself and the mother who abandoned her years before. On top of everything else, she finds she's obligated to share her practice with handsome physician's assistant Zach Gibson, who, unlike Callie, knows exactly what he wants from his life. And one of those things he knows he wants is Callie.

Will Callie be able to have it all? A career, a love of her own, a happy life in White Pine Lake? Will she be able to weave all these tangled strands of family and romance into a seamless loving whole, or will it all be too much? Will she end up with her happy-ever-after or will Callie turn her back on everything and everyone she cares about rather than risk it all for love?

We hope you enjoy reading *Family Practice* as much as we enjoyed writing it.

Sincerely,

Marisa Carroll

(Carol Wagner and Marian Franz)

HARLEQUIN HEARTWARMING

Marisa Carroll

Family Practice

Recycling programs
for this product may
not exist in your area.

ISBN-13: 978-0-373-36633-0

FAMILY PRACTICE

Copyright © 2013 by Carol I. Wagner and Marian L. Franz

This is a work of fiction. Names, characters, places and incidents are
either the product of the author's imagination or are used fictitiously,
and any resemblance to actual persons, living or dead, business
establishments, events or locales is entirely coincidental.

This edition published by arrangement with Harlequin Books S.A.

For questions and comments about the quality of this book,
please contact us at CustomerService@Harlequin.com.

® and TM are trademarks of Harlequin Enterprises Limited or its
corporate affiliates. Trademarks indicated with ® are registered in the
United States Patent and Trademark Office, the Canadian Trade Marks
Office and in other countries.

Printed in U.S.A.

MARISA CARROLL

Marisa Carroll is the pen name of sisters Carol Wagner and Marian Franz. They have been writing bestselling books as a team for more than twenty-five years. During that time they have published more than forty titles, many for the Harlequin Superromance line and Feature and Custom Publishing. They are the recipients of several industry awards, including a Lifetime Achievement Award from *RT Book Reviews* and a RITA® Award nomination from Romance Writers of America, and their books have been featured on the *USA TODAY,* Waldenbooks and B. Dalton bestseller lists. The sisters live near each other in northwestern Ohio, surrounded by children, grandchildren, brothers, sisters, aunts, uncles, cousins and old and dear friends.

Books by Marisa Carroll

HARLEQUIN SUPERROMANCE

HARLEQUIN NASCAR

To Marsha Zinberg

For all your years of excellent editorial advice,

steadfast friendship

and your uncanny ability

to choose the restaurants with the best crème brûlée.

CHAPTER ONE

CALLIE LAYMAN STEERED her eight-year-old Jeep off the pavement and into a small, scenic turnout. Luckily, it was momentarily devoid of camera-wielding tourists and their bored offspring, and so for a precious few minutes she had the parking lot and the spectacular view of the Sleeping Bear Dunes to herself.

She had a love/hate relationship with this season. Tourism was the mainstay of the economy for this semi-remote region of Michigan's northern Lower Peninsula; it was also its bane. Tourists came for the unspoiled natural beauty and the opportunity to commune with nature. They stayed, in droves, to complain that their internet connections were too slow, their cell-phone reception was spotty at best and nonexistent at worst, and that the nearest Starbucks was more than an hour away. Through it all, the citizens of White Pine Lake, her hometown, smiled and nodded and kept their opinions on city folks' strange ways to themselves, as their cash registers jingled and the motel rooms and rental cottages filled up.

The problem for Callie was she felt like one of those city folks these days, one of those barely tolerated outsiders. She'd been gone from White Pine Lake for over a decade, attending college and medical school. She wasn't ready for what she had agreed to do this summer—assume responsibility for the health and well-being of the citizens of her old hometown. What if she wasn't up to the challenge? What if she failed them? Luckily, just days before she headed north, she'd gotten another job offer—an escape plan if things here didn't go well.

She had left Ann Arbor in the early afternoon. It was now a little after eight in the evening. Five hours with only one stop. Not bad travel time on the two-lane state highway. Especially on a late-July weekend when mud-splattered RVs pulling all shapes and sizes of boats and trailers loaded with camping equipment slowed traffic to a crawl.

She was tired and stiff, but she'd managed to arrive a day ahead of schedule. No one expected her until tomorrow, and she was in no hurry to resume her journey. So she unhooked her seat belt and rested her forearms on the steering wheel, soaking in the quiet and the view. Below her the ruffled blue water of White Pine Lake was dotted with fishing boats and the red-and-white sails of small sailboats. The occasional Jet Ski cavorted among them, rooster tails streaked with iridescent rainbows shooting high in their wakes. The sun was just dropping behind the horizon, painting the sky with a dozen shades of red and gold. At the far edge of the lake was the town of the same name, the place where she'd grown up.

She loved this view, especially at this moment in midsummer when the sky was so high and blue, the trees a dozen shades of green, from the darkest pine to the palest silver-green of birch and poplar—"popples," as they were called this far north—and the last of the warm golden sunlight shining bright and benign on the cottages that dotted the shoreline.

Even from this distance, she could tell that Lake Street was crowded with cars, a good sign in these hard economic times. It appeared as if McGruders' Bait and Tackle was doing a brisk business in minnows and night crawlers to tempt the lake's wily perch and walleye onto anglers' hooks, and Kilroy's ice-cream parlor had a line at the takeout window. Only three streets deep and half a mile in length, the town where she'd been raised was so small it could be viewed in its entirety from her vantage point.

The year-round businesses were clustered at the intersection of the county highway and Main Street: a hardware store, the grocery and pharmacy, a single gas station, a pizza shop and an auto-repair shop. Across the street, rental cottages and three or four motels turned their back sides to the pavement so their patrons could enjoy the lake views from decks and shaded porches. Further to the north, where the street narrowed and clung to the shoreline, tourists strolled along, window-shopping at the galleries and gift and fudge shops that comprised the "historic" district. A few miles south, toward Traverse City and the Leelanau Peninsula, the land grew more rolling and fertile, home to dozens of boutique wineries and the sweet-cherry orchards the area was world famous for. White Pine Lake tended to cater more to families and retirees, so there were no casinos or tasting rooms to lure the upscale and trendy, and that suited Callie just fine.

She let her attention be drawn to the place she had always loved best in the world, a three-story white clapboard building with a steeply slanted roofline, topped by a glassed-in widow's walk with an oxidized copper roof. The White Pine Lake Bar and Grill had been sitting foursquare and solid on that slight rise above Lake Street since the 1930s. It was the business that had sustained her family for three generations, and it was her childhood home.

She couldn't quite make out the details from this distance, but the memory was clear in her mind. Six double-hung windows guarded by faded green shutters were spaced across the second floor, above the long, covered porch. Stone steps, bordered by flowerbeds filled with cascading petunias, daisies and lush green ferns, led from the sidewalk to the wide porch set with small tables and chairs. The building's tall double doors always stood open whenever the weather permitted, as it did today. The wood-framed screen doors that kept the mosquitoes away banged shut behind customers with a satisfying snap when they stepped into the native white-pine foyer that separated the family-oriented dining room from the bar.

Callie had always been fascinated by the history of the place, too. Over a hundred years old now, the building, once a railway hotel, had been moved to its current lakeside location by teams of huge draft horses. The black-and-white photos taken by her grandfather Layman in his youth chronicled the fifteen-mile journey and still hung in the taproom. When her father was a child, the town's historical society had published a little booklet documenting the move and sold it for three dollars a copy. For as long as she could remember, the booklets had been kept in a stack by the cash register.

She wondered if they were still there or if they had been moved or just plain done away with. There was no telling what kind of changes Ginger Markwood Layman had made to the place since Callie's last visit at Christmas. She wouldn't be a bit surprised if nothing was the same as it had been. Her dad certainly wasn't.

Callie straightened and refastened her seat

belt, ashamed of her lapse into uncharacteristic spitefulness. J. R. Layman was exactly the man he'd always been: honest, hardworking, thoughtful and soft-spoken. What was different about him was that at forty-nine years of age, the staid, upstanding, fifteen years-divorced CPA had fallen head over heels in love with a woman a dozen years younger than he was, gotten her pregnant and married her.

Consequently at twenty-nine Callie was going to be a big sister. Well, technically, she already was a big sister, she amended as she shifted out of Park and checked her side mirror for traffic coming up behind her on the narrow, curving road. Her new stepmother had two children by her first marriage—eleven-year-old twins, a boy and a girl, Becca and Brandon. At least they were fraternal twins, so she didn't have any trouble telling them apart, but she was very much afraid she would have trouble relating to them once she was home permanently.

Their first meeting had been during her last visit at Christmas. It hadn't been a roaring success. The gifts she'd chosen for the twins hadn't suited their interests and had only been grudgingly acknowledged, and the awkwardness of all of them being thrown together, virtual strangers to each other at the most family-oriented time of the year, had made the visit even more painful.

Still, she had to get used to being around preteens and babies. Not only because she had stepsiblings and a new half brother or sister on the way, but because in less than forty-eight hours she would begin practice at White Pine Lake Community Health Center, and that meant treating everyone, young and old, who walked through its doors. Whether she felt ready for the challenge or not.

And Callie truly had no idea what she was walking into. Gail Wilberforce, the fifty-something veteran certified nurse practitioner at the clinic, had up and eloped with a golf pro and moved with him to North Carolina. So a physician's assistant she'd never met was staffing the clinic—one Zach Gibson, former navy combat medic.

Her dad said Zach was one heck of a nice guy, but the practice required more than just one PA. They needed a doctor—they needed Callie.

Since Callie had the summer off—her first

ever, she thought with a pang—and since the clinic was dedicated to her grandparents, who had worked for years to see it built and staffed, and since her dad was now the president of the Physician's Committee, she couldn't say no. Even though it was the last place in the world she wanted to start her professional life.

But she was a Layman. There had been Laymans in White Pine Lake for a hundred years, and all of them had done whatever they could for the town. So here she was, a freshly minted M.D. with no real-world experience to speak of, about to step into the most frightening situation she could imagine—being responsible for the health and well-being of people she'd known all her life on top of being thrust into partnership with a man the whole town considered a bona fide war hero.

Describing Zachary Gibson as battle hardened wasn't a cliché. It was the plain, unvarnished truth. After two tours of duty in Afghanistan and an honorable discharge from the military, he'd moved to Petoskey and begun working with one of the staff surgeons at the hospital there. He had military decorations and commendations and a

4.0 grade-point average during his medical training, as well as glowing recommendations from his boss, a hotshot neurosurgeon.

Her dad had told her all of this, proudly believing such a résumé would sweeten the deal for Callie to take over as the clinic's doctor. Unfortunately, it only added to her insecurity. On paper, at least, she was the physician in charge, the boss, but deep down inside where it really mattered she wasn't so sure of herself. She was the rookie, the one with no street smarts and little small-town-practice experience. She was afraid it wouldn't take long for her combat-tested PA to figure out he was the one really running the show.

ZACH GIBSON WONDERED what the hell else could go wrong today. It was Saturday. He was supposed to be out on the lake in the small aluminum boat that came with the tiny, amenity-scarce cottage he rented, watching the sunset, swatting mosquitoes, hoping to latch onto a keeper walleye or a couple of nice bluegill and perch to fry up for his dinner. Fishing usually put him in a great mood, let him concentrate on his thoughts, and this afternoon's outing was supposed to have given him a chance to make a game plan for Monday morning. Should he show up for work in khakis and a nice shirt to impress the new boss, or stay with his usual T-shirt and fatigues beneath his white coat, silently making a stand for doing his own thing right from the start?

Instead he was ankle-deep in water in the middle of the clinic lab, wielding the hose of an industrial vacuum cleaner in hopes of keeping the floor tiles from buckling, ready to duck and cover if the ceiling caved in. From the size of the increasing bulge in the tiles above his head, his buddy Rudy Koslowski hadn't yet found the leak in the sprinkler system that had caused the damage in the first place and shut it down.

So much for making a gonzo first impression on the new M.D. He'd be lucky now if they could even open the clinic for regular hours Monday morning. Mercifully the plastic cover they used to keep dust off the X-ray machine had saved it, but the computer system was gone and all the supplies in the lower cupboards were waterlogged and probably ruined. They would have lost all the temperature-sensitive medications and vaccines stored in the ten-year-old fridge as well if he hadn't decided to come check on a few things before he went fishing. And he didn't even want to think about what kind of mess they'd be in if the water had gotten high enough to reach the shelves of patient records stored in the room next to where he was standing. Thankfully, only the oldest records, the ones waiting to be purged and shredded, had gotten wet, and then only the plastic containers that they'd been stored in. Still, the containers would have to be checked to make sure there weren't any cracks in the plastic or partially opened lids that had let water get inside.

Any plans he had of spending the rest of the weekend fishing sank like a stone tossed into the waters of White Pine Lake.

When he'd come in and discovered the flooding, he'd shut off the electricity and the propane supply and called Rudy. That was four hours ago. He'd been on damage control ever since.

Cold water began dripping on his head. He flipped the switch on the shop vac and took a prudent step to one side, wondering how much the exam rooms would have to be dried out. The emergency shutoff system seemed to have done its job in that part of the L-shaped building, and hopefully Burt Abrahms from the hardware store would show up soon with some extra extension cords and a couple big fans to hurry along the process. If the ceiling didn't collapse first.

"Rudy," he yelled. "Why the heck isn't the water off? The ceiling's ready to cave in. It's looking like the last few minutes of the *Titanic* in here."

"Good heavens," a shocked female voice responded—not his handyman's. "What happened?"

Zach didn't make the mistake of thinking she was a tourist who had wandered inside. Though they'd never been introduced, he'd noticed her picture on the wall in the White Pine Lake Bar and Grill, and most recently on the front page of the White Pine Lake *Flag* in an article announcing her graduation from the University of Michigan Medical School.

Dr. Callie Layman, M.D., wasn't supposed to arrive in town until tomorrow. But here she was.

He'd been wondering what else could go wrong. Now he had his answer.

"Broken water line in the sprinkler system, ma'am," he said, eight years of military protocol kicking in. "Situation's under control."

She raised one hand to shield her eyes from the glare of the harsh emergency lighting and gave him a skeptical look. "It doesn't appear to be under control at all, as far as I can see."

Something in her cool, detached tone and her equally cool, detached appearance—despite the fact that she had apparently just driven over three hundred miles in hot July weather—rankled, but Zach stopped himself from snapping his reply. "We'll be open for business by Monday morning. I give you my word, Dr. Layman."

She gave him another sharp glance. "Have we met?"

"No," he admitted. No reason to be churlish. He held out his hand after wiping it dry on his shorts. "I'm Zach Gibson, your PA. Welcome back to White Pine Lake."

She wasn't as tall as he was, but she wasn't a short woman, either. He guessed about five foot seven or eight, maybe a hundred and thirty pounds. Her mouth was thinner than he preferred on a woman, but a rounded chin and a nose that could only be called "pert" softened the overall contours of her face, framed by cinnamon-brown hair. Her eyes were hazel, big and fringed with long, gold-tipped lashes, and saved her from being plain. She wasn't drop-dead gorgeous. Many wouldn't even call her pretty, but for some reason he'd found her face interesting in photographs—at least in the rare ones where she'd been smiling—and now, in person, he found her even more appealing.

"Thank you," she said. Her tone was dubious, and frankly he couldn't blame her, considering the condition of her future workplace. "How do you plan to clean up this mess?"

"My buddy's got a construction business. He's here hunting down the source of the leak and hopefully shutting it down."

"Only the two of you? You need to get more people in here."

Zach didn't let the judgmental remark goad him into a retort. "I called your father. He's rounding up some volunteers." She had grown up in this town. Surely she realized people would pitch in to help once word went out? Or had she been living in the rarified world of a Big Ten medical school so long she'd forgotten her roots?

She might have blushed but he couldn't be sure with the lousy lighting. "Of course they'll come."

Though she didn't offer to pitch in and grab a mop herself. Great, was she going to be one of those kinds of doctors, the ones with the God complexes and the egos to go with it?

"We weren't expecting you until tomorrow," he said as the ominous sound of dripping water filled the silence between them.

"I left Ann Arbor a day early." She peered around at the boxes of rescued lab supplies and disintegrating cartons of exam gloves, the empty, wide-open refrigerator with the remains of a collapsed ceiling tile still piled on top, balanced precariously on the carcass of the shorted-out police scanner. A frown drew her arched brows together. "Do you have an assessment of the damages?" She didn't bother to make eye contact this time, just clipped out the question. "Will we be able to see patients on schedule Monday morning?"

Great, she *was* going to be one of those

ramrod-and-ruin kinds. It was going to be a long summer. But two could play at her game. "We lost the computer system and the police scanner, ma'am. That's the worst so far. I don't believe there's any structural damage to the building."

"But the mess." She made a little sweeping gesture with her right hand. "There's water everywhere—"

"Incoming," Rudy yelled from the doorway. Zach reached out and wrapped his fingers around Callie's wrist, hauling her forward and almost into his arms as three overhead tiles crashed to the floor, splattering Zach and Callie with water and soggy, cardboardlike shrapnel.

He was wearing old cargo shorts and an even older T-shirt, and he was already wet through, but his new boss hadn't been expecting a dousing. She let out a shocked gasp as the cold water cascaded down her back and soaked her to the skin.

"SORRY ABOUT THAT, Doc."

Callie shifted her attention to the man in the doorway, a short, ruddy-faced, stocky guy with a buzz cut not doing anything to hide his receding hairline, and laughing blue eyes. He was wearing a faded red T-shirt emblazoned with U*S*M*C in equally faded gold letters, and shorts that exposed the prosthesis that replaced his left leg below the knee. His leather tool belt hung low on his hips, as if he were an old-time gunslinger. Rudy Koslowski. She remembered him from high school, even though he'd been a couple of years ahead of her. He'd joined the Marines immediately after graduation and lost his leg in a suicide-bomb attack in Afghanistan.

"Hi, Rudy," she said, swallowing a sharp comment about the inadequacy of his warning. Rudy had always been a gossip even as a kid. She doubted he'd changed much over the years, and the last thing she wanted was to be reported to all and sundry as a bitch her first day on the job. "Quite a welcome home you arranged for me."

"We aim to please. You still got the moves, Doc," he said next.

"I beg your pardon?" But Rudy wasn't looking at her; he was grinning at the man beside her.

"Oops." Rudy chuckled, his expression

as mischievous as Callie remembered from high school. "Guess we're going to have to figure out another nickname for you, Corpsman. Can't have two Docs in the place, can we?" He paused as if waiting for his barb to strike home.

Rudy was smiling, but Zach wasn't. "Stow it, Rudy. She outranks us."

"Sure thing." Rudy raised both hands, signaling surrender, but his grin grew a little wider as he stared pointedly at their joined hands. "Whatever you say." Belatedly Callie tugged herself free of Zach's grasp. Why hadn't she noticed Zach was still holding her hand before Rudy did? Maybe because she had enjoyed the feel of Zach's long, strong fingers wrapped around her wrist. He had big hands, but his hold on her had been gentle. He would have no trouble setting a bone or reducing a dislocation with those hands and that strength, even in a combat situation. Experience she certainly didn't have.

"Zach's patients may call him whatever they and he are comfortable with," she said, appalled at how condescending the remark sounded. She hadn't meant it that way. She avoided speaking to colleagues in that manner, although she'd been talked down to plenty of times herself. Medicine, for the most part, was still a man's world.

"Sure thing, Dr. Layman," Rudy said. He wasn't smiling anymore.

"What can I do to help?" she asked, hoping to make some kind of amends. This was not how she'd wanted to start her relationship with Zach Gibson, especially not with a witness as talkative as Rudy.

"Nothing, ma'am."

She wished he wouldn't call her that, but she could hardly ask him to call her Callie so soon, and insisting on being addressed as Dr. Layman would only add insult to injury at this point. "I want to help," she said. "It's my practice now," she couldn't stop herself from adding.

Zach's face hardened momentarily. "You don't know where a bloody thing is yet, or where it goes." His tone softened, probably when he remembered he was talking to his boss. "You're soaking wet and covered with fiberglass. Go on over to the White Pine and get changed. Besides, Leola and Bonnie are on their way to lend a hand." The two women, both of whom Callie knew from her childhood, were the clinic's nurses and receptionist/bookkeepers, both essential to the efficient functioning of the practice. "Everything's under control here, ma'am."

"I wish you wouldn't call me that," she snapped before she could censure her words.

"Yes, ma'am." A corner of his mouth ticked up in what might have been a grin, but it was so fleeting Callie couldn't be sure. "Go, Dr. Layman," he said, the words just shy of being an outright command. "Let your dad and your new stepmother know you're in town. Get yourself settled in and we'll have this place ready for business on Monday morning."

So this was the way he wanted things to go. Where he continued to call the shots and she had no say in the decisions.

Zach Gibson didn't want her here; that was easy enough to figure out. The problem was…he was right. She would be more of a hindrance than a help to these people, who were used to working together as a team. She was the outsider. And the one thing she could never let any of them guess, especially her new PA, was that she was afraid she would never fit in.

CHAPTER TWO

THERE WAS NO PARKING space in front of the White Pine Bar and Grill, though Callie would have been surprised to find one on a Saturday evening in midsummer. She drove on by, turned left at the corner onto Perch Street, climbed the low hill, turned left again and angled her Jeep into the narrow gravel alleyway that ran behind the building. Her stepmother's minivan was parked in the spot next to her dad's SUV, but there was just enough space alongside the storage shed to park her car, if she didn't ever need to open the passenger-side door.

She wiggled out of the Jeep and brushed at the front of her slacks. The fiberglass had made her itchy, not to put too fine a point on it. She wanted a hot shower and a change of clothes. She tugged her overnight bag out of the car and headed toward the kitchen entrance. There was an outside stairway leading to the family quarters on the second floor but she didn't have a key to the door at the top, so the back stairs through the kitchen was her only option. She just hoped the White Pine's longtime head cook, Margaret McElroy—Mac to everyone who knew her—would be too busy to question Callie on her unexpected arrival and bedraggled appearance.

She was in luck. As Callie entered, Mac, pushing sixty, wiry-haired, and as short and round as a fireplug, was haranguing her staff of college students and long-suffering grill cooks like the army drill sergeant she used to be. The high, screened windows, although open to the cooling evening breeze, did little to dispel the heat and humidity in the too-small room. The dishwasher was rumbling away, fire flared in the grill, and the smell of seared beef and hot grease caused Callie's stomach to rumble. She hadn't eaten since she left Ann Arbor and she suddenly realized just how hungry she was. The White Pine served great steaks, but what the restaurant was really famous for was the all-you-could-eat perch and bluegill dinners.

She'd return to the kitchen for some of each as soon as she was clean and dry. She grabbed her duffel, holding it to her chest, and hurried up the steep, narrow stairs. In the days when the building was a hotel, the stairs would have been used by the maids to carry hot water to the patrons in the rooms above. Nowadays it led to a door that opened into the family kitchen she and her dad had seldom used. She hesitated for a moment before the closed door. Should she knock? After all, it really wasn't her home anymore. It was her father's—and Ginger's. She was only a guest. She settled on a quick, light tap, the kind of combined warning and greeting you'd give anyone before you opened a closed door in a house. No response. She opened the door. The kitchen was empty. The light was on, since it was now almost nine and the windows faced away from the lake into the lower branches of the pines and maples on the hillside. Ginger hadn't gotten around to changing much in the small, functional room beyond painting the old pine cabinets a creamy white and adding a colorful valance above the utilitarian white blinds on the windows. Although the changes were minimal, Callie had to admit the room was a lot more inviting than it had been in the past.

"Hello, anybody home?" Callie called out. She didn't really expect her dad or her stepmother to be here. They would be downstairs, her stepmother overseeing the dining-room operation and her dad behind the bar, where he still helped out during busy weekend evenings. But her stepsiblings might be hanging around. "Brandon? Becca?"

Silence. Maybe the twins were busing tables. She'd been younger than they were when she'd started busing, under the less than enthusiastic supervision of her mother. Free-spirited and fun-loving, Karen Layman hadn't wanted to work in the grill when her in-laws retired to Arizona, but business hadn't been good enough to warrant the expense of another full-time employee. So Callie's mother had reluctantly filled the role of manager until the long hours, tight money and long, cold winters she hated had drained all the joy from her life and her marriage.

At least, that was what she'd told Callie when she'd taken off to rethink her priorities three weeks after Callie's sixteenth birthday. From then on it had been just Callie and her dad...at least until a little over a year ago when Ginger Markwood had come into the White Pine inquiring about a job. She'd found not only employment but a place in J.R.'s heart. Now she was his wife, and her two children—three, soon—called Callie's old home their own. The realization was more disturbing than she cared to admit.

"Hey, kids? Anyone here?" Callie called out again, moving from the kitchen into the big, high-ceilinged great room that had once been a dormitory for male guests. A huge river-rock fireplace dominated the wall to her left, twin to the one in the dining room that helped make it so inviting. The three double-hung windows covered in long, sheer panels of voile that were currently moving in the breeze faced Lake Street and also had a view of the lake, as did the window in her bedroom. What had once been six smaller private rooms bisected by a hallway leading off the wall opposite the fireplace had now become a master suite and small bathroom on the hill side and three bedrooms along the lake side. Her old room, the first on the left, was above the foyer on the main floor, the others above the dining room. When she was little, Callie had often lain in bed and listened to the muffled sounds of laughter and low conversations and the chiming of silverware against the edge of a china plate downstairs.

The living area with its worn, overstuffed leather furniture—she remembered what a production it had been to get it up the stairs—was empty, the TV turned off. She had the place to herself. The bar was directly below her but the ceiling had been sound-proofed years before, so unless there was a live band playing on the occasional Saturday night, the room was as quiet as any other home's main living area.

She hurried into the hallway toward the bathroom. The itching was getting worse. She didn't carry a black doctor's bag in this day and age but she did have a very well-equipped first-aid kit in the Jeep and she'd transferred some cortisone-based skin cream to her duffel before she came upstairs.

A nice hot shower, clean hair, dry clothes, and relief from the itching on her feet and calves, and she'd be ready to face her new family. She opened the door of her bedroom and swung the heavy walnut panel inward. But it wasn't her bedroom anymore. Gone were the pale pink rose-strewn sheers and matching comforter her mother had helped her pick out the year before she left. The walls were newly painted a cloudy gray, and the drapes at the windows were heavy and pleated and almost black, casting the room into shadows now that the sun had set. Her brass bed had been replaced by a futon with a blood-red throw scattered with half a dozen pillows in jewel tones. The walls were plastered with posters of dragons and gryphons, elves and sorceresses, and hard-muscled, broad-shouldered mystical warriors in armor and chain mail that oddly enough reminded Callie just a tiny bit of Zach Gibson as he'd been earlier, legs spread wide, wielding his shop vac instead of a magical sword.

"Hey, what are you doing in my bedroom without permission?" a voice demanded. Callie gave a little yelp of surprise. Her new stepsister had come up behind Callie without her noticing and was standing in the hallway, hands on hips, her chin thrust out at a stubborn angle.

Becca was not a pretty child. She was tall and reed thin with long, straight strawberry blond hair, freckles, and a nose that was too big and too sharp for her face. Someday she would grow out of this awkward stage and become a striking, if not classically beautiful, woman. But today, dressed in a pine-green T-shirt with the White Pine logo on the left breast pocket and khakis—the uniform of the restaurant's waitstaff—she was just plain homely. Her expression was as belligerent as her tone of voice.

"I'm sorry," Callie said, shutting the door. "I…I didn't realize you'd moved into my… into this room."

"The new baby's getting my room," Becca said. She was still scowling and Callie wasn't able to tell if she was happy with the move or not.

Her twin, Brandon, stuck his head around his sister's shoulder and stared at Callie's bedraggled appearance. "What happened to you? You're all wet."

He had the same strawberry blond hair and blue-gray eyes as his sister, but the resemblance ended there. He was three inches shorter and twenty pounds heavier than his sister, with a linebacker's build and a round baby face that would be the bane of his existence well into his thirties, Callie guessed.

"Hi, Brandon." She smiled, and it wasn't quite as forced as when she'd greeted Becca. Brandon was a lot less hostile than his sister, even if she had disappointed him at Christmas by buying him a Detroit Tigers baseball jersey when his favorite team was the Cleveland Indians. Lesson learned, she'd promised herself. From now on she would consult Ginger before picking out gifts for her children. "I stopped at the clinic. There's a broken water line in the ceiling. There's water everywhere."

"We heard," Becca said. "Zach called us. Mom and your dad are going to the clinic to help as soon as the dinner rush is over."

"You weren't supposed to get here until tomorrow," Brandon said. His blue-gray eyes were clouded with worry. "Everything was supposed to be cleaned up. You weren't supposed to see the mess."

"I wish I hadn't," Callie said frankly. Brandon seemed to be one of those kids who always felt as if everything that went wrong around them was their fault. Another reason she found it easier to relate to him. She remembered being the same way at his age. "It was an accident. We'll get it all squared away." She smiled again, although she wasn't all that confident of her own words.

"Oh, dear, Callie? It is you." The light, musical voice belonged to her stepmother. "Mac thought she saw you sneaking up the stairs. I sent the twins up to check, and when they didn't return, I figured she was right."

"I wasn't sneaking," Callie said, defending herself. "Hello, Ginger." She spread her hands. "I wasn't too keen on being seen this way."

"Goodness." Ginger took Brandon by the shoulders and moved him out of her way. Becca flattened herself against the wall, pointedly avoiding any contact with her mother's protruding belly as Ginger moved forward to get a closer view of Callie. "What happened?" Her eyes narrowed as understanding dawned. "You've been to the clinic."

"The door was open. There were cars in the parking lot when I drove by. It seemed unusual for this late on a Saturday. I thought I should check it out."

"It's lucky Zach stopped in when he did. It could have been a lot worse."

"He seemed to have things pretty well under control when I left." The way he'd dismissed her offer of help still bothered her slightly, but she didn't say anything more. It was obvious her stepmother held the man in high regard—as did her father, she reminded herself. Professional courtesy and self-preservation warned her to keep her less flattering opinion of the PA to herself.

"Nothing's going the way I planned it," Ginger lamented. "Nothing's ready for you." She furrowed her brow, as if trying to figure out what to do next. She was a small woman, several inches shorter than Callie, with strawberry blonde hair the same shade as Becca's but cut short and feathery, and with Brandon's rounded face and snub nose. There were tiny laugh lines at the corners of her generous mouth and blue-gray eyes, another trait she shared with her children. She was pretty and petite and she laughed a lot. Maybe that was why her dad had fallen head over heels in love with her, even if she did come with a ready-made family in tow.

"Should we tell Dad she's here?" Brandon asked.

A tiny needle prick of jealousy shot through Callie, an unsettling sensation. It was the first she'd heard either of Ginger's children refer to her father that way. She hoped her involuntary reaction hadn't been evident on her face or in her eyes. She was a grown woman. She could share her father's love and affection. It was just going to take a little getting used to, that was all. "No, Dad's probably busy behind the bar. I'd rather he not see me this way. Really, all I want now is to shower off this fiberglass and get into some dry clothes. I didn't know where else to go. I'll call around and find a motel room." Callie was mortified. "It was thoughtless of me not to call you about the change of plans."

She belatedly remembered that the Physican's Committee had arranged a place for her to live, but no one had given her the details. She'd been so busy packing away her things and finalizing the sublet on her tiny apartment in Ann Arbor that it had slipped her mind to inquire further. If pressed she'd admit she just assumed she'd be staying in her old room until she got settled in. A miscalculation in line with everything else that had happened today. She had nowhere else to go except to her mother's, and she wasn't up to dealing with Karen tonight.

"Don't be ridiculous. You'll stay right here.

No more arguing. Of course you'll be wanting a shower." Ginger laid her hand on her stomach, glancing across the hall at the bathroom door. She was wearing a pine-green top over slim white slacks. The top was fitted below her breasts and elasticized at the bottom so that it flared gently over her baby bump and fitted snugly on her hips. The shade of green that washed out her daughter's pale skin tone flattered Ginger's warmer complexion.

Her stepmother was getting quite big, Callie noticed, but she *was* already in her third trimester.

Callie wouldn't be delivering any babies while she worked at the clinic—the hospital was too far away to make that practical, and to be truthful an ob-gyn practice had never been what she wanted—but she would be seeing prenatal patients and coordinating their care with the obstetrician in Petoskey. Ginger, however, was family, and medical ethics prohibited her from treating or prescribing medications for family members. If she was honest with herself, she was relieved not to be forced into such an intimate relationship with her stepmother, who was, when she got right down to it, a virtual stranger. And sleeping with her father to boot.

"Mom, our bathroom's trashed, remember," Becca said acidly. "We were going to clean tomorrow. You and J.R. made us work on the cottage today." She shot Callie an accusing glare as though the messy bathroom was somehow her fault. So, her dad evidently hadn't made as much progress with Becca as he had with Brandon.

"I'm not fussy," Callie said. "A few dirty towels lying around won't bother me." She'd only stayed with her new extended family on the one previous occasion—the not-so-successful Christmas visit—and then only for two nights. The apartment had been spotless. Callie had been impressed and said so. Neither she nor her dad were particularly good housekeepers but evidently Ginger was.

"I wanted everything to be just right," Ginger said under her breath. "I'm sorry. We changed Becca's room because I wanted the one closest to us for the baby. Your dad hasn't been sleeping well lately. I…I decided it would be better for the little one to be in a room of his or her own."

J.R. and Ginger had decided against learning the sex of the new baby. That was fine with Callie, but she was disturbed to hear that her dad wasn't sleeping well. Was it stress or, worse, some kind of health problem he was keeping from her? It seemed every few minutes something else served to remind her just how long she'd been away, how little she was aware of what went on in her dad's life these days. It hurt.

But she could begin to do something about it now that she'd returned to White Pine Lake. Being close enough to spend time with her dad was one of the reasons she'd taken the job. She had to keep reminding herself of that.

"It's fine. I don't care what the bathroom looks like. I'm the one who should be apologizing for not telling you I was coming early," she repeated, sincerely remorseful. "If there's a clean towel and hot water, I'll be fine."

Ginger smiled and almost got it right. "Stop apologizing for wanting to come home a day early. Just pretend you're the first person to take a shower after a hurricane blew through the bathroom, okay?"

"I promise not to notice a thing."

"Have you eaten?" Ginger caressed her stomach absently as though soothing herself as well as the baby inside her.

"No, and I'm starved," Callie said, grinning. "I hope you aren't sold out of the bluegill tonight."

"I'll go down right now and have Mac set some aside."

"And a spinach salad," Callie said, "oh, and a baked sweet potato. I've been craving one for a couple of weeks."

"Cravings have taken over my life," Ginger said, seeming to relax a little.

"You're craving sweet potatoes? That's a new one."

Ginger laughed. "Nothing so healthy, I'm afraid. Anything salty and crunchy and sweet." She threw up her hands. "Every kind of junk food. It's driving your dad crazy. Thank goodness we live above a restaurant. I can always raid the snack rack by the cash register, even in the middle of the night."

"She set off the alarm once." Brandon snickered. "The fire department came and everything. You can ask Dad."

Ginger flushed an unbecoming red. "Oh,

let's not," she said. "Go tell Mac that Callie will want dinner in, oh, about twenty minutes or so?"

"Twenty minutes. Great."

"And I'll remind her not to forget the cinnamon butter for your potato," Brandon offered. "It's my favorite."

"Mine, too."

"All right." Brandon gave her a thumbs-up and took off at a trot.

"Are you sure it's not too much trouble for me to shower here? I could drive out to Mom's farm." She was embarrassed. Ginger must assume she was as unreliable and unprepared as her mother. She didn't appreciate the comparison one bit.

"That was going to be part of the surprise tomorrow," Ginger said. "The elderly couple who always rent half the double cottage for six weeks had to cancel due to health issues. It's small but so much nicer than the 'mini suite' at the Commodore Motel the committee picked out for you." Her tone of voice when she said "mini suite" suggested the Commodore Motel wasn't the nicest in town by a long shot. Callie was relieved she wouldn't be staying there. "The cottage is all ready for you to move into as soon as you've cleaned up and eaten dinner. Peace and privacy. Well, a place of your own, anyway," she added cryptically.

"Thank you." She couldn't quite keep the relief out of her voice. She loved the tiny duplex cottage on the lakeshore. And it was within walking distance of the White Pine and only half a mile from the clinic. She could bicycle to work—if her old bike was still hanging from the rafters in the garage.

"I'm glad you're pleased. Your dad said you would be." Ginger didn't sound as convinced as J.R. apparently was. "The other side is rented, so it won't be all that private, but it's the only property not booked solid for the season."

"It is my favorite, and I'll love it, neighbor or no neighbor." But the duplex was income for her dad. She couldn't just move in during peak tourist season. "I'll make up your shortfall on the rent. I'm sure the Physician's Committee bullied Dad into giving them the same rate they were getting from the manager at the Commodore."

"Settle that with your father over dinner," Ginger said, waving off Callie's suggestion.

Dinner with Dad. Callie couldn't believe how much she wanted just that. There would be no expansive emotional display from J.R. when she came into the bar. When he caught her eye, he would smile at her, jerk his head in a signal to meet him in the kitchen at the old Formica table with its eight well-worn chairs—the "Cook's Corner," as her grandmother had named it years before Callie was born—where the staff ate. He would give her a quick, awkward hug, pull out her chair, set a steaming plate of fish before her and straddle the seat beside her so he could watch her eat. He wouldn't scold her for not calling to say she was coming a day early, but she would apologize anyway because she had caused Ginger distress. He would tell her not to worry, that it was okay. *It's good to have you home, Callie girl,* he would say. And that would be all she needed to hear. She would be home, and everything would be right with the world, because J. R. Layman could make it so.

At least, it had seemed that way to her when she was a child. But she wasn't a child any longer, and J.R. had new responsibilities and a new family to keep safe from the big, bad world. She was on her own now, and that was the way it should be. She couldn't pretend it didn't hurt to be the outsider in this new family grouping—it did hurt—but that didn't mean she intended to stand aside and do nothing to improve the situation, if for no other reason than to make things easier on her dad. She would do what she could to make them all a family.

"C'mon, Becca, you're on the clock until nine, remember." Her stepmother's strained voice brought her back to the moment at hand. Ginger held out her arms, attempting to gather her daughter close. Becca sidestepped the embrace. Ginger hesitated a moment, her arms still outstretched, and then she dropped them to her side. "We really are happy to welcome you home, Callie." Her smile didn't falter but her eyes were bleak. So, the unhappy vibe Callie had picked up on when Becca had told her about switching bedrooms hadn't been her imagination. There *was* some tension between mother and daughter over the new baby's arrival, and perhaps between her father and his new wife, too?

Suddenly all the insecurity she'd been experiencing since she'd agreed to take the position at the clinic returned in a rush, almost overwhelming her determination to help her family. Developing relationships with her stepmother and stepsiblings and finding her own place in a new blended family was yet another complication to add to the weight of uncertainty over her sojourn to White Pine Lake. At least she had options if she couldn't stay.

It was going to be a very long summer.

CHAPTER THREE

THUNDER RUMBLED OVERHEAD and Zach swung his feet over the edge of the bed. He rested his elbows on his knees and dropped his head into his hands, staring down at the scarred pine floor. It was barely daybreak but he wouldn't be sleeping any more. Something about the long, rolling rumble of a storm coming in off the big lake reminded him of Afghanistan. There weren't a lot of thunderstorms in that far-off, arid country, but there was a lot of gunfire. The one aspect he didn't like of living near a big body of water was the really loud thunderstorms. Occasionally, they still triggered a bout of PTSD, and he didn't want that happening with his brand-new roommate just on the other side of the wall.

He'd grown up on the edge of the California desert, shuffled from one foster home to another. He had no idea who his parents were, his people, but he suspected somewhere in his lineage there had been at least one sailor. He'd been fascinated by the sea as a child, and now as an adult by the great inland seas so nearby. The day after he graduated from high school, he'd left the last foster home he'd been placed in and joined the navy. He'd thought he'd spend the next four years surrounded by water, maybe even assigned to an aircraft carrier, but instead he'd ended up in Afghanistan. Twice.

In White Pine Lake there was water everywhere he looked, exactly as he'd envisioned as a child, but he still didn't like thunderstorms.

He pulled on a pair of sweats and a T-shirt. Rudy had advised him early on not to wander around in his skivvies while he was living in White Pine Lake, and his old Marine buddy had been right. It wasn't unheard of for someone to come knocking on his front door at any hour of the day or night for free medical advice. He wondered how his new neighbor, the uptight Dr. Layman, would handle that aspect of a small-town practice. Not well, he'd guess. He wondered what she was doing here at all.

Actually, the answer to that one was easy

enough. She was a Layman. Knowing J.R., hearing the praises of J.R.'s father and—from the old-timers who remembered that far back—*his* father sung throughout the town, it was because of an overdeveloped sense of duty, not because practicing medicine in a small town was what she wanted most in life.

Well, it was what *he* wanted, and he intended to hang on to this job with both hands, even if it meant butting heads with her at every turn.

He'd been willing to make amends after their less-than-stellar first meeting when he'd heard her Jeep pull into the parking space behind the duplex that first night. He'd gotten up off the couch, even though he was bone tired, and walked out into the cool, humid night to greet her and offer a hand to help unload her Jeep. He could hear a radio playing in a nearby cottage, and traffic sounds from Lake Street intermittently drowned out the chirping of crickets and the eerie wail of a loon calling for its absent mate. A small tingle of uneasiness prowled at the edge of his consciousness. A motorcycle going by had masked his footsteps on the gravel, so she whirled in surprise when he spoke, hitting him in the thigh with a big overstuffed duffel bag as she swung around.

"Oof," he said.

"Good heavens, you scared the life out of me. What are you doing here?" She dropped the duffel with a thud, barely missing his foot in the process.

"I was coming to offer my help unloading your Jeep."

They were standing under a streetlight. He could see her face clearly. Surprise at his appearance had widened her eyes momentarily. Now they narrowed with suspicion. "Where exactly did you come from?"

He hooked his thumb over his shoulder toward the duplex. "Didn't your dad explain? We're neighbors. Real close neighbors."

"No." Her lips thinned. "He did not. He just said he knew the cabin was my favorite place and since it had become available—" She put her hands on her hips. "This isn't acceptable," she said.

"Why not? You just said how much you like the place."

"What I am worried about is what people will think of us living so close. It's…it's not professional."

"Come off it, Dr. Layman. This isn't the Middle Ages. You're not giving your friends and neighbors enough credit. Why should they care?" She had a point, though. There would be some small-minded people who would raise their eyebrows and wag their tongues—there always were in a town this size. "It's no different from a coed dorm. Are you saying you've never lived in close proximity to a man?"

"I..." she sputtered. "Of course I have."

Did that mean she'd been in a serious relationship? Did she still have a boyfriend? Somehow he didn't like that idea, although he couldn't pinpoint exactly why. He didn't pursue the topic, however, for the same reason he hadn't elaborated on town gossips. Now that she was here, he didn't want to scare her off. "Do you believe your dad would have sent you down here if he didn't trust me to behave myself?" He was beginning to enjoy this. She was so easy to rattle.

"Don't be silly," she said, but she sounded as if the fight had gone out of her. For the first time he noticed the dark circles under her eyes and the droop to her shoulders. She'd had as long and as hard a day as he had. He ought to be ashamed of himself for goading her. "Good. Then that's settled. You're staying. It's late. We can work out some ground rules for sharing the place in the morning so we can both have our privacy."

He bent to pick up the duffel and so did she. They both straightened with a hand on a strap. He tugged and she had the grace to let go without a struggle. "I don't need ground rules," she said. "I just believe it's better if I find another place. We'll be together quite enough during office hours." She didn't give up easily; she'd hold her ground in an argument or a fight.

"Whatever you say, Dr. Layman," he replied as formally. "But don't count on finding anything better. It's high season. The town's booked solid. No landlord in his right mind will accept the stipend the Physician's Committee's willing to pay, except for that old coot at the Commodore. If you're determined to make up the difference out of your own pocket, you might as well stay here."

"Fine," she said, throwing up her hands. "You have made your point, and it's too late to argue with you any more tonight. Just be careful with that duffel. It's got my coffee-maker in it and I don't want it to get broken. I can't function in the morning without my caffeine."

That scene had taken place Saturday night. Now, four days later and three days into their working relationship, it was still the longest conversation they'd had so far.

It was shaping up to be a long summer.

He punched the button to start the cof-feemaker he'd found in the thrift store and headed for the closet-size bathroom to shower and shave.

Ten minutes later he was on the porch, one shoulder propped against the stone pillar that supported the roof, drinking his coffee while he kept one eye on the leaden skies. He heard the door on Callie Layman's side of the du-plex open. He shifted position slightly so it wouldn't seem as if he was hiding from her as she sat down in one of the two pine rock-ers that matched the set on his half of the porch. She was already dressed for her day at the clinic in slacks, a tailored shirt and the long white lab coat that he thought was an attempt to look as much like a man as possible. It didn't work, though. The curves beneath the layers of fabric were all female.

"Good morning, Dr. Layman," he said, lifting his mug in salute—might as well be neighborly. He wasn't going inside just so she could have the porch to herself.

She jumped a little in surprise and hot liquid sloshed over the rim of her coffee mug. "I didn't see you there," she said with a hint of accusation in her voice, holding the mug out so it didn't drip on her slacks.

"Just checking on the weather." The duplex was about the size of a two-car garage, with doors at opposite ends of a shared front porch. The porch was divided by a screen made from an old pair of folding doors that offered about as much privacy as adjoining hotel balconies. In the past the building had been a garage, then a bait shop and finally used for boat storage before Callie's dad had remodeled it into two one-bedroom rental units. It was built of native river rock and, with its weathered wood trim and faded green shutters, was solid and sturdy and rooted to its spot on the lakeshore. It was small and cramped and lacking in all kinds of creature comforts like internet service and cable TV, but it suited Zach just fine.

"Looks like the storm might miss us." He gestured out over the lake with his mug. The air was cool, and mist shrouded the far shore of the lake and clung to the tops of the high dunes in the distance, but when the sun eventually broke through the clouds, it would be a warm day.

"It will," Callie responded confidently, scanning the dark rolling clouds at the far edge of the lake. She wrinkled her nose. "I can't smell the rain, so it's not coming this way." She tilted her head slightly as though waiting for him to contradict her.

"You think so?" Why couldn't he just agree with her? What was it about her that made him want to challenge everything she said?

"I know so. I grew up on this lake, remember. And I come from a long line of avid weather watchers."

"Can't argue with that," he conceded.

She nodded, satisfied she'd won the argument. "Just a light show in the sky giving the fishermen time for another cup of coffee before they head out onto the lake," Callie said as a three-pronged lightning strike arced out of the dark clouds and disappeared behind the dunes. Thunder rolled on like a giant's chorus of kettledrums. Zach tightened his grip on the handle of his mug and worked to slow his too-fast heartbeat. He forgot the retort he'd been going to make. "Where did you grow up?" she asked before he could come up with another.

"California. Little town in the desert."

"That's a long way from White Pine Lake. How did you end up here?"

"I like water," he said, "and Rudy boasted they had lots of it where he came from. He was right."

"You and Rudy served together?"

"He was my buddy and my patient," Zach said. Now, why the hell had he said that? The storm had shaken him more than he realized. He didn't want to talk about Afghanistan and the things that had happened there. If Rudy wanted to tell her about the IED attack that had cost him half his leg, that was his business, but Zach wasn't going to. He set his teeth and remained silent.

She tilted her head and gave him a long, straight look, then nodded slightly. "I see.

Afghanistan is off-limits. I accept that." She reverted to their previous subject. "We could use some rain, though. It's pretty dry."

Maybe he'd been too quick in judging her; she'd picked up on his reluctance to talk about his past and hadn't pressed him on it. He just hoped she did as well with her patients. He relaxed, confident he had himself under control again. It was getting easier as time went on and the flashbacks became fewer and less intense. "Yeah, we could use a good shower or two." Last winter there hadn't been a lot of snow, so too-little rain in the summer months increased the danger of wildfires in the heavily wooded national parkland surrounding the town. "I'll water the planters before I leave this morning. That should guarantee at least a little rain."

The corners of her mouth turned up in only a slight smile, but it was enough. It transformed her face and made him catch his breath. He wondered what she would look like if she really let go. Spectacular, he suspected.

"Same with washing your car. Works every time," she said. "I'll take my turn later in the week."

"It's no trouble. I've been taking care of them all summer."

"So I've noticed," she said drily. "When was the last time you deadheaded the petunias?"

"Uh, you've got me there." Did she always have to be in charge? Be the one to give the orders? But her next words surprised him.

"We've got joint custody of the landscaping now, so I'll do my share. How's this for a division of labor—you water, I'll weed. Deal?"

"Deal." He considered holding out his hand to shake on the agreement but found himself reluctant to do so. He remembered how the softness of her palms against his that first day had electrified his nerve endings and then refused to fade away. Better not to touch her at all, no matter how casual the contact. Anyway, she'd probably take it as an insult, call it inappropriate conduct. She kept both her hands wrapped around her coffee mug as she rose from her seat. "Good. That's settled. I'd better go. I have some things I need to research before office hours start."

He considered taking the reference to office hours as an opening to talk about their working arrangements. The situation was awkward for all of them at the clinic right now, as most of the patients were on his schedule and there was little chance to discuss which of those patients would be least upset to be moved to her care, as the doctor in charge.

So over the past couple of days, he'd taken the established patients while Callie had dealt with the walk-ins. She'd spent the rest of her workday reviewing their procedure list, making notes on her laptop, discussing with Bonnie and Leola the changes they would like to see when the clinic was remodeled, and generally avoiding being alone with him.

This practice wasn't as structured as the military. The chain of command was clear as mud. Outside of the mandatory guidelines and protocols the hospital imposed on them, they had to work out their own routine, and Zach preferred to do that in private. The sooner the better. He opened his mouth to start the ball rolling but he'd waited too long.

"I'll see you at the clinic," she said, her hand already on the screen door handle as another long, low peal of thunder rumbled out over the lake, fainter than before and even farther away, as she had predicted. "It will be a zoo today with the carpet cleaners in the waiting room and the electrical inspector coming at noon. We'll have to keep a pretty strict schedule this morning to have room for him."

"I don't like to rush my patients," he said. There was no way he was going to turn into a clock-watching corporate sawbones just because she wanted to clear the schedule over the noon hour.

Nonetheless, he had to admit she was right—he was heavily booked. He was going to have to keep people moving through at a steady clip, whether he wanted to or not.

"I'm not asking you to rush any of your appointments, but I also don't approve of patients sitting in the waiting room for too long," she said, all starchy and nose-in-the-air. She was very much on her high horse again, no hint of the incandescent smile he'd witnessed earlier, no softening of her professional demeanor. The humorless and by-the-book Dr. Layman had returned.

"Neither do I."

"Good, then we do agree on something."

It wasn't quite a question but he chose to respond as if it was.

"Yes, Dr. Layman, I guess we do."

"HI, DAD, WHAT ARE YOU doing here?" Callie looked up from the chart she was attempting to decipher. The White Pine Lake Community Health Center had not yet gone digital in its record keeping. Zach Gibson might not be entitled to an M.D. after his name but he sure had the chicken-scratch handwriting that usually accompanied the title.

"Ezra Colliflower asked me to sit in on the electrical inspector's walk-through. He'll be gone all day delivering a load of lumber to the mill in Gaylord."

"Good. I'd rather have you here than Ezra. He's scared me ever since he caught me and Gerry Forrester mushroom hunting in the woods out by his place and threatened to come after us with his chain saw. I still say we were on the other side of his property line, but he acted as if we were stealing his family jewels or something."

"You did have a heck of a bag of morels," J.R. reminded her. "I've never tasted better. Worth their weight in gold."

Callie sighed, remembering her haul of succulent fungi. "Hmm. Maybe he did have a reason to be angry, but I still say we were on the right side of the line on state ground. Twenty years hasn't mellowed him, either. He's still bad-tempered and cranky."

"He wouldn't be Ezra if he changed his habits," J.R. said with a grin. Her father was a handsome man, just under six feet tall, with a full head of steel-gray hair and skin permanently bronzed by years of exposure to wind and sun and the cold temperatures of long northern winters.

"Rudy and his gang finished the subfloor in the lab section this morning. Hopefully they'll have the new laminate flooring installed as soon as the electrical inspector gives the okay on the additional wiring. Bonnie and Leola are thrilled by the layout for the new electrical outlets. They're tired of running extension cords all over the place whenever we get a new piece of equipment."

"I'm glad you brought it to my attention. Zach said he'd intended to bring the subject up himself but you beat him to it."

Zach hadn't mentioned any of that to her. But to be fair she hadn't spoken to him about her conversations with the female staff. She should have. They were on the same team, after all. Something she had difficulty remembering whenever she was in the same room with him.

J.R. crossed his ankle over his knee. He was dressed in jeans and a green White Pine polo, so she guessed he was taking the early shift behind the bar today. The middle of summer wasn't a busy time for his CPA business but it was for the bar and grill. It usually worked out well for him, but today he seemed tired and there were new lines around his hazel eyes, the same color as hers. She wondered briefly if the new baby would share their eye color, Ginger's blue-gray or a shade unique and entirely his own? "How are you and Zach getting along?" J.R. asked before she could start her own line of questioning about his health.

"Fine," she said automatically.

"Hmm," he said, leaning back in his chair. "So not very smoothly, huh?" He knew her too well.

Callie cut her eyes to the open door. Her new office had been doing double duty as a storage area since the sprinkler malfunction, although she couldn't complain; she only had the occasional interruption to deal with, not patients funneling in and out for blood tests and weights and measurements as Zach did. "He's good at his job," she said, determined to put the best face on it. "We have different styles of interacting with our patients, that's all."

"Coming from the military, he's had a lot of responsibility thrust on him from a young age. He's used to being his own boss," J.R. said. "But I'm confident you two will work it out."

"Of course we will. We're both professionals."

"I know it hasn't helped that you're in the other half of the duplex," J.R. said with a frown. "It's just...well, things are complicated right now. I didn't plan far enough ahead. All those years of the two of us rattling around alone at the White Pine, I never realized it could get overcrowded, but it has. Becca's too old to share a room with her brother, and I assured Ginger I was fine with the baby being in our room, but—"

"It's a huge improvement over the mini-suite at the Commodore." She gave an exaggerated mock shudder and was rewarded with a quick smile from her father. "But it's as much my fault as yours. I should have planned where I'd be staying before I ever got here," Callie said. "Dad, is everything all right between you and Ginger?" She waited, not quite sure how he would react to such a direct personal question from her. Her father was a very private man.

"It's not easy getting used to the idea of being a new father when you're staring your fiftieth birthday in the eye," he said candidly. He shook his head ruefully, one side of his mouth lifting in a grin.

"Or being a sister when you're twenty-nine," Callie admitted, returning the smile. She waited but he didn't add anything further. "We'll figure this blended-family thing out together. Deal?"

"Deal," he said. "Your mother has plenty of room out at her place if it gets too uncomfortable being in such close proximity to Zach Gibson day and night."

"The prospect of moving in with Mom and the goats and the chickens should be all the incentive I require to come to a truce with my PA."

She'd made peace with her mother over the years, accepting the reality that Karen could only be happy marching to the beat of her own drummer. J.R., however, had never come to that same acceptance. He might have forgiven Karen for leaving him and their marriage, but never for abandoning Callie. Her parents were civil to each other these days but by no means friendly. Juggling birthdays and holidays without causing hard feelings was stressful for Callie—for all of them, really. Deep down she had to admit that continuing animosity between her parents was the biggest reason she hadn't come home as often as she could have these past few years.

"That's settled, then." J.R. relaxed in his chair, but she knew him too well not to notice that the tension hadn't completely left him.

"You are okay with the new baby, aren't you?" Overcoming a lifetime of reticence on her dad's part—and on hers—wasn't going to happen overnight, she realized.

"Sure," he said a little too quickly. "Especially if I get another great little girl like you."

MARISA CARROLL 69

"Come on, Dad. You can admit you really want a boy."

He dropped his foot to the floor, not reacting to her smile. "Either one is fine with me as long as he or she and Ginger are both fine." He stood up. "I'm going to go check in with Rudy and the inspector and see what's going on. Want to come along?"

"I don't know anything about electricity, and I don't *want* to know any more than it hides in the wall and comes out when you plug something into a socket. Don't you dare tell anyone I said that. Especially Zach." She stood up and straightened her shoulders. "But when duty calls, we Laymans step up to the plate." J.R. opened his mouth and Callie was afraid he might broach the subject of her staying longer than the three months she'd agreed to. "While we're at it, I could use another receptacle or two in here."

J.R. took the hint. "We don't have an unlimited budget, remember. Especially not until we find out how much the insurance company is going to pay for the water damage."

"Not enough," Zach's voice said. Callie glanced away from her father to find her

PA standing in the doorway. Her first day in the office he'd worn khakis and an open-throated pale blue dress shirt, but since then he'd shown up in camo-patterned fatigues and olive-green T-shirts beneath his long white lab coat. She didn't approve of the casualness of his dress but she had to admit the clothes suited his warm skin tone, dull gold hair and military bearing.

"Is something wrong?" She came out from behind her desk as she noted Zach's grim expression with a sinking sensation in her chest.

"We've got wiring problems," Zach announced.

"Oh, boy," J.R. muttered under his breath. "That's not good news."

"You're right. It's not. Evidently the breaker box is going to have to be changed."

J.R. whistled softly. "That's going to cost a pretty penny. Are you sure?" Zach nodded. "Well, it can't be helped. Let's go hear what the man has to say."

The two men stepped back so that Callie could lead the way into the staff room at the back of the building. They joined Bonnie Highway, copper-skinned, dark-haired and stout, and Leola Townley, tall and fair with light brown hair and the sharply etched features of her Finnish logger ancestors. They were both staring at the open circuit box as though it contained a nest of snakes. Callie hid a grin.

Rudy, whom she remembered owned a construction business in town, and a middle-aged balding man in jeans and a wrinkled cotton shirt were discussing the wiring, the inspector pointing out problems with the beam of his pencil-size flashlight, Rudy shaking his head and jotting notes on a clipboard. They broke off as the newcomers entered the room. Zach made a quick introduction, Callie first and then J.R.

"We have a serious problem here, Dr. Layman," the man explained. "Whoever put this box in must have wired it up blindfolded."

"The building's over twenty years old. I don't even remember who the original electrician was," J.R. admitted.

Rudy lifted his shoulders in a brief shrug. "Before my time."

"It has to be replaced," the inspector said, his voice pleasant but implacable. "There's no way I can approve any upgrades to this box. It's a miracle you haven't had a fire before now."

"How long will it take?" Callie asked. "We're trying to run a medical practice here."

"Three days," Rudy replied. "Have to go to Petoskey for a bigger box. Then get hold of the power company to shut off the juice. Replace the box, run new wire, run new ground wire, too, put in the new receptacles, then get Art to okay all of it before we get the power switched on again."

"Is that as quickly as it can be done?" Callie asked, dismayed. "We're already behind schedule because of the water break."

"I'll do my best," Rudy promised.

"I'll give you my home phone and my cell number," the inspector offered. "I'll come as soon as I can get here when Rudy calls."

"Thank you," Callie said, smiling in relief. "We're grateful for your cooperation. Can we finish seeing patients this afternoon, Rudy, or do you have to shut off the electricity right away?"

"I'll head to the electrical supply place in Petoskey once I figure out everything we need. You go ahead and finish out your day."

"Shall I start rescheduling our Friday patients?" Leola asked Callie after Rudy and the inspector had gone outside with J.R. to mark the location of the underground electric cable.

"That's a good idea. Don't you agree, Zach?"

"Yes, unless you want to set up a tent and examine patients in the parking lot."

She wasn't certain if he was joking or not, so she decided to respond as if it was a serious suggestion. "I don't believe that's necessary."

"I'll make sure the meds are taken care of, Dr. Layman," Bonnie promised. "I've still got plenty of room in my basement fridge from the first go-round. Is there anything else you want us to do?" She included Zach in the question.

"No," he responded. "Why don't you switch on the answering machine and take a lunch break while you have the chance?"

"Yes," Callie agreed, wishing she'd thought of suggesting it first. "It's almost 12:30. You both are already late for your break. Our afternoon patients will be showing up before you know it."

The phone at the reception desk rang and both women rolled their eyes. "You get our lunch bags out of the fridge," Leola said, "and I'll answer the phone."

"I'll call the Petoskey hospital and inform them what we're up against," Zach offered, pulling his stethoscope out of his coat pocket and wrapping it around his neck. For a split second as she watched his movements, Callie remembered the heat and strength of his touch on her arm and she shivered. "We'll have to get their okay to close the office Friday."

"I guess we have no choice. We can't function without electricity." More work-arounds, more improvising, more confusion, more failures. "I should never have left Ann Arbor," she said before she could stop herself.

Zach gave her a long, steady look. "Hey," he said. "Rudy's the Marine, not me, but it's time we apply a little Corps philosophy to the situation."

"What philosophy would that be?" she asked suspiciously.

"Improvise. Adapt. Overcome," he said.

"Improvise? Adapt? Overcome? I don't

understand." She hated how uptight and prissy she sounded, but she was not in the mood for word games.

"We're improvising like hell right now, right?" He grinned, a very appealing, very handsome grin.

"I suppose we are," she admitted reluctantly.

"Next we adapt so we can overcome this latest cluster…fluff," he said, hesitating until he came up with a sufficiently mild substitute for what he'd obviously really wanted to say. "We just got handed Friday off whether we wanted it or not. Do you have plans?"

"My plans were to be here doing what I was hired to do."

"Now you have room on your calendar to do something else."

"What do you suggest?"

"Go fishing with me."

"Absolutely not," she said. "That's an absurd suggestion. If we do anything together it will be to discuss which of our patients you'll be assigning to my care. We have put it off long enough."

"Why can't we do that after we've gone fishing?"

A little curl of anger stirred inside her. He'd avoided discussing transitioning some of his patients to her, as if he didn't want to give them up, as if he didn't think she could hack it. This man was getting on her nerves.

"Stop making light of the situation, Zach. We'd get more done here working in the dark than we would after we've been out on the lake in a boat."

The humor faded from his eyes. "I'm sorry, Dr. Layman. You're right. It was a bad idea. If you want to talk about the patients, we can do that from home. We don't need the internet or access to the hospital network. We'll do it low-tech. I'll give you thumbnail sketches of our patient roster and you can choose the ones you consider the best fit. Is that acceptable?"

"Yes." She was ashamed of losing her temper. It was unprofessional. She hated appearing unprofessional. "Yes, I agree that would be a better solution. We should have done it days ago."

"In a perfect world we would have. This is not a perfect world. I'll be over at eight."

"Eight?" She'd hoped she might be able to sleep in for an hour or so in the morning.

"Improvise, adapt, overcome, Dr. Layman. Remember? I still plan on going fishing. So the earlier we get started, the earlier we get done." He gave her a two-fingered mock salute and strolled off toward his office, leaving Callie without a word to say.

CHAPTER FOUR

CALLIE SAT QUIETLY, moving the base of the old-fashioned garden swing with her feet, letting the sunlight shining through the leaves of the big maple in her mother's yard dance against her closed eyelids.

She had never imagined her mother would end up returning to White Pine Lake, and certainly not to the farm her bachelor-farmer great-uncle had left her. But as always, Karen Freebeing—the name she had chosen for herself when she joined a commune in Oregon—had defied expectations and done just that, raising Angora goats and free-range chickens, and making videos of her off-the-grid lifestyle that were surprisingly popular and even profitable.

Today Callie was just very glad to have a place to get away from the clinic—and Zach Gibson.

High summer was her favorite season on the farm. The warm breeze whispered overhead, in the distance a tractor started up in a neighboring field, but it was a long way off and didn't interfere with her drowsy thoughts. In the paddock by the barn, her mother's Angora goats grazed, the babies bleating in high-pitched alarm whenever their mothers drifted too far away. Closer by, bees buzzed among the flowers, and the long-handled well-pump creaked and groaned as it settled a little in its sleep.

A nap would be nice, just a quick one. She hadn't been sleeping all that well. The duplex seemed smaller than she remembered and the soundproofing not quite as good. On some level, she seemed to always be aware of the man on the other side of the dividing wall. So it was nice to have a couple of hours to unwind after the hectic morning of electrical malfunctions and yet more rearranging of schedules and appointments at the clinic. She had to admit she was looking forward to the day off tomorrow, at least the part that would come *after* her meeting with Zach Gibson.

"Penny for your thoughts," Karen said, setting a tray of lemonade and a crockery bowl of popcorn down on a rusty wrought-iron table beside the swing.

"Oh, Mom, I didn't hear you coming. I must have dozed off for a minute or two."

"You work too hard. You always have. You should slow down and smell the roses."

"I am taking your advice, although it's mint I smell and not roses."

"The Girls have been looking for grubs in the mint patch, I suspect."

"Yes, they have. They've been giving me the evil eye ever since I sat down here."

"Must be Miss Fancy Pants and Evangeline, then. This swing is their favorite spot." Her mother's Buff Orpington chickens all had names and, Karen swore, personalities. They were pets as well as a source of income. Karen sold their eggs and they also starred in a series of their own videos.

"They don't take kindly to trespassers," Callie said as she accepted the cold glass of lemonade and scooted over a little to make room for her mother on the glider. When Karen sat down, the glider swayed harder, and Callie held out her vintage water-lily-patterned glass to keep lemonade from splashing over the edge.

"Sorry," Karen said. "I've put on a couple of pounds the last few weeks. Too much strawberry shortcake." Her mother was tall and long-legged, full-figured but not overweight. She favored long skirts, peasant blouses, and vests and sweaters she knitted herself from the fiber of her goats. Her hair was long and straight and today she had it piled on top of her head, held in place by a leather-covered comb.

The two big red-gold hens they'd been discussing bustled forward from beneath the sunflowers and began eating the popcorn kernels Karen tossed to them.

"Mmm, the lemonade is wonderful," Callie said, closing her eyes as she savored the cool drink. "Just what I needed to sweeten my day."

"You're welcome to move in here if being too close to J.R.'s new wife and kids is too much of a strain."

"It's not Ginger and the twins that are stressing me out." That wasn't precisely the truth, but close enough. "And you know you and I are too different to get along well even in a house this size."

Karen didn't press the invitation. Their relationship had improved as Callie matured. In her own way Karen had done her best to make amends for the years she'd been away, and Callie had done her best to try to forget how much her mother's desertion had hurt. But there was still a thin, transparent barrier between them, and so far neither of them had made an attempt to strip it completely away. Perhaps they never would.

"What possessed that man?" Bitterness seeped into Karen's tone and she threw the next handful of popcorn hard enough that the kernels overshot the hens and landed in an overturned bushel basket planted with yellow and white daisies and pink waterfall petunias. The chickens clucked in annoyance.

Callie didn't have to ask what Karen meant. "He fell in love with her, Mom."

"And where has it gotten him? Fifty years old and about to become a father again. He's the laughingstock of White Pine Lake—"

"Mom, change the subject." She wasn't going to go that route with her mother today. She suspected that Karen was still a tiny bit in love with J.R. But there was no going back for any of them and Callie had stopped indulging the fantasy of reuniting her parents many years ago.

Karen sighed and patted Callie's hand. "Sorry, baby. Letting the bad vibes get the better of me today. I should fire up the sauna and indulge myself in a good purging. What's on your agenda for the weekend?"

"House hunting," Callie said, although she hadn't actually planned on it until that moment.

"Hmm," Karen said, aiming the next handful of popcorn so it fell like a puffy white shower on top of the hens' heads. "Too close for comfort with Doc Hottie on the other side of the wall, huh?"

"What are you talking about?" Callie hoped she wasn't blushing. "No, it's not Zach. Well, *mostly* it's not Zach. The duplex is income property, after all, and sort of out of my price range now that it's high season." She could afford the rent on the duplex for a couple of months, but as she suspected he would, her father had refused to accept it. "And besides, it's too small."

"Too small? Don't try to flimflam me." Her mother rolled her eyes. "It's Zach. He's a hottie," Karen repeated, fanning herself with one hand. "Every premenopausal woman within twenty miles flocks to him for sympathy and hand-holding. And a bunch of the older ones who ought to know better, too."

Callie took a moment to consider what her mother had just said. Karen had spoken lightly and more than half-teasingly, but there was probably a lot of truth in her observation about the town's ladies. She wondered how Zach handled the unwanted attention. Very professionally, she was certain, and probably with good humor, she admitted grudgingly to herself, but would he be trying to transfer a gaggle of disappointed female patients onto her shoulders? Did he want her to take them to avoid the hassle and not because he recognized her skill? She would have to make it perfectly clear to him that she wanted a mix of patients of all ages and both sexes, not just women's care. She would have to be very firm on that point when they met in the morning.

"Of course, if he was in a relationship, they wouldn't be quite so pushy," Karen continued, and Callie caught herself tilting her head just slightly to listen to what her mother had to say.

"He's dating someone?" She wished she had enough self-control not to ask the question but she didn't.

"Not that I'm aware of," Karen admitted. "And I would have heard, believe me. The gossip chain in this town moves at the speed of light."

"I don't know anything about him, really," Callie confessed. "Just little things. He grew up in California and served as a navy medic attached to a Marine unit for two tours in Afghanistan. That's how he met Rudy and eventually ended up here."

Karen nodded. "I don't think he has family, or if he does they are all out west. He eats most of his meals out. That's another favorite pastime for the older women in town, feeding him. As for some of the younger ones, like I said, it's not his stomach they're interested in." She sighed a little wistfully. "Although I have to admit it's a very nice flat one. And those shoulders—"

"Hang on, Mom, I'm getting up," Callie said, forestalling any more comments on Zach Gibson's physique. She put one foot onto the floor of the glider and the other on the ground before she scooted off the seat.

The glider rocked, forcing her to take a quick step to avoid landing with her face in a pot of nasturtiums. "I will never get the hang of getting out of this thing," she grumbled.

"You're going already? I hoped to talk you into staying for supper." Karen sounded disappointed.

"I promised Dad I'd have supper with him and Ginger and the kids," she said cautiously. She had to be careful how she handled these kinds of situations with her mother. Luckily she'd had a lot of practice over the years. "I haven't spent any more time with them than I have with you this week." She wasn't overly thrilled about the prospect of making small talk with her stepmother and stepsiblings after the day she'd had, but she hadn't been able to refuse the invitation, just as she hadn't been able to convince her conscience that a visit to her mother could wait a few more days. "I'll come out any day next week you want me."

Karen's expression lightened. "The kale is ready to pick and I've been hungry for creamed kale and new potatoes."

Callie made a little face. Karen rolled her

eyes. "All right, I'll add some ham. How does that sound?"

"Better," Callie said, grinning. Karen ate little meat. Callie had nothing against vegetables but she preferred some protein mixed in with them.

"And I have a strawberry-rhubarb pie in the freezer. I'll bake that for dessert."

"I'll bring ice cream from Kilroy's. I might not be able to get here early enough to make our own."

"Wonderful." Karen shooed the chickens back toward their enclosure. They went, tails high and fluffed, ships under sail. "Call and let me know what day is good for you."

"I will, I promise. But it will probably be later in the week. Everything's still pretty hectic at the clinic, and since I'll be seeing regular patients for the first time, the visits will take longer than usual. I'll probably be running behind schedule the first few days." She hoped she sounded more confident than she felt.

"Good luck with your negotiations with Doc Hottie," Karen said with a little half smile that could be interpreted in all kinds of ways. Callie chose not to notice the open-ended comment.

"Thanks. Love you." She let Karen enfold her in a quick hug and then headed for her car before her mother could say anything else.

THE OTHER HALF of her family, she discovered, wasn't averse to asking her questions about Zach Gibson, either; they were just a little slower getting to the subject. The five of them were eating at the cook's table in the restaurant kitchen instead of upstairs. Ginger had no problem admitting she couldn't hold a candle to Mac's cooking and wasn't about to try.

"I helped Mac prep the vegetables today," Brandon announced, proudly indicating the sautéed fresh green beans on Callie's plate. He had evidently decided a grown-up stepsister was preferable to a new baby in the family and had attached himself to Callie as soon as she walked through the door, even offering to help her with chores around the cottage to earn money for a new computer game. Becca, however, had kept her distance. "Mac won't let me use a knife until

I'm thirteen, but I'm thinking I might be a chef someday," Brandon chatted on.

Becca snorted. "Last week you wanted to be a fireman. The week before that you were going to be a professional gamer and make a billion dollars designing computer games." Callie noticed the girl had eaten two servings of the green beans and most of her fish, but hadn't touched the fresh-baked rolls dipped in honey butter or the sweet-potato casserole.

"I changed my mind," Brandon responded. "The good chefs make a lot of money, too, and write books and have their own TV shows and everything."

"You'll be a good chef if you listen to Mac," Callie said. Mac had given her a solid grounding in the culinary basics when she was barely older than Brandon and Becca, but she hadn't had much opportunity to put what she'd learned to practical use after she entered medical school.

She'd enjoy cooking again. Maybe it was something she could do with the twins, or at least with her stepbrother.

Callie pulled her thoughts up short. There was a very real chance she wasn't going to be here that long. And if the position she'd been offered just days before she left Ann Arbor came through, she'd have all her meals provided for.

"Did you have a nice visit with your mom?" Ginger asked politely, pushing green beans around on her plate. She'd eaten very little and Callie noticed her fingers were puffy as though she were retaining water, not an unusual occurrence for a woman seven months pregnant in warm weather, but something to keep under observation. Her stepmother appeared tired, too. When Callie met with Zach tomorrow, she would ask him his opinion of Ginger's overall health. There was nothing out of line in that.

"Yes," Callie responded equally politely. "She showed me her goats and we had lemonade with Miss Fancy Pants and Evangeline."

"Those are funny names," Brandon said, pausing with a forkful of green beans halfway to his mouth. His round face wrinkled up in a frown. "Are they old ladies? Who has names like that?"

"They're chickens," Callie said, smiling at him across the Formica tabletop. "My mom raises chickens and Angora goats."

"I've never seen a goat up close. Can you take me to visit them someday?" He shoved the green beans into his mouth and chewed lustily while spearing a piece of whitefish for his next bite.

"I suppose," Callie said. She appealed to her father for guidance. J.R. looked at his wife. Callie moved immediately to reinforce Ginger's authority. "If it's all right with your mother, that is."

"How nice of you," Ginger said pleasantly, although her expression was troubled. "But please don't feel obligated to entertain Brandon."

"Oh, no," Callie assured her. "My mother loves to show off her animals. All the chickens have names, and the goats, too. And she'd be happy to demonstrate to Brandon… and Becca, too, if she's interested…how she spins the fiber. I'm just not sure how soon I'll have a free day. There is so much to do at the clinic."

"Weird," Becca muttered. "Who names chickens?"

"My mother, I guess. She's a little odd that way."

"How can you name something you're going to eat?"

"She says it's a sign of respect and affection to a noble breed of bird," Callie said with a grin. Her dad snorted but didn't raise his eyes from his plate.

"It's creepy," Becca said and put her fork down with a clatter. "But I suppose I might be interested in how she does that spinning thing." She didn't sound overly excited by the prospect of a trip to the farm, but Callie took even her lukewarm interest as a hopeful sign.

"We'll plan a trip as soon as I can work it into my schedule."

Becca shrugged. "Okay, but I said maybe, remember. I'm finished eating, Mom. Can I leave the table?"

"*May* I leave the table," Brandon said in a superior tone. "*Can I leave the table* is bad English, right, Mom?"

"*May* I leave the table," Becca shot back with a look that boded ill for her twin when they were alone.

"Don't you want dessert?" Ginger asked.

"No. I'm stuffed." Becca folded her thin arms across her chest. "I don't want anything sweet. I'll get an apple or a banana later. Fruit is better for you than a bunch of stuff made with refined sugar."

"Mac's desserts are very good."

"We'd all be better off with the fruit," she said stubbornly. "You're a doctor, Callie. I'm right, aren't I?"

"I approve of eating fruit," Callie said diplomatically. "But I love Mac's desserts. As long as you don't have them at every meal—"

The art of diplomacy was wasted on Becca. "I still just want an apple."

Ginger broke the awkward little silence. "Then, yes, you may leave the table."

Becca left the kitchen without another word.

"Sorry, I apologize for my daughter's bad manners," Ginger said, color staining her cheeks.

"She's practicing to be a teenager a couple of years earlier than normal," J.R. said with a rueful shake of his head.

"It's nothing," Callie said.

"What is for dessert?" Brandon asked above the clatter of a tray full of dirty dishes being loaded into the dishwasher behind them.

"Whatever's on the menu. You know that." Ginger began fanning herself with her hand. "It's so warm in here."

"Why don't I commandeer us a table on the porch?" J.R. suggested, taking Ginger's barely touched plate and stacking it on his own. "We can have orange sherbet and chocolate cookies out there. Mac baked a batch today when I told her Callie was coming for supper. It was always Callie's favorite dessert when she was the twins' age."

"It's still pretty high on my list."

Callie was tired and would have preferred to go back to the cottage to be alone for a while, but this was more or less her official welcome-home dinner, so she had to do her best to make it as much of a real family occasion as she could. In the old days, she and J.R. would have taken their cookies up to the cupola room at the top of the building and eaten them while they "spied" on the tourists and townspeople unsuspectingly going about their business on the street below. Now that wasn't an option. The cupola room had been off-limits since a big storm a few years earlier had damaged the floor. And anyway, it wasn't just her and her dad anymore. The realization was bittersweet.

"Great, sherbet and cookies all around, then. I'll ask Mac—"

"I heard!" the older woman hollered from her station behind the grill, where a trio of steaks sizzled and flared. "Orange sherbets and chocolate cookies coming up," she said, never taking her eyes off the steaks as she moved them off the heat for a short rest before plating.

"Thanks, Mac." Callie whisked across the kitchen and planted a kiss on her old friend's cheek. "It's good to be home."

Mac brushed off the sentiment with a wave of her spatula. "It's good to have you home, too, Callie. Really good. The town needs you and so does your dad." She moved away and began berating the hapless college student who was serving as her sous-chef before Callie could ask her what she meant by that last part of her statement.

"C'mon, Callie," her dad said, sticking his head around the swinging door that separated the kitchen from the rear of the dining room. "Brandon says there's a two-top open on the porch. It'll be a squeeze but we'd better snag it while we can."

"Coming." Callie called goodbye to Mac and headed toward the door. She wished they had had a chance to talk before this, but no opportunity had presented itself. Soon, though, she would get her friend's insights on how things were going between J.R. and Ginger.

"I'll grab an extra chair," J.R. said, "and when we're settled you can fill us in on how you're getting clinic schedules worked out with Zach."

THE SUN WAS GONE, the long midsummer twilight fading into night along the eastern shore of the lake. Zach heard the call of the little pond frogs start up along the marshy strip of shoreline just outside the business district. Music spilled out of the open doors of the White Pine, filtered by some quirk of atmospherics over the rooftops of the motel and cottages on the water's edge out to where he was fishing. A country song, all guitars and bass. He couldn't make out the words; it was more sensation than sound, anyway, far less of a disturbance than the trio of Jet

Skis returning to the marina dock a quarter mile away.

He shut the lid on his tackle box, secured the hook on his pole, laid it across the seats and unshipped the oars. The bluegills had quit biting and the mosquitoes had started up. Time to call it a night, Zach decided as he freed the anchor of weeds and started rowing toward the dock. He'd been fishing the secret hole J.R. had told him about in the spring. Formed by an underground spring bubbling up from the sandy bottom of the lake, it attracted bluegills and pumpkinseeds of truly awesome size, but he hadn't kept any fish this time. Too late to start cleaning them tonight.

He could have used the motor on his boat, too, but the exertion and the pull of the oars through the dark water felt good. He hadn't been getting enough exercise lately. Maybe that was why he wasn't sleeping as well as he usually did. If he was smart he'd row the full length of the lake, work out the kinks and make himself good and tired, but he didn't have lights on the little boat, so that option wasn't going to work tonight.

Instead, he figured he'd better get himself

home to the cottage and into the shower before Callie returned from dinner with her family. He knew that was where she was because Brandon had tracked him down a couple of hours earlier with a message from Mac. The cook had been running short of bluegill fillets and had been willing to pay fifteen bucks a pound if he had any in the freezer of his refrigerator. He did have a couple of bags and he'd told Brandon he'd trade them for a steak dinner or a couple of burgers some night when he didn't feel like being by himself. Or when the duplex walls seemed to be closing in on him.

That seemed to be happening more often lately, and it wasn't because of the PTSD. It was because of Callie. He'd thought the soundproofing was pretty good. The two or three short-term renters earlier in the summer hadn't disturbed his rest, or his peace of mind. But the new resident sure did. He swore he could even smell her shampoo through the bathroom wall if he put his mind to it when he stepped into the shower in the morning.

He pulled deeper on the oars and the boat shot over the water, skirting the lily pads that grew within fifty feet or so of the dock. They were closed for the night, their white and yellow petals furled over their waxy hearts, waiting for the touch of morning sunlight to open again.

Yep, he'd make it an early night. He understood the physician in charge well enough now to realize he'd need all his wits about him in tomorrow's early-morning face-off with Dr. Callista Layman.

CHAPTER FIVE

"Is it necessary to keep two appointment spaces available in the morning and the afternoon for unscheduled cases? We only left one open in the clinic where I worked during my residency."

"You probably did—but I bet there were several doc-in-a-box clinics and hospital emergency rooms close by, right? And how many of you were there on staff?"

"There were three physicians and two nurse practitioners on staff."

"And here there's just the two of us," Zach pointed out, spreading his hands. "When there are a lot of tourists in town, even that block of time gets used up fast. Usually it's just sniffles or a sunburn or poison ivy, but no one wants to be sick on vacation in the first place, so to spend half a day driving to Petoskey or Traverse City to the emergency room just makes it worse."

"Point taken," she said. And another point

lost in their latest sparring match. She bet he was keeping score. She shouldn't have tried to equate her experience at a busy urban clinic with what went on in White Pine Lake.

"Did you ever consider setting up practice here, I mean before your dad's SOS brought you back?"

The question caught Callie off guard. "Sure," she said. "Once I settled on family practice as my specialty, it seemed the logical thing to do, but then, as time went on I realized there were other opportunities out there I wanted to explore." And by then she had been away from home so long it seemed less familiar and more intimidating.

"For instance?"

He was sitting across from her at the little table positioned by the front window of her half of the duplex, and he seemed to take up a lot of space in the small room. She'd had to stop herself from scooting backward in her chair when he'd sat down twenty minutes earlier, and she still felt as though he was encroaching on her space.

Doc Hottie. She wished her mother hadn't called him that. It was far too close to the truth. Maybe if she had been able to keep a bit more distance between them she would stop noticing that he smelled like pine soap and fresh air and a hint of some kind of masculine aftershave that she couldn't name.

"Well, traveling, for one." She took a quick breath. She was going to have to start telling people sooner or later. "I've got an offer for a two-year contract with a cruise line. They sail the Caribbean in the winter and Mediterranean and Europe in the summer. The salary is minimal, but if I agree to a two-year commitment, they'll retire almost half my student-loan debt."

He whistled softly. "That would be a sweet gig."

"Yes, it would, though I haven't accepted it yet."

"Have you mentioned the offer to your dad?"

"No, I haven't. Not yet, and I'd appreciate it if you keep the information to yourself." The question struck a nerve; it was just another indication of how her relationship with J.R. had changed since Ginger had arrived on the scene. Before, she would have been on the phone to him the moment she had hung up on the cruise-line headhunter. Instead she had kept it to herself to spare him another thing to worry about, because having her halfway around the world for the next two years would definitely cause him stress.

"I won't mention it. You'd be a fool not to accept it, though."

"That's what everyone says."

He cocked his head and regarded her with unblinking eyes. "Not sure you'd be advancing your career sailing around the Med for two years in a floating hotel?"

More as if she wasn't sure she could handle the responsibility alone; she hadn't done such a great job with the clinic or with her family. Not that she'd admit that to him. She took the opening gratefully. "Possibly. I'm not sure overseeing the aches and pains of overweight, overindulged and overfed tourists is what I put myself through eleven years of medical school for."

"Ouch," he said. "Pretty much sums up what I've been doing since I got to White Pine Lake?"

"I'm sorry, I shouldn't have said that." Callie hadn't meant to sound so condescending and dismissive. She was only trying to protect herself. She, too, had trained for this

kind of a family practice; if not in White
Pine Lake, then somewhere else. Was that
why she hadn't jumped at the cruise-line
offer the moment her application was accepted? Was that what she really wanted—
a rootless, uncommitted lifestyle that didn't
put her skills to the test?

She chose her next words with care. "It
isn't the same at all. What you do here at the
clinic is completely different. You treat the
whole individual and build a rapport with
them and do your best to help them live a
long and healthy life."

"Apology accepted." His expression was
set, though. He didn't look as if he'd forgiven
her tactlessness.

"Would you care for another cup of coffee?" she asked to change the subject.

"Thanks," he said, standing up, making
her even more aware of how completely he
dominated the space around him. "I'll get
it myself. Stay sitting." He took his time
pouring a mug from the French press cof-
feemaker he'd helped her carry in that first
night.

She'd done it again, said something to
put them both on edge. What was it about

the man? She could usually get along with almost anyone. And she couldn't blame it solely on his alpha-male tendencies. Being an alpha personality was practically a prerequisite in the medical profession.

She found she was staring and decided it would be best to concentrate on something besides the way he moved, all harnessed strength and quiet efficiency. She gazed out the window. A couple of middle-aged guys in a high-end bass boat were casting lures just a few yards from the tethered wooden raft she'd played on as a kid. She wondered if Ginger let Becca and Brandon play on it as she had back in the day. Ginger didn't seem like a helicopter parent who would consider jumping off an anchored wooden raft too dangerous, but Callie wasn't sure.

As she watched out the window, two hummingbirds arrived simultaneously to argue over possession of the feeder she'd hung from a hook above the porch railing, swooping and dive-bombing each other. It amazed her how much noise the tiny birds could make. The sound of their wings was the buzzing of a hundred bees. They chattered like angry little squirrels as each of the two females attempted to gain control of the feeder for herself.

"Want a refill?" Zach asked, returning to the table. The movement behind the glass startled the hummers and they took off for the pine trees down the shore, continuing their rivalry in an aerial dogfight that would have impressed a WWI flying ace.

"Thanks, no. I've had two. That's enough for me."

"Suit yourself." He was wearing shorts and a T-shirt, not khaki colored today, but a warm coppery shade that picked up the highlights of the same hue in his blond hair and the day-old stubble of beard on his chin. A faded scar sliced across his left calf.

Callie suppressed a shiver. The scar came from a bullet wound. She'd seen enough of them working her emergency-medicine rotation. Was that the source of the Purple Heart listed on his service record? She'd come across his résumé while making sure the employee files hadn't been damaged in the office flood, and she couldn't resist taking a peek. When had it happened? How? She wondered if they would ever be comfortable enough with each other for her to ask or for him to tell her.

"I really am sorry for that remark about overfed tourists," she said.

"Don't worry about it. I'm a PA, remember. I can't go out and practice medicine on my own. I have to go along to get along. I'm used to dealing with M.D.s and their God complexes."

"I suppose you are." There was no use denying the truth of what he said. Physician's assistants were required to be affiliated with an M.D. or a hospital to practice their profession. "Regardless, I don't care to think of myself as one of those God creatures. It still doesn't make it right."

"If had to guess, I'd say I struck a nerve. Playing doctor on a cruise ship? Is it what you really want to do?"

His question startled her into an honest answer. "I'm considering it. I have some time to decide."

"You realize the committee will probably ask you to stay on. They'd be fools not to. You're a good doctor. But if you're determined to go, it will influence the patients I assign to you. I can work with just about any

M.D. I get handed, but some of our patients aren't as flexible. They're older. They don't adapt well to change. They've already lost Gail, and she was the physician here almost from the day the clinic opened."

"Everyone is aware I'm only here temporarily."

"It won't stop them from being upset when you leave."

"I understand. I'll try not to get too close."

He blew out a breath. "That's not what I was getting at."

"Wasn't it? It doesn't matter. It's a good reminder. I'll keep you informed of my plans." She pulled her laptop in front of her and opened the lid. "We should get started. I'm ready when you are."

He hesitated a moment, staring down at his coffee mug before raising his eyes to her face. "Okay. We might as well get this out of the way up front. I would appreciate it if you take…a few…of my more…"

"*Difficult* patients?"

"You could call them that."

"More specifically, your difficult *female* patients," she finished for him.

"Yes." He pushed his coffee mug aside and

picked up a pencil, twirling it between his fingers as he avoided her gaze. She had been prepared to stand her ground when the subject came up, but she found the sudden look of discomfiture on his face and the slight reddening of the skin of his throat disarming. "The, um, the ones of a…certain—"

Good heavens, he was blushing. Zach Gibson, uncomfortable, embarrassed, knocked off his stride. She felt sorry for him but it was difficult to keep a smile from sneaking onto her face. Her mother had been right. He was being…*sexually harassed* was probably too strong a term…but certainly he was uncomfortable in at least a few patient relationships. "Premenopausal? Hormonally challenged?"

"You're enjoying this," he said, his eyebrows drawing together above those incredibly blue eyes. The color was hard to describe—twilight on a summer day just before moonrise, maybe? Oh, man, what had gotten into her? She sounded as besotted as the women they were discussing. That was not acceptable. "It isn't only women doctors who find themselves in uncomfortable situations with patients. Let's just say a couple of them have…boundary issues…"

"Bonnie stays with you in the exam room, doesn't she?"

"Of course, but let's just say they're inventive. I suspect they check her schedule, have emergencies on her day off, that kind of thing."

"I see," Callie said.

"In different circumstances I'd refer them to a women's clinic or an ob-gyn, but that's not what you do in a rural practice. We're here to make health care more accessible, not more difficult. And that's not a dig at your cruise-line offer. It's the truth, plain and simple."

She hadn't considered what they were doing in precisely those terms, but Zach had summed up their specialty very well in a single sentence. "I'll be happy to take over any patients you believe would be better off under my care, no questions asked." She sat up a little straighter in her chair and stared fixedly at her laptop. "Want to give me their names?"

He spelled out four names and she dutifully typed them in. Two of them were almost old enough to be his mother, if she remembered them correctly. No wonder he was uncomfortable treating them. "Anyone else?"

"No," he said. "I'll inform you if anything else comes up." He seemed relieved and picked up a dog-eared notebook. No laptop for him but she'd noticed his cell phone was state-of-the-art. "Okay, let's move on to your other patients. Shall we start with the *A*'s?" Twenty minutes later she had several pages of names and personality sketches, idiosyncrasies, phobias, and likes and dislikes to add to the patient histories she'd find in their charts. A little thrill of excitement danced across her nerve endings. It was as if she had her own well-run practice.

"Now, as far as the acute cases and walk-ins," he said, breaking into her mental celebration. "I imagine you'll be handling most of those since your schedule isn't going to be as full as mine, for the next few weeks, at least."

"Well, yes, I suppose I will." She wondered if he really wanted those cases for himself. Deep down inside she couldn't blame him if he did. He had been trained to cope with situations beyond anything she had ever experienced. He must grow weary some days of encountering nothing more interesting than routine blood pressure and cholesterol checks, but nothing of the kind showed on his face.

Improvise. Adapt. Overcome. He was good at taking things as they came. She wished she was better at it. It would make her life easier all around.

"Bonnie's a rock when it comes to emergencies. She's seen it all, and Leola is no slouch at triage. If she says someone has walked in complaining of chest pain and she thinks it's an MI, you can be darned sure it's a heart attack, not indigestion from the all-you-can-eat fish fry at the White Pine." He paused, waiting to see how she would handle that little zinger he'd tacked on to the end of his sentence, but she was ready for him and didn't react.

"I'll remember that." She relaxed her shoulders and smiled.

WHAM! IT HIT Zach right in the gut, that quick, incandescent smile. It nearly took his breath away. He recovered enough to ask, "Any other questions, Dr. Layman?"

"Not right now. If I have any later, I'll send you a text."

He found himself trying to find something witty to say that would make her smile again. He hadn't been this fixated on getting a girl to smile since eighth grade. He couldn't remember that girl's name anymore after so many years, but she had been his first real crush. He might have actually gotten up the nerve to ask her out if he hadn't been shuffled to yet another foster home halfway through the school year. After that he hadn't put too much effort into attracting girls, instead concentrating on sports and fantasizing about owning his own car. By the time he was sixteen, he found they were starting to come after him, anyway. That was pretty much how he'd operated in the romance department ever since. Nothing serious. Nothing permanent.

But he suspected Callie Layman didn't fit into the category of women who were no more into long-term than he was. He'd better watch himself. And if none of those rationalizations helped when she turned that fabulous smile on him, the cold, hard fact that she was his boss should do the trick.

"We should be able to hit the ground run-ning Monday morning, then," he said.

"A week behind schedule, but who's count-ing?"

"But what a week. You have to admit it hasn't been boring."

"It certainly has not." Another quick smile, but he was ready for it and avoided the punched-in-the-gut wallop the last one had produced.

They'd made some progress today. Sure, she was still as prickly as a cactus, always standing on her dignity, but heck, he'd dealt with newly minted M.D.s a lot pricklier than Callie Layman.

He couldn't fault her for considering the cruise-line job. She hadn't figured out what she wanted to do with the rest of her life like he had. And a chance to work on a cruise ship would be hard for anyone to refuse. It would be a real temptation for anyone who hadn't already found the one place on earth he wanted to be for the rest of his life.

"I'm sorry for oversleeping this morning and getting us off to a late start. Did it ruin your plans to go fishing?" she asked as she powered down her laptop and closed the lid. Everything she did was precise, but still somehow completely feminine and underscored by a quiet strength he wondered if she even knew she possessed.

She'd overslept and he'd had to knock to wake her up; still, when she reappeared a half hour later, apologizing and offering Mac's incredible chocolate cookies and coffee as a very good peace offering, she'd looked as cool and composed as always. He wondered how she did it.

"I don't have a choice." He grinned. "I've got an order for three pounds of bluegill fillets from Mac. Last night I let those fish believe they were getting a free lunch. Today they're going on the stringer, and tonight some lucky guy from Detroit will be dining like a king at the White Pine."

She laughed and the sound was silvery and cool—raindrops on birch leaves—and even more enticing than her smile.

Zach stood up and walked the few feet to the tiny kitchen area and set his coffee mug in the sink. The bathroom was only three feet away. The door was half-open. A shampoo bottle sat on the shelf right in his line of vision. A field of purple flowers graced the label. Lavender. One of his foster mothers had been an avid gardener. She had raised lavender, and whenever he smelled it, he recalled sunlight and summer days. But no longer; now he would always associate the scent with Callie.

He stopped himself. Definitely letting his thoughts get too personal. Not good. Not good at all. So though he wanted to add *Want to come along?* he didn't.

She had stood up when he did but didn't move away from the table, keeping it between them. Okay, he got it: *Don't come any closer. Don't get any more personal.* Just as he'd been warning himself not ten seconds earlier.

"What are your plans for the rest of the day?"

Man, why couldn't he just say *Thanks* and head out the door? Maybe because today he hoped they'd taken a step forward in their relationship and for once had avoided the "two steps back" portion of the routine? Or maybe he just wanted her to smile again and know he had something to do with it.

"I'm meeting a friend for lunch and to ooh and ah over her new baby. Gerry Forrester.

I mean, Gerry Seamann. We grew up together. We've been friends since preschool." She grinned and he suspected her sense of humor could hold a very sly edge. "She and Kayla, her little one, and her other three children are patients you won't be seeing while I'm here, even if I did forget to mention their names earlier."

Her words jiggled his memory bank. There was something he'd forgotten to tell her about the patient list also, but he couldn't remember what it was. She went on talking and the thought drifted away.

"And then I'm going to drop by the White Pine and visit with Mac during her afternoon break."

"She'll probably put you to work."

"I don't mind. I like cooking. I just never get much chance to do any. You know how it is when you live alone."

"And have a sixty-hour workweek."

"Closer to seventy these last eighteen months. I imagine it was the same for you in the military."

He stiffened. It wasn't sixty or seventy or even eighty hours a week when you were in a war zone. It was 24/7/365. With death and dying coming at any moment of the day or night. "Yeah," he said shortly. "It could be a bitch. Well, I have to be going."

"Zach...I...I'm sorry. I was just making small talk. I didn't mean to pry—"

"Not your fault," he said, wishing he could keep the tightness out of his voice, but he couldn't seem to do that, either. "Just not a place I want to go."

"Of course, I understand." She glanced down at her laptop. "Well, I won't keep you."

"The sun's getting up there. If I want to get Mac's order filled, I should get out on the water. I'll—" He'd started say *I'll see you bright and early Monday morning,* but of course, he'd probably run into her half a dozen times before then. "I'll see you later," he finished lamely.

"I'm sorry I brought up the subject of the war," she said softly as he headed for the door.

"Let's just say I didn't make the best choice. 'Join the Navy and See the World.' It didn't happen that way. Kuwait, Iraq and Afghanistan. I spent some time in all those places. The Middle East's a long way from home. Long way from the water. Just a lot of war and suffering and pain and dying." He snapped his mouth shut before he said any more. Before she heard the demons he kept mostly locked away these days fighting to get out. He didn't want her to diagnose him as unstable...although, once in a while—but not too often anymore, thankfully—he still worried he might be.

"But in the end that decision led you to your career in medicine. It brought you to White Pine Lake."

"Yeah," he said. "It did do that." He felt a small measure of serenity return.

Her expression was stricken. "You don't have to worry. I won't mention Afghanistan again." She'd tried to reach out and he'd slammed the door in her face. It was a warning to him. He was attracted to her but she was a healer, same as he was. She would push to find the cause of his pain, his misery, and he didn't go there. Not now. Not ever.

He should have said *It's all right. It was no big deal. I'll get over it.*

Instead he nodded his head and walked out the door.

Two steps back... And this time it was no one's fault but his.

CHAPTER SIX

"HI, GINGER. HOW are you today?" Callie lowered herself onto the desk chair positioned alongside the narrow counter in the newly refurbished exam room. Three weeks ago when she arrived in town, it had been a cool, sterile blue, the floor awash in floodwater. Today it was a creamy buff color, which contrasted nicely with the off-white counter and the shiny new simulated-hickory laminate floor. The new decor was a collaborative effort between the female staff—with input from Rudy, Zach and her father on what type of flooring surface and paint finishes would wear best. Maybe her dad and Rudy being there had helped keep the sessions upbeat and not too serious, or maybe they were all beginning to learn to function as a real team. She hoped so. She was doing her best to make it happen.

Over the past week, Rudy Koslowski and his crew had labored tirelessly to get the clinic back in shape. The electrical upgrades had been accomplished without a hitch, and three members of the White Pine Physician's Committee had volunteered their evenings to help paint. Callie had even managed to find time to help wallpaper the children's corner of the waiting room.

The committee members on the wallpaper crew had been gracious in accepting her help, and since only one of them had known her as a child— the straight-A student voted most likely to succeed, the girl whose mother had walked out on her family to join a hippie commune in Oregon—the evening had passed pleasantly enough. Gerry Seamann's mother-in-law, Doris, had donated a set of almost-new colorful plastic child-size table and chairs she'd found at a thrift shop in Petoskey. And as quickly as that, there was a bright, cheerful place for little ones to stay occupied while they waited to see the doctor.

Being away from her hometown for so many years, Callie had forgotten how quickly the townspeople could all come together for the betterment of the community and how satisfying it was to be part of such an effort.

Lately she had been reminded in ways large and small how good it was to be home.

Unfortunately, the examining room's warm color palette, chosen for its calming influence, didn't seem to be having the desired effect on her stepmother. Ginger perched uncomfortably on the edge of the paper-covered exam table, her distended stomach very evident beneath her lightweight summer top. The baby was moving, and vigorously, too, it seemed, by the grimace on Ginger's face as she pushed gently on a protruding elbow or knee, hoping the little one chose a more comfortable position to settle in.

Callie stared for a moment, distracted by the realization that the tiny being was her blood, too. Her half brother or sister, tied to her forever by the love they would share for the man who was father to them both. Usually she could consider the situation with some detachment, but not today. It was Friday, the end of a second busy, stressful week, and her guard was down.

"I assumed I'd be seeing Zach," Ginger said.

"You will be," Callie assured her. "I just stopped in to say hello and make sure you're okay and to apologize for having to cancel dinner the other night." The clinic had been swamped with patients on Wednesday. A nasty summer virus had decided to pick White Pine Lake's population as a "target of opportunity," as Zach described it. They'd had to squeeze half a dozen unscheduled appointments in that day and then do a hurried disinfect of the exam rooms after the last patients left.

Callie had been exhausted by the time she finished dictating her patient notes. Zach, on the other hand, had returned to the clinic that night to help Rudy and his crew lay the flooring in this very room.

"Don't mention it," Ginger said, visibly relaxing. "You've been swamped here. Rumor has it you've put in nearly as many hours decorating as the Physician's Committee."

"I really didn't do that much," Callie insisted, although she was pleased that her effort hadn't gone entirely unnoticed in town.

"You've done wonders. You'd never guess two weeks ago this place was a disaster area."

"Just about everything's up and running again."

"It's one of the good things about living in a small town," Ginger said with a little edge to her voice, as if there were other aspects of small-town living she didn't appreciate quite as much. "Brandon was disappointed. He missed you the other night," she said, changing the subject.

"I promised to take him to meet my mother, but I couldn't find a spare moment. Perhaps this weekend." Karen had dropped off a half-dozen eggs from The Girls' laying earlier in the week. Desperate to find some way to connect with her stepsiblings, Callie had asked if she could bring the twins to visit. Karen had appeared surprised at the request, then shrugged and said sure. Callie appreciated her mother's help in making progress with the twins. She doubted Karen would be as generous helping her find common ground with Ginger, however.

"Please don't feel as if you have to entertain my son," her stepmother said.

"I want to. And I hope we can persuade Becca to come, as well."

She didn't hold out a lot of hope in that regard. Her young stepsister hadn't seemed very enthusiastic about the proposed visit, or anything else to do with Callie, for that matter.

Ginger sighed. "I hope so, too, but please don't be offended if she refuses to go. Preteens can be difficult."

A knock sounded on the half-open door and Zach's face appeared around the edge. "Hi, Ginger." He walked over and held out his hand. Ginger gave it a quick shake. "Sorry to keep you waiting."

"Callie and I have just been catching up." Ginger scanned their faces. "Is there some reason other than small talk that Callie's here? You aren't considering transferring me to her care, are you?" She must have realized how ungracious the words sounded because she lifted her hands in apology. "I mean, I understood Callie wasn't supposed to treat family members. I'm sure I remember J.R. telling me that."

"That's true," Callie agreed with a smile she hoped wasn't as tight as it felt on her face. She had anticipated this was going to be an awkward conversation, but it was even more difficult than she had imagined. She wanted to be on good terms with Ginger; she hoped that they could grow close enough to call each other friend and mean it. But so far they hadn't made much progress. Between the hints of a rough patch from Mac, her mother's gossip and the tension she'd sensed for herself between J.R. and Ginger, she didn't want to be forced into a more intimate relationship right away. So far her good intentions of repairing any cracks in J.R. and Ginger's relationship hadn't amounted to much. She hadn't even had a chance to talk more with Mac. She'd been too busy working on her own relationships with Zach and the clinic staff. "It's clinic policy that staff not treat family members, except in emergency situations."

"Callie is also the physician in charge here, though," Zach said, his hands thrust deep into the pockets of his white coat, his head cocked a little to one side, that darn, gorgeous half smile just visible at the corners of his mouth. And try as she might, Callie couldn't hear any patronizing undertones in his statement about her being in charge. "So I would like your permission to be able to consult with her if I have any concerns about your pregnancy."

Ginger laid her hand protectively on her

stomach. "Concerns? What concerns are you referring to? Is something wrong? Bonnie did say my blood pressure's up slightly, and my ankles are swollen, and my hands, too, but it's been so warm, and I'm on my feet a lot—"

She glanced at Callie, who kept her expression pleasant but unreadable despite her own worries. This was the first she'd heard of Ginger's blood pressure being elevated. She didn't like the sound of it.

"There's nothing to be alarmed about today, Ginger," Zach continued, "but we've been over this before. A woman in her late thirties is considered at high risk for complications during pregnancy."

"But this is my second pregnancy. Everything's checked out fine so far, all the blood tests and the ultrasound. And the baby's active. Very active." She grimaced as a wave of movement rippled over her distended belly. "See, and he's strong, too. And I'm not really so old these days—lots of women over forty have babies, and I have given birth to twins, remember." She tried to make it a joke and almost succeeded.

"That's a second complicating factor, a

multiple first pregnancy, although we all know there's only one baby this time."

"He's right, Ginger," Callie said soothingly, hiding her own disquiet. "And you are only eight weeks from your due date. Dr. Carmichael is already bending the rules for you. You should be seeing her in Petoskey weekly."

"But she agreed—if I see Zach twice a week here I only have to go to her once a month until September. She has a lot of confidence in Zach. She said so herself."

"Then you have to have confidence in Zach, as well." She could give credit where credit was due without diminishing her own authority. "He is an excellent PA."

"Thank you, Dr. Layman," he replied with equal formality.

Ginger missed the slight stiffness in the exchange. "I really don't want to spend most of a day coming and going to a doctor's appointment," she said fretfully. She began twisting her wedding ring around on her finger. The gold band was tighter than it should be. Something Callie had noticed before, but then she hadn't realized how serious the situation might be. "We're shorthanded at the

White Pine. I'd have to leave the kids alone with J.R." Her face flamed. "I only meant to say he's busy, too, and the twins can be a handful." She tried to explain. "We've been alone since they were babies. Their father died so young. It's hard for them to have a man in the family." She made a little gesture of defeat. "They're good kids, and your dad's great with them, Callie, he really is, but we're all still adjusting. And the baby coming makes everything that much harder." She stopped abruptly.

Callie didn't have any trouble getting her smile right this time. Even if she had taken offense for her father's sake, which wasn't the case, she couldn't let any patient continue in such distress. "It's okay, Ginger. I understand what you meant to say, but Zach's right. You are at a higher risk than you were eleven years ago when you were pregnant with the twins. It's simply a fact of life, especially if we can't keep your blood pressure under control. But if we can, everything should be fine."

"And if we can't control it?"

"Dr. Carmichael will probably want you to go on bed rest," Zach said. "As a precaution."

"Oh, no, I can't do that again. I had to go on bed rest with the twins, and I only had to take care of myself then. Well, me and my late husband, who was about as much trouble as a child. How will I ever manage now? Please, what do I have to do to avoid that?"

"Watch your salt," Zach began. "Get off your feet as much as possible. Take a nap in the afternoon. And stop worrying."

Ginger stared at her clasped hands. "I'm not very good at that."

Callie rose, sensing her stepmother wanted her to go so she could talk to Zach in private. "Ginger, remember, I'm only on board to consult on your physical condition. Anything else you discuss with Zach is totally confidential. You're still Zach's patient. We both want you and the baby to have the best care possible."

"Thanks, Callie, I appreciate your concern."

Callie opened the door. "I have some patient notes to dictate. I'll leave you two alone now."

"Mac baked cookies today," Ginger said to Callie as she took a step into the hallway.

"Brandon said I should tell you. He's hoping to bribe you into stopping by."

Callie laughed. "He's going to be a heart-breaker in a few years. He's already discovered the best way to wow the ladies is to offer them Mac's triple-fudge chocolate-chip cookies."

"He takes after his father in that respect. He was a real charmer, Kyle was. But when all is said and done, I hope Brandon grows up to take after your father and not his own."

Callie nodded, touched by her stepmother's words. "Dad is a good man and a great father."

"He is." Ginger smiled brightly, but anxiety still clouded her eyes. "And thanks for watching over us."

"You're welcome." Callie closed the door softly behind her. Maybe she couldn't give J.R. and Ginger a happy ever after all by herself. But she would do her best to not be part of the problem. She'd try harder to have a better relationship with Ginger and the twins for J.R.'s sake—and her own.

"GOT A MINUTE?"

"Of course, come in."

Zach stepped inside and closed the door of Callie's office. There were still a couple of stacks of plastic storage bins containing old records shoved in one corner, with a pyramid of boxes of salvaged supplies stacked on top, but for the most part the small space no longer looked as if it was part of a disaster zone.

When the committee had decided to repaint the entire clinic, Callie had picked a rich, warm brown for this room. White mini-blinds covered the single window, and she was planning to order sheer curtains of the same color to soften the look and frame the view of the wildflowers in the overgrown meadow bordering the narrow strip of lawn behind the building. Other than that, the walls were bare. Her diploma was on the wall above the reception desk where everyone could see it, next to Zach's. Leola had insisted they be prominently displayed, and she and Bonnie had badgered Rudy until he hung them precisely where they wanted them. But when she found a free hour, Callie was going to visit the galleries on either side of the White Pine to find a print or two. With the finishing touches of the framed prints, the little room would truly be her space.

"What can I do for you?" she asked, motioning Zach to a chair. For a moment she feared he might refuse the offer and continue to stand with his shoulder against the door frame, taking up more than his fair share of the space. He was just a little scruffy after a long, hard day and week, but nowhere near as wrung out as she must appear. It wasn't fair that men could look sexy and desirable when they were tired and women just looked tired.

As he came near she caught a whiff of his cologne. It was suddenly hard for her to take a breath. "Please, have a seat," she said a little more forcefully than she'd intended.

He didn't appear to notice her tone and she relaxed slightly. She was simply going to have to get used to having so much high-octane testosterone so close at hand—day *and* night. She leaned forward on her elbows and rested her chin on her crossed hands. "What can I help you with?"

"First of all, thanks for backing me up in there with your stepmother."

She nodded. "You're welcome." She almost added something about partnership but didn't. They weren't really partners, not in the way most people used the term. And as far as she could, see they probably never would be, although surprisingly she hadn't even thought about the job with the cruise line for almost a week—she simply hadn't had time the past week, she excused herself.

"I got Ginger to agree to cut some of her hours at the White Pine and to try to get off her feet at least two hours every afternoon."

"But will she follow through?"

He shrugged. "I hope so." He rested his forearms on his thighs and stared down at the floor between his spread legs. After a moment he straightened, giving her the full effect of those rain-cloud-blue eyes. "Callie, do you think your father is aware of how dangerous a situation his wife and baby could be in?"

"I…I'm not sure," Callie said. "We've never talked about it in any detail. It was an unplanned pregnancy, but that's about all I know. I've been home so little these last eighteen months."

He waved off her explanation. "I get what the final year of a family-practice residency can be like."

"My dad's a smart guy, but I can't say he has a lot of experience with pregnant women.

He probably isn't aware of the extent of the risks for both Ginger and the baby. I noticed she was retaining water, but as far as her blood pressure being elevated, no one mentioned it." High blood pressure could lead to premature birth and even death for both Ginger and the baby if the condition wasn't kept under control. She shuddered, letting the sentence trail off. They were coming close to the boundaries of patient/practitioner confidentiality. But they were also talking about her family, her flesh and blood. J.R.'s greatest fear was that something might happen to Ginger or the baby. She made up her mind. "Should I talk to him?"

Zach shook his head. "Not unless he brings up the subject. We don't want Ginger to think we've gone behind her back."

"No, I certainly don't want that. Perhaps I should talk to her instead?"

"Are you comfortable doing that?"

"No," she said ruefully. "Not as a doctor and not as a stepdaughter. If there are problems between Ginger and my father, I'd much rather they come to you with them. Perhaps she's kept them from him so he doesn't worry about her. Or she might simply be blocking it out of her mind?" She made it a question.

Zach nodded. "She wouldn't be the first person to behave that way."

"It's complicated all around," she said. "My mother says there's talk in town about them."

"There's bound to be some jokes and teasing when a man your father's age finds himself with a new baby on the way. I imagine it's good-natured ribbing for the most part."

"Are you sure?"

"Your dad's a popular guy. He's got a lot of friends. He can take care of himself. But I'm not so sure about Ginger. She might believe she has a lot to prove to the residents of White Pine Lake." He shrugged. "I'm a PA, not a psychologist. But just so we're on the same page—if I think the situation warrants it, I'll call J.R. and Ginger in for a consultation. She'll listen to him if he's the one insisting she slow down and take it easy. And he'll make sure that she does."

Callie smiled, relieved. "He will do that."

"Can I share a little observation of my own?" he asked.

"Certainly." She sat a little straighter.

"I understand the delicacy of your situation, but your stepmother's still new in town," he said, one big hand closing around the bell of the stethoscope hanging around his neck. "I said I'm not a shrink, and I'm not, but it doesn't take one to see Ginger could use a friend."

"I'm trying," Callie said honestly. "I'll do my best."

"But…?"

"I'm not sure where to start. I don't know very much about her," she said, ashamed to admit all the things she'd never asked.

"I'm not sure anyone around here does, except your dad."

"I'm not so sure he does, either. It was a whirlwind romance. Love at first sight, I'd guess you'd say."

Zach picked up on the skepticism she hadn't been able to filter out of her voice. "Don't believe it's possible?" he asked, just a tiny hint of his killer smile flickering across his mouth.

"I might if I'd ever experienced the phenomenon."

"I can't fault you there, although I believe love at first sight is possible."

"My dad is convinced of it. He said he felt that way about my mom, too. But it's still so out of character for him. He's methodical and reasoned in every other aspect of his life."

"There's nothing wrong with letting your heart take the lead now and then."

"My mom's heart led her to leave us. Was that the right thing to do?"

He shrugged. "People grow apart. And it's been my observation that marriage is hard work."

Did that mean he was for it or against it? But she wasn't going to start wondering what Zach's Gibson's views on marriage and happy ever after were. It might keep her awake at night. So she just nodded. "Is that all you wanted to talk about?"

"On that subject, yes. Moving on, I'd like to congratulate the two of us for having made it through a hell of a couple of weeks." He grinned, full wattage this time, and propped one foot on the opposite knee. "A modest celebration is in order, Dr. Layman. Would you care to join me for a drink at the White Pine after we finish here?"

Callie couldn't have been more surprised

if he'd transformed into a bat and flown out of the window as she watched. "A drink?"

"Yes. A beer or a glass of wine, or we can get really wild and crazy and order a margarita. I've been known to drink one or two in my day."

"The clinic doesn't have a policy on after-hours socializing among staff, does it?"

Zach grinned. "Come on, Dr. Layman, are you saying you haven't read the handbook?"

Callie was determined not to let on how surprised she was by the unexpected invitation. They had been finding their footing on a professional level this past week, but socially? *Good morning* and *Good night* and *I see you deadheaded the petunias today. They look good* was about the extent of their conversations. She'd cultivated a pretty decent poker face during her years of medical school. She put it to use now. "I haven't had a chance, but I assume you *have* read the handbook and there's no specific prohibition against it. Am I correct?"

"You are."

"I—" She hesitated, still uncertain it was the smart thing to do.

"Let's consider it a team-building exercise,

then," he continued before she could marshal her arguments against the plan.

"I don't suppose I could object to that." Why not have a drink with him? It was a lovely evening. She had nothing else to do. "Are you sure the White Pine's a good choice, though?"

"If we're lucky, we can snag a table on the porch. Best place in town to watch the sunset."

"Second best," she said automatically. "Number one is our front porch."

"That's another possibility." His eyes darkened slightly, and immediately she imagined moonlight on still waters and the privacy of the shadowed porch of the duplex.

Team-building exercise, remember, she scolded herself. Not a date. "I'll meet you at the White Pine," she said hurriedly. "I have a few errands to run after I leave here. Is six-thirty okay?"

"It's great." He uncoiled from the chair and stood up, forcing her to raise her eyes to meet his. "I'll see you there."

HE WAS PLAYING with fire, Zach decided, staring at himself in the mirror. What had possessed him to invite the lady doc for a drink to celebrate the fact that they'd made it through the workweek without coming to blows? He decided he didn't really want to self-diagnose the impulse. They were just two colleagues unwinding after a busy week. Getting to know each other a little better. Team building. That was all.

He rubbed his hand over his chin, wondering if he should shave. No, she'd just have to take him as he was. He didn't want to be late, and he also didn't want to make too big a deal out of a glass of wine and a little conversation.

It was already a few minutes after six. It would take him ten minutes to walk to the White Pine. No use getting the truck out to drive the short distance; he'd never find a parking space anyway.

He'd meant it when he said he wanted a table on the porch of the bar and grill—in full view of passersby. People seeing them together after clinic hours would reinforce the notion they were a team. A good one, maybe even one that could last a lot longer than the three months Callie had signed up for. And since he was being so incredibly honest with himself, he might as well admit he wanted to be sitting there when she walked up the big, sloping stone steps so he could enjoy knowing she was going to be joining him and no one else. He wanted to be relaxed enough to have let go of the workaday tensions no doctor could avoid, and experience the full force of her smile when she spotted him waiting for her. He wanted her to relax, too, so they could talk without her measuring every word he said or calculating her own responses to fit what she thought his expectations would be. He wanted her to be spontaneous and open, the way some sixth sense told him she would be with a man she trusted and respected.

Maybe more than merely respected.

Zach stared down at the rust stain rimming the drain in the old-fashioned pedestal sink. He'd never had a home, not a real one, and he wanted White Pine Lake to be that elusive place. Over the past few days he'd come to realize he wanted Callie to start thinking the same way. He wanted her to remember that once upon a time she'd planned on returning to White Pine Lake to practice medicine and make it her home—the way he had.

A future that included Callie Layman.

Was that really what he wanted? Or was she just another patient he wanted to help? He was a healer. It was what he did, what he'd been trained to do. It didn't matter that he was a quack when it came to healing himself. He was very good at doing it for others. And Callie Layman needed healing, at least her family did.

He didn't have a family of his own. He'd never had one. Maybe he never would, but he understood that Callie was struggling to find a way to bring together the disparate elements of the one she'd been handed. It was going to be one hell of a job. But despite the differences in their approach to their common goals, where it counted, deep down, he and Callie were more closely aligned than they'd expected.

So he was going to do everything he could to help her achieve her goals: a happy marriage for her father and a happy blended family for herself, whether she recognized that was what she was striving for or not.

He lifted his head and stared at his face in the mirror for a long few seconds.

Just think of her as a patient. That's the answer.

"Liar," he said under his breath. "Man, you'll never learn. When you start lying to your own face in the mirror about why you're interested in a woman, you're already too far gone to save yourself."

CHAPTER SEVEN

"HERE, CALLIE, you take the baby while I go rescue my father-in-law from the clutches of the other three kids." Callie held out her arms automatically as Gerry Forrester Seamann handed her the squirming form of her three-month-old daughter. "Jacob needs his diaper changed, and Grandpa Seamann is not going to appreciate spending the rest of the evening with a big wet spot on his pants." Her friend gave Callie an impish grin perfectly suited to her elfin features, pale skin and fiery-red hair, and bustled off without waiting for a response from Callie.

"How does she manage?" Jen Koslowski asked, dropping into the rickety lawn chair next to Callie. "She's a baby machine. Four kids under six. Two of them in diapers and one still breast feeding. I'd have left Rudy and run away to Paris or Rome by now if it was me. Oh, man," she said, rolling her eyes and clapping her hand over her mouth. "I shouldn't have said that. Forgive me, I forgot about your mom."

"It's okay," Callie said. "It was years ago. We're good now." Jen was from Ohio. She hadn't been born and raised in White Pine Lake. The scandal of Karen running off and leaving Callie and J.R. had happened long before she met and married Rudy.

Callie repositioned the baby in the crook of her arm so that she could see her sweet little face and let her wrap her tiny fist around Callie's finger. "Gerry's always loved dolls. I remember when we were little, she'd bring a whole suitcase of them with her when she came to spend the night. We had to sleep on the floor because there wasn't room for both of us and all of them in my bed, and heaven forbid they had to sleep on the window seat by themselves."

Jen laughed, recovering her poise. "I believe it. She definitely has the mommy gene. I'm exhausted by the end of the day and I've only got two. And they're potty trained and almost civilized." She was a plump, easygoing woman who worked part-time at one of the town's gift shops and managed the bookkeeping and scheduling for Rudy's construction business. She also didn't have an ounce of shyness in her personality. Everyone she met was an instant friend. Her children were middle-school-aged—two boys who at this moment were riding their bicycles up and down the long dock that stretched out through the shallow reed bed in front of Jen and Rudy's home into deeper water. The boys' first couple of trips up and down the narrow wooden planks had brought Callie's heart into her throat but didn't seem to upset their parents or grandparents, so she'd pushed aside visions of greenstick fractures and concussions and tried to enjoy herself. And surprisingly, she had.

She still wasn't certain how her not-a-date quiet drink with Zach on the porch of the White Pine had morphed into a backyard barbecue at Jen and Rudy's, but it had. One minute they were sitting at their small table watching the world pass by, and the next Zach's phone was chirping. Callie had immediately thought it was an emergency or an accident, but it was only Rudy Koslowski.

She'd had no trouble overhearing the conversation because Rudy, like many of White Pine's inhabitants, never knew if his cell-phone calls were coming through loud and clear or were filled with static and barely audible, so he always assumed it was the latter and spoke accordingly.

"I just drove by and saw you two sitting on the porch," he had yelled. "Have you ordered food or are you just having a drink?"

"Just a drink," Zach replied, far more quietly than his friend.

"Great. We want you and Callie to come on down. I thawed a couple of packages of steaks and Jen got inspired and made enough potato salad to feed an army. Gerry and Ron Seamann are coming over. And both sets of our parents and one or two of my guys and their wives. It will be a chance for Callie to meet them and catch up with the rest of us. Join us and we'll have a beer or two to celebrate what a great job Koslowski Construction did on getting the clinic up and running again."

Callie had been a bit dismayed by the out-of-the-blue invitation, but when she'd heard Rudy say he wanted to toast the clinic and his crew, she had to accept. She didn't want to appear ungrateful for all their hard work. "But we don't have anything to take," she said. She may have been away from White Pine Lake for years and years, but she was certain one thing hadn't changed. No one went to dinner at a friend's or neighbor's without bringing something along to share.

"I heard that," Rudy bellowed. "Bring a six-pack of beer and a couple dozen of Mac's cookies and you will be welcomed with open arms."

Zach regarded her before responding, one eyebrow slightly elevated. She nodded, doing her best not to let her discomfort show. She wasn't comfortable with being spontaneous, but she could try.

"It's a deal," Zach said. "We'll be there in half an hour."

"Can I get you anything?" Zach said, pulling her thoughts back into the moment, taking the seat Jen had vacated moments earlier to referee a heated argument between one of her boys and another child over who was going to be in charge of the game of hide-and-seek. The sun was about to go down and the shadows of the big pines that lined the property on two sides had crept out into the yard.

"No thanks. I have everything I want right

here," she said, snuggling the baby under her chin as she gently patted her back. The little one turned her tiny face into Callie's shoulder and nestled against her neck, falling asleep between one breath and the next.

"You're an expert at that," Zach said, gesturing with his hand.

"Babies are the joy of family practice," Callie said, placing a featherlight kiss on Kayla's fuzzy head.

"Gerry's a great mother. It shows. All her kids are happy and well-adjusted."

"Jen and I were talking about Gerry a few minutes ago. She was born to be a mother. It's all she's ever wanted to do. She excels at it."

"You two are old friends."

"We bonded the first day of kindergarten. I was her maid of honor at her wedding and I'm godmother to her second. The one who's standing over there, crying his eyes out because his sister stole his cookie." It was one of the best things about coming home to White Pine Lake. With Gerry and Ron she never felt as if she didn't belong. It didn't matter if Gerry and Callie hadn't seen or talked to each other for six weeks or even six months—they always took up where they had left off, as if they had been apart only a few hours or days at most.

"Those kinds of friendships are hard to come by," he said.

"Are you still in touch with any of your high-school friends?" she asked.

"No," he said. "I attended six high schools in four years. You get moved around a lot in the foster-care system. I didn't make any long-term friendships." It was one of the few details of his life he'd volunteered. She waited for him to say more but he didn't.

"But you made friends in the military." She indicated Rudy, who was bending over the fire ring as he showed his oldest how to stack firewood in a tepee shape.

"Good friends," he said, flicking a mosquito away from his ear with a wave of his hand. "But they're scattered all over the country, busy with their own lives. An email now and then is about all the contact we have these days."

"You could have all the friends you want here in White Pine Lake." A steady stream of people had stopped by their table while they'd been sitting on the porch at the restaurant. He had been at ease and friendly with all of them.

"Yeah," he said. "There are great people in this town."

"I agree."

"You handled yourself pretty well tonight. You didn't let old Ezra Colliflower rattle you with that question about how much money you'd have to be paid to stay on permanently."

She gave a little laugh. "Well, it did startle me," she confessed, "although I suppose I should have been ready for it."

"Does that mean you'd consider it if the committee makes a formal offer?"

The direct question surprised her. Was he asking because he wanted her to stay and make their partnership permanent, or because he didn't want her as his superior? She didn't have the courage, here and now, to ask him which it was.

"I'm not sure," she replied truthfully. Two weeks ago the answer would have been a categorical no. Tonight, here among old and new friends, with a baby in her arms and the sounds of children laughing and boats out on the lake returning to shore for the night, a loon calling eerie and beautiful off in the distance, she wasn't so sure. But would they want her?

"Come on over here closer to the fire, you two," Ron hollered. "If you stay there under the trees, the mosquitoes will eat you alive."

Callie had already draped Kayla's lightweight blanket over the baby's head so she didn't get bitten, but the steady drone of the insects around Callie's own head signaled it wouldn't be long until they found a way to get past her defenses. She stood up as Gerry came toward her, arms outstretched to retrieve her daughter.

"You didn't really answer my question," Zach said quietly, rising when she did.

"Because I can't."

"WELL, YOU'VE FINALLY gotten around to showing your face to your oldest friend, have you?" Mac straightened from inspecting the huge roaster of oven-baked chicken that she had just taken out of the oven. Callie's stomach rumbled, but she fought the temptation to ask for a piece. Callie and the twins were going to Karen's farm later, and her mother would be disappointed if Callie didn't do justice to the lunch she was preparing for them. Still, she'd only had a single slice of toast for breakfast, and that had been hours ago. She'd fully intended to sleep in this morning, but the bell of St. Timothy's calling the faithful to early Mass had awakened her earlier than she planned.

"I could flatter you and say I saved the best for last but we both know that wouldn't work," Callie said, batting her eyelashes. Mac snorted and began transferring pieces of golden-brown chicken from the roaster to a warming pan. "I'm well aware of how much you hate to be interrupted when you're busy." You couldn't let Mac get the upper hand or she ran roughshod over you.

"I'm always busy, but that doesn't stop me from carrying on a conversation. You're the one that flits in and out of here like a dragonfly. Are you going to light a spell this time?"

"I'm lit." She grinned, resting one hip on a stool. "For a little while, anyway, I'm supposed to be bonding with my stepbrother and stepsister today," Callie said. "We're going out to the farm to have lunch with Mom."

Mac raised her steel-gray eyebrows. "Bonding means you take them to a movie or to the water park in Traverse City. I find it hard to believe that woman invited them at all." Mac's words were heavy with suspicion. Callie felt a little stab of guilt. The invitation had been her idea and it was true Karen hadn't been all that enthused.

"Well, she *did* invite them, and even more surprising, Becca agreed to go."

"I hope Karen cooks something they'll eat. None of that hunter-gatherer leaf-and-berry stuff she touts on the internet." Karen's tutorials on everything from carding and spinning to making soap and canning pickles were surprisingly popular, racking up amazing numbers of hits a day. She had attracted several sponsors and was actually making money at the enterprise.

"She promised me the twins would love the meal." Callie recalled the menu of creamed kale and new potatoes Karen had mentioned on her first trip to the farm and wondered if she should wrap up a couple of peanut-butter sandwiches to take along.

Her hesitation must have showed on her face. Mac sniffed. "She *is* planning on twigs and berries, isn't she? I'll fix a little something for the kids, just in case."

Callie smiled her thanks. "You're a treasure, Mac."

"Your mother's sure changed her tune. She couldn't even wait for you to grow up enough to take care of yourself before she hightailed it out of here," Mac grumbled on, shaking a large metal spoon in the air for emphasis. "I can't get my head around the idea of her warming up to the second wife's children."

"Hush, Mac, someone will hear you." Mac didn't have children of her own. She'd arrived on the scene when Callie's grandparents retired to Arizona when Callie was thirteen. Soon after, Callie's aunt and uncle—her father's only sister—and their three children had followed her grandparents to Arizona, and Callie, bereft, had spent even more time with the gruff middle-aged chef. Mac had watched Callie grow up, watched J.R. and Karen's marriage crumble and fall apart. She'd done her best to comfort both Callie and her dad after Karen left, but she had never forgiven the younger woman for abandoning her family. Callie suspected she never would. Most of the time Mac just pretended Karen was a thousand miles away

from White Pine Lake, but now and then she
couldn't help herself and let her acid tongue
get the better of her.

"Not saying anything but the plain truth."

Callie glanced away. One of the summer college kids who made up the waitstaff
and kitchen gofers was prepping vegetables on the far side of the room. Two more
were manning the dishwasher, so there was
enough background noise to make their conversation private. The breakfast crowd had
thinned out and the early lunch crowd hadn't
yet arrived. It was as quiet as the White Pine
kitchen ever got. "What can I do to help you,
Mac?"

"Not a thing. Just making sure the chicken
will be rested and ready for the early lunch
crowd. The Catholics are up at the crack of
dawn and walk through the front doors right
on the dot of eleven-thirty for the baked-
chicken special. Then comes the Method-
ists, and then the slugabeds and the all-night
partiers." Mac raised her eyes to the ceiling.
"May they see the error of their ways, Lord."

"Amen," Callie said, trying not to smile.
"Don't forget the tourists."

"Never do," Mac said. "Pray for them

every night to be fruitful and multiply and keep our four-tops filled, or at least to go home and give us fantastic word of mouth."

"Amen," Callie repeated, grinning irreverently. Tourists were what kept the White Pine in the black eight months out of the year.

"So how was your night out with the handsome Doc Gibson on Friday? Heard you ended up back here after the barbecue at the Koslowskis'."

"You don't miss much around here, do you?"

"When I do it'll be time to hang up my spatula and head for Florida."

"You'd really move to Florida?"

"In a heartbeat. Well, for March and April, anyway. Lousiest weather of the year then."

"We did come in for a nightcap. With Ron and Gerry, Rudy and Jen, and a couple of the guys who work for Rudy. Their wives took their kids home so they'd be ready for church this morning. But I was home and asleep by midnight. Cross my heart. Yesterday I slept in—the first morning since I returned. Then after lunch I drove to Petoskey, got my hair cut, got a manicure and bought myself a bathing suit and some new sunglasses."

"A bathing suit?"

"It's been really hot. I like to swim when the water's warm."

"When was the last time you went swimming in this lake, warm water or no?"

Callie laughed. "You're right. I haven't even bought a new bathing suit in years. But I haven't gone native yet. Ask me that when I show up in a new snowmobile suit." She closed her mouth abruptly. When snowmobile weather rolled around, she would be sailing the Caribbean.

"Since they're singing the Benediction hymn about now, I'll go out on a limb and say you didn't make it to church this morning."

"Next week, I promise."

"I'm off next Sunday, I'll pick you up at nine forty-five. We'll sit together. Now, back to Friday night. You're not giving me the slip that easy. What all'd you do?"

"Rudy's parents offered to babysit so we could all come down and have grown-up talk, that's all. The porch wasn't crowded so we sat outside, talked about sports and the plans for the Labor Day fireworks, and tried not to get eaten alive by mosquitoes."

"Shirley Koslowski is a braver woman than I gave her credit for, for offering to babysit six little ones," Mac said, referring to Rudy's mother. It might seem as if Mac had finished her interrogation, but Callie didn't dare relax. It was probably a feint.

"Well, she did raise five of her own."

"True." Mac eyed Callie from beneath her white paper chef's cap. She only wore the cap on Sundays when she deigned to leave her kitchen and make a couple ceremonial rounds of the dining room. "Sounds as if you enjoyed yourself. Especially being all cozied up to Doc Heartthrob like you were."

Here it comes, Callie thought, *be ready.* "It was a pleasant evening out with a group of friends. That's all." And a man who, if she was honest with herself, she had already started thinking of as more than just a friend.

"You could have evenings like that whenever you wanted if you took the committee's offer and stayed here where you belong."

Callie's mouth flopped open. She shut it with a snap, taking a moment to absorb

Mac's bombshell. "The committee hasn't offered me anything."

"They will," Mac insisted, waving a wooden
spoon she'd been using to stir gravy in a huge
cast-iron skillet that took both hands to lift.
"They've wanted to since the day you graduated from medical school. Your dad wouldn't
let them. He's afraid you'd say yes because
you felt you had to, being a Layman and all.
Sun wouldn't rise in the east every morning if
there wasn't a Layman looking after this town
one way or another."

"Are you sure of that?" Though, now that
she thought about it, J.R. had never in all
these years tried to influence her to practice
in White Pine Lake. Whenever the subject
came up, which it had in the early days but
not so much lately, he had always said he
would leave the decision up to her.

"If you mean have I been eavesdropping
on the committee's doings when they meet in
the small dining room—no. If you mean do I
figure that's what's going on in those meet-
ings—yes. You'd best be ready with your answer when they do ask. Especially if you're
going to be having more of those friendly
nights out with Dr. Heartthrob in tow."

Callie ignored the jibe about Zach. "I will think about it, Mac." How naive had she been? She'd been so exhausted and stressed out for the past year and a half she'd let herself be swept along by events without really examining the repercussions. She'd been willfully blind. Of course, she couldn't just come home, hang out her shingle, start treating friends and neighbors, then pull up stakes in three months and go sailing off to the far corners of the earth without explanation or hard feelings. She needed some advice. Now. "Where's Dad?"

"He's working the front. Marcie Butler's got the bug everyone else had last week." Marcie was one of the year-round waitresses that had been at the White Pine almost as many years as Mac and usually worked the early Sunday shift and took over the kitchen on Mac's one Sunday a month off. "Evidently Ginger's sleeping in this morning. Becca and Brandon are busing tables for your dad. They should be in here any minute. I just sent the eleven o'clock shift out onto the floor." Mac had barely closed her lips on the words when her dad and the twins came through the swinging double doors that led to the dining room.

"Hi, Callie," J.R. said. He was lean and handsome in his green White Pine polo and khakis. It seemed the bar and grill's signature color suited the whole family except for Becca—and herself, Callie thought with a little smile. Pine-green was not in her color palette, either.

"Hi, Dad." She gave him a little wave, hoping she didn't seem as off balance as she felt right now.

"Hi, Callie," Brandon said, bounding up like an eager puppy. "I got tips! Ten dollars!"

"I'm impressed. You must have really hustled."

"We were slammed," Becca said, pulling off her apron and going to the sink to wash her hands. Neither one of the twins were in uniform. Brandon was wearing jeans and a Green Bay Packers T-shirt, and Becca was dressed in white capris and a floaty top in a mixture of blue and taupe that suited her far better than the restaurant's signature color.

"Your dad shared his tips with us. He says the owner never accepts gratuities. That's a fancy word for tips, in case you're wondering."

"Thanks for telling me."

"Don't be stupid, Brandon. She's a doctor and ultrasmart. Besides, she used to work here. She doesn't need to be told what *gratuities* means." Becca leaned her hip against the deep stainless-steel sink, where the big pans were washed, and crossed her arms across her flat chest, distancing herself from the group around the prep table. "We were shorthanded because my mom's sleeping in." Her expression was fiercely disapproving, but Callie sensed fear lurking deep in her blue-gray eyes.

"Do you want me to go check on her?" Callie asked her father as he stood with his hands on Brandon's shoulders. He used to do that with Callie, making her feel special and safe and protected with him standing tall and strong behind her. But she wasn't eleven anymore. She was a grown woman and capable of taking care of herself and making her own life decisions. Still, right now she wished for those long-ago days so she could ask him to tell her what to do with her future.

J.R. shook his head. "She's fine, just couldn't

sleep. The heat's getting to her. I've been meaning to upgrade the air conditioner in our bedroom but haven't had a spare minute." He'd spent a couple evenings working at the clinic, Callie recalled, giving of himself for the betterment of White Pine Lake. The way Zach had done.

The way she had done, too.

"If it doesn't cool off pretty soon, I'm going to sleep in the widow's walk room," Becca said defiantly. "I bet there's always a breeze up there. You went up there a lot when you were living here, didn't you, Callie?"

"I did," Callie agreed, "but I haven't been in years."

Callie had found the small glassed-in room at the top of the building a magical place as a child. She'd spent hours and hours, reading and stargazing and dreaming a young girl's dreams—and crying her eyes out the summer Karen left. But the stairs to the widow's walk room were steep and narrow and warped from years of temperature change and leaks in the roof. With so much maintenance to be done in a building the age of the White Pine, J.R. hadn't gotten around to repairing the room.

"It's hot up there, too," J.R. said with his usual patience. "Not nearly as nice as you imagine. But mostly I don't want either of you going through a rotten floorboard or missing a step and breaking your leg."

"Or worse," Mac said, rolling her eyes. "Okay. That's settled. The boss has spoken. No sneaking into the widow's walk room. Now, listen up! Everyone out of my kitchen. It's 11:17. In ten minutes this place will be crawling with the early bird lunch crowd. Shoo."

"C'mon, guys," Callie said, suddenly nervous as she prepared to head out with her stepsiblings alone. "My mother's expecting us for lunch at noon."

"We're ready. We can still go with Callie, can't we?" Brandon asked J.R.

"That's up to Callie," her father said noncommittally, glancing across the room at her. "Your mother gave her permission." J.R.'s disapproval of Callie's scheme, though, was evident in the furrow drawing his eyebrows together above his hazel eyes. He clearly wasn't in agreement with Ginger in allowing her children to be brought into his ex-wife's orbit. Callie suffered a momentary stab of disloyalty, but she pushed it aside. She was trying to forge her own bonds with the twins, and Karen was her mother; there was no getting around that.

"Yes, she did."

If J.R. thought it through with his usual clearheadedness, he would understand Callie's reasoning. But he wasn't entirely clearheaded when it came to Karen. Callie would have to take this blending business slowly. Still, White Pine Lake was just too small a town to try to keep the twins strangers from their stepfather's ex-wife. Ginger understood that, and despite their differences, Callie appreciated her stepmother's support.

"We really should be going. We don't want to be late." Callie smiled, hoping he could read her mind as he'd seemed to be able to do when she was small.

J.R.'s expression softened as though he indeed knew exactly what she was thinking. He nodded slightly before giving Brandon a little shove. "Get going, then," he said, "and have fun. All of you."

"Thanks, Dad. You go spend some time

with Ginger, okay? It will be good for both of you," Callie urged.

J.R.'s expression lightened a little and he smiled. "I plan to do just that."

Though she wished she could take J.R. aside and beg for his advice on what she should do about staying in White Pine Lake, now was not the time or place. For the moment at least, their roles were reversed. It was her dad who needed someone to take some of the burden from his shoulders. The possibility of her staying in White Pine Lake for longer than she had originally planned could be dealt with later.

CHAPTER EIGHT

CALLIE WATCHED ZACH come up the path from the dock as she rocked lazily on the porch. On the table beside her, Karen's natural citronella candles cast flickering shadows in the darkness. It was a little past ten, but there was enough light out on the water for Zach to dock his boat. He'd been fishing again but he wasn't carrying a stringer, nor had he paused to drop any fish into the wire cage beneath the dock that served as a live well for those awaiting the fillet knife and frying pan. Either the fish hadn't been biting or he hadn't landed any he wanted to keep. He'd used the electric trolling motor to come in off the lake, so there was no sound to disturb the quiet of the summer evening. No wash of waves on the shore. The night was warm, the water still and calm. There was no breeze rustling through the branches of the pine trees next door, only the buzzing of mosquitoes waiting in ambush just beyond the range of the candles' scent.

"Catch anything?" she asked. He was wearing a Detroit Tigers baseball cap and a Ski Michigan T-shirt that portrayed a man wearing a snowmobile suit waterskiing behind a powerboat in a snowstorm with the Sleeping Bear Dunes in the background. Her dad had had a shirt like that when she was a kid. It had always made her laugh when he wore it. Zach's appeared worn and faded enough to be from the same time period.

"There's probably a cave painting in France somewhere of a woman asking her man that same question forty thousand years ago," he said, lifting the baseball cap to run his fingers through his short blond hair. The cut wasn't precisely military but it was certainly one that didn't require much fussing in front of the mirror. Whatever the reason he'd chosen it, the style suited his rugged features and broad-shouldered build.

Callie laughed but her pulse ticked up at the thought of having a man like Zach come home to her each night, to call her own. She'd felt a similar little shiver of longing when she'd held Gerry's baby at the barbecue. She wanted all the things other women did: a husband, children, a home of her own. She just hadn't let herself think about those things too much during medical school. But since she'd been home again, they were more often on her mind. "Well, did you catch anything?"

"Nope. The only things biting tonight were mosquitoes."

She tilted her head to one side, listening. "I can hear them out there in the darkness, waiting for me to put out the candles so they can swoop in when I open the screen door and torment me for the rest of the night."

"And at least a half dozen of them will manage the feat."

"Bloodthirsty beasts." She shivered and hugged herself in mock terror. "I used to call them vampire mosquitoes when I was a kid."

"Rudy calls them Michigan's state bird." He grinned and leaned one hip on the porch railing. "How was your day?"

"Very nice," she said. "Would you care for a glass of wine?" she asked, lifting her own to her lips.

"No, thanks," he said. "I'm not much of a wine drinker."

"I've noticed. Sorry, I don't have any beer. The fridge is too small to keep them both cold at the same time."

"What all did you do today?" he asked, leaning against the porch railing, hands outstretched on either side.

"I spent most of it bonding with my stepsiblings."

"And?" he asked. She couldn't read his expression in the faint light of the candles, but she sensed he might be smiling a little.

"It wasn't a complete failure, considering I took them out to the farm to visit my mother."

Zach whistled through his teeth. "Gutsy move for a first attempt."

"I was nervous, I'll admit," she confessed. He was a good listener. And she knew him well enough now to trust his discretion. It was no wonder his patients thought the world of him. "I can't say that Becca and I are going to be BFFs, but she didn't demand to be returned to town fifteen minutes after we got out there. I doubt she'll admit it, but I think she truly enjoyed watching my mother spin. Karen's spinning wheel is an antique. She found it in a corner of the attic when she moved out to the farm. She says it was a sign from Gaia—the earth goddess, you know—that she was supposed to buy the Angoras. I'm not sure what sign pointed her to the Orpingtons but the omelets she fixed were excellent. Ham and cheese for Brandon and me, fresh tomato and cheese for Becca. She also served creamed kale and new potatoes."

"Yuck." Zach leaned forward enough for the candlelight to bring his handsome features into focus. Callie caught her breath. His expression was comical. It was the exact replica of the one Brandon had made when a spoonful of the creamed kale and potatoes had been put on his plate.

She laughed, pleased that Zach could make fun of himself. She relaxed a little, even though the tingling in her nerve endings remained. "Brandon was a good sport about it. And there was the lure of homemade ice cream for dessert. We made it ourselves, just the two of us. I haven't cranked an ice-cream freezer in years."

"I can't say I ever have. What flavor?" Zach asked, looking interested.

"Vanilla bean."

"Sounds delicious."

"We had all the fixings, too—homemade fudge sauce, homemade wild-strawberry jam, nuts, bananas."

"Stop! You're making me envious. What was Becca doing while you and Brandon were cranking away?"

"Talking to my mother," Callie said. "Surprisingly Mom seemed to enjoy her company and Becca was interested in the spinning, which helped. I think Mom's getting ideas for a blog entry on kids working with fiber."

"How do you know?"

"From the way she watched Becca, the questions she asked."

"Maybe she was just remembering doing those kinds of things with you when you were a kid?"

"She wasn't into that kind of thing when I was young. That all came after she found herself."

"I see." He shoved his hands into his pockets, watching her from slightly narrowed eyes. "Not only were you bonding but maybe getting your first taste of sibling rivalry?"

She laughed. "I guess it might sound that way. I didn't mean it to."

"Or was it regret I heard?" His eyes were

dark, shadowed like the porch, but somehow she understood he was speaking as much of the loneliness of his own childhood as of hers.

"We did a lot of fun things together when I was a kid," she insisted, somewhat defensively. "She was a good mother in her own way." But she didn't want to talk about what had been, only what might be. "She offered to teach Becca to knit, but that was a step too far. Knitting is not cool, as far as Becca is concerned, although she might change her opinion one day. I took pictures. I'll print them off at the clinic tomorrow."

"Uh-oh." Zach waggled his finger at her. "Wouldn't that be unauthorized use of office supplies and equipment?"

"I plan to put money in the petty-cash drawer."

"Yes, boss," he said.

"I most certainly will." Man, there she went sounding all starchy and humorless when everything had been going so well. She felt herself flush and stood up so quickly her chair skidded backward and hit the wall.

"Callie, slow down. Don't get all fired up. I was only teasing." He reached out and closed his hand around her wrist, just as he'd done that first day in the clinic. And just as it had done that first day, his touch threw her off balance.

"I know you were teasing. I overreacted. I seem to have misplaced my sense of humor, probably somewhere around the third year of medical school."

"You've had a lot on your plate."

"That's no excuse. I've been rigid and humorless. That's not the real me. Truly it isn't. Do you know I agreed to this job and never even considered asking where I'd be living? I just showed up at the White Pine and expected my old room to be ready for me. How thoughtless is that?"

"Give yourself a break. You've been under a hell of a lot of stress for years. You're bound to slip up once in a while. And why shouldn't you assume there'd be a place for you at the White Pine until you get settled in? It's your home."

"And I never expected them to offer me the position permanently," she said, brushing aside his excuses for her behavior to get at the heart of her dilemma.

His eyes narrowed. "Have they? Made a formal offer, I mean."

"Well, no. Not yet. But Mac says they're going to, and Mac is never wrong."

"What are you going to say when they do?"

She lowered her eyes to his hand, still clasped lightly but firmly around her wrist. "I don't know," she whispered. "I just don't know."

"Callie." His voice was a low, rough growl, more sensation than sound. It was late; there were no boats on the water to see them outlined by the candles' glow, no one nearby to overhear their words, but he tugged her closer and into the shadows on his side of the porch anyway. "Do you want to stay here? Do you want to make this your home again, not just for now but forever?" His words sent shivers up and down her spine. He smelled of warm skin and cold lake water and a little of seaweed. He smelled just right.

"I want to fit in again. I want to be useful, to be respected. I want to help people, to heal them, and I want to be part of what goes on around me. I want my family to be strong and whole and happy. Is that all too much? Am I capable of all of that? Am I setting myself up to fail?"

"Family is always worth a big risk."

"I hope so. I feel like a hamster on a wheel these days," she said, trying to lighten the mood, to gain a little distance from her problems, from him.

"You've got a 'yours, mine and ours' thing going on that even the folks at Disney would have a hard time finding a happy ever after ending for."

"Don't make fun of me. You don't know how hard it is."

"You're right. I don't have a family. None. Nada. No one. But that doesn't mean I didn't try. Man, how I tried with every foster family they put me with." His face hardened for a moment and his mouth snapped shut. "Sorry, I didn't mean to go off on you like that."

"No, I'm sorry, Zach. I should have never said that. You should have a family of your own, the one you deserve. I hope you do someday."

He didn't move a muscle. His expression didn't change, but he drew her closer. "I do, too. I always have," he said very low.

She swallowed hard to ease the sudden tightness in her throat. She could imagine him young and alone, trying to fit in with strangers, to make it work, to be one of them. Maybe he was right. Maybe she couldn't spin all the separate ends of her family ties together into a long, strong yarn that could be woven into a whole, but she had to make an attempt. "I have to try," she said, low but forcefully. To convince herself as much as him?

He lifted his hand and touched her lips, just a brush of his fingertip, but it felt as if her skin had been seared by fire. "I wouldn't expect anything less of you. You want what's best for everyone. That doesn't always happen, Callie. And that's not your fault. Sometimes you can't make it all come out right. It doesn't mean you're a failure."

Tears blurred her vision. She blinked them away. She didn't want to be this vulnerable. She didn't want her innermost hopes and dreams exposed to a man as perceptive as Zach Gibson.

She sensed what was going to happen next. He was going to kiss her. And dear heaven, she wanted him to even though she knew it would mean too much. "Zach, please—" She laid her hand against his chest, felt his heart beat strong and just a shade too fast beneath her palm. She had meant it to be a barrier, a warding off, but instead it seemed more like a caress.

"Shh—" he said and leaned into her hand.

She couldn't move into his arms but neither could she pull away. It was too late to prevent what was going to happen next.

He lowered his mouth to hers. The kiss was long and sweet and the world tilted just a tiny bit on its axis, and she sensed she would never be quite the same again.

"Zach," she whispered when he lifted his head. It sounded as though she were pleading even to her own ears. This was wrong. He knew exactly what she wanted, and she was too conflicted, too confused. Besides, workplace romances were bad news. They almost always ended badly. She'd seen it happen to friends and colleagues often enough.

"You're right," he said, reading her mind. "It won't happen again. You have my word, but please, don't expect me to say I'm sorry. I'm not." He stared down at her in the near darkness for a long moment, his eyes the same dark blue as the lake before a storm, and then he smiled. "Sleep well. See you in the morning." He touched his lips to her forehead, turned on his heel and left her alone.

CHAPTER NINE

HE HAD SCREWED UP royally. It was Friday again. D-day plus five, and he was still pinned down at the water's edge taking heavy fire. He had thought he'd handled that out-of-nowhere kiss pretty well Sunday night, even though it had shaken him to the soles of his feet. No use denying it. He was falling for her, and it couldn't be happening at a more inopportune moment.

It wasn't that she was his boss. He suspected they could grow into a heck of a medical team with time and trust. But being a team meant staying together. He had no intention of leaving the town he'd come to regard as home, no matter what other opportunities might come his way. But Callie wasn't as certain of her future as he was. He knew, and he suspected she did, too, that long-distant relationships didn't work. So where did that leave them?

Plain and simple, kissing Callie Layman

was playing havoc with his peace of mind and keeping him awake at night. But he'd managed a smile that wasn't a grimace and kept it all as light and casual as humanly possible when he'd left her. He'd even convinced himself it had worked.

He'd been wrong.

She'd been gone when he woke up Monday morning. He couldn't explain how he knew she wasn't there, on the other side of the too-thin wall, but she wasn't. And she'd stayed away as much as possible since, spending her evenings at the White Pine, or out at her mother's place, or doing some shopping in Petoskey and at the town's galleries with Gerry Seamann and even once with Ginger.

It didn't take Sherlock Holmes to figure out what she was up to. He'd spotted her heading out of town toward her mom's place after office hours with a basket of laundry under her arm. He'd glimpsed her climbing the outside stairs to the family quarters above the White Pine as he drove by in his truck. Two watercolors he'd previously noticed hanging in the gallery beside the bar and grill had appeared on her office wall. Since they were a pretty good size, in heavy rustic-style frames, he figured she'd asked her dad to help hang them.

Last night he'd watched from his porch as she and Becca and Brandon had canoed out to the raft to catch the heavenly light show of the Perseid meteor shower. He'd been watching the fire in the sky, too, from the shadows of the porch and saw them sneak down to the dock, flashlights bobbing, the twins arguing as usual, Callie shushing them with a silvery giggle that lifted the hairs on his arms and made him long to feel her lips beneath his again.

He'd been happy to see her getting along so well with the twins, but their little expedition gave rise to darker musings. Had that been her first trip to the raft? Or had she been out there before, maybe with her old high-school boyfriend or a lost love from college?

He didn't know where she was every hour of the night when she wasn't at the clinic. He just knew where she wasn't—home.

In the office, it wasn't a lot different. She wasn't cold or unfriendly; she simply avoided him as much as humanly possible. Bonnie and Leola noticed the lengths Callie went to avoid being alone with him, though he was pretty sure none of the patients did.

And there had been a lot of patients over the past week. It was the time of year for high-school athletic physicals, so members of the football, basketball and volleyball teams, as well as cross-country runners, had Callie and Zach hustling to stay on schedule. If anyone caught them together in the hallway or jotting patient notes at the reception area, she always had something to say to him, a little joke to pass on or small talk, the kind strangers on a bus might share, otherwise he got the silent treatment. As for her patients, she was charm personified. She was working very hard at gaining the respect of the citizens of White Pine Lake, and she was doing an excellent job of it.

But did that mean she'd decided to stay when the position was officially offered, as he was convinced it would be? Did it mean he had a chance with her?

On that thought, her laughter drifted down the hall. He'd been standing in the reception area, reading lab reports. Bonnie was with his next patient, the White Pine High School's Loggers quarterback, taking his vi-

tals and medical history. Leola was checking the appointment log for someone she was
talking to on the phone. She hadn't seemed
to notice the strain beneath Callie's soft, rich
laughter. But he did; and he realized he was
going to have a lot of explaining to do. Soon.

Callie had just ushered an elderly couple
in their late seventies out of one of the exam
rooms. Eno and Miriam Amstutz had lived
on a small farm outside White Pine Lake
since Eno had returned from Korea with a
bright-eyed, soft-spoken USO girl from Al-
abama on his arm.

"If you call him up in Arizona, your
grandfather will tell you I'm speaking the
gospel truth," Eno was saying to her. "No
one, including your grandfather old Jack
Richard, would believe my Southern belle
would last through that first bad winter."

"But I did," Miriam said with a sad, sweet
smile that faltered a little and echoed the sorrow he saw lurking in Callie's eyes. "Even
though there was snow up to the eaves and
no indoor plumbing and me with a baby on
the way."

"And she's stuck it through sixty more
since then," Eno said with pride.

"I tried to call my grandparents yesterday," Callie said, her tone bright, the distress she must be experiencing completely under control. "I got their answering machine. I forgot their euchre club meets on Thursdays."

"Old J.R.'s been playing euchre since he was a boy. He's hard to beat, especially when he teams up with your grandma."

"I'm afraid I take after my mother when it comes to playing cards. The Layman card-sharp gene was left out of my DNA," Callie said with a grin.

He should have talked to her about Eno and Miriam before this. He had figured they would want to be assigned to Callie's care, but somehow he and Callie hadn't discussed the couple that morning at the duplex, and that was his fault, too.

Eno and Callie's grandfather had been friends for nearly seventy years. Their children had grown up with Callie's father and her aunt, he'd learned from the couple. Callie had probably gone to school with one or two of their many grandchildren. It was the sort of intertwining of generations and families you found in small towns everywhere.

And Callie had just discovered Eno was dying. And very soon; most likely he would not be alive to celebrate another Christmas with his beloved Miriam and their large family.

Zach didn't have to have been present in the exam room to guess what had happened. Callie would have opened the old man's chart and glanced over the most recent blood-test results, and her brain would have given her the diagnosis in a matter of seconds: a chronic form of leukemia, caused by a gradual shutting down of the bone marrow.

It would have taken longer for her heart to come to grips with the evidence before her. So she would have bought herself a little breathing room by leafing through the past few months of test results, all the while aware two sets of wise old eyes were following her every move. And in Miriam's eyes, a silent plea for Callie to tell her something other than what they all knew to be the truth. Then she would have asked Eno all the questions Zach himself had asked the old man every two weeks for the past several months: How was he sleeping, how was he eating, was he in pain? Eno's answers were always the same: good, good, how could he not be eating with the best cook in White Pine Lake fixing his meals and no, he was not in pain. If his red-cell count was too low, Zach would make arrangements for an appointment with the specialist in Petoskey for a blood transfusion. If the numbers were stable, Zach would send him home to sit on his porch and play with his dogs and his great-grandchildren for a few more weeks or months.

Through the door, Zach could see Eno leaning against the counter. He was a tall, stooped man with the telltale bruising and pale skin that telegraphed his illness to an educated observer. "When are your grandparents coming back this way?" he asked as Callie approached.

"In the fall." Callie smiled, but Zach noticed the strain was beginning to wear on her. "He's planning on being home for Thanksgiving and the opening of deer season. It depends on Grandma's arthritis, though. She's not used to the cold weather anymore."

"We hope Evelyn's well enough to travel," Miriam said, lifting her chin as if defying anyone to contradict her. "We're anxious to have them home again. Aren't we, Eno?"

"Yes, dear," he said, patting her shoulder. She shifted a few inches closer, her hand lightly touching his arm. "We're always happy to see Jack and Evelyn. It's like old times when they're back in town."

"Yes, and you two can remember the days when you were randy young bucks out chasing all the pretty girls in town," Miriam teased.

"Those days ended for both of us the day we met the loves of our life." Eno smiled down at her and in his eyes he obviously still saw the beautiful young Southern belle he'd fallen in love with so many years earlier.

"Save your breath, Eno. I'm too old to fall for that sweet talk at my age." But she blushed as though she was still nineteen and ready to fall in love.

"You come along to visit, too, when Jack Richard and Evelyn come out to the farm," she said to Callie. "Promise?"

"I wouldn't miss it," Callie said.

"We'll see you around," Eno said, then, noticing Zach, he lifted his hand in a half wave. "You, too, Doc."

"Take it easy, Eno." Zach gave the old man a two-fingered salute.

"Remember you have blood work scheduled first thing Tuesday morning, Eno," Leola said, handing Miriam an appointment card. "Don't forget or I'll have to come out to the farm to get you," she teased, but there was strain in her voice, as well.

"She never lets me forget," Eno groused but the look he gave his wife was filled with close to six decades of love and respect. "She started bossing me around two hours after we met."

"And I intend to keep doing just that as long as the good Lord's willing." She took his hand and they walked slowly across the reception area to the exit, nodding and speaking to everyone on the way, pausing long enough to admire Gerry Seamann and the baby, who had just arrived for a vaccination. A minute later Eno pushed open the glass doors and let Miriam precede him out into the warm August afternoon. Everyone was quiet a moment, watching them walk down the wooden ramp to their car, all of the staff aware it could be the last time they saw them together this way.

"Oh, dear," Leola said, her eyes darting between Callie and Zach. "I—" But she didn't finish what she'd been going to say, as Gerry arrived at the reception window to sign herself and the baby in for their appointment.

Callie's face was a mask of studied calm. It was the expression every medical student achieved early on in their career to hide their true emotions. She avoided Zach after one quick, icy moment of eye contact. "I'll be in my office, Leola," she said. "Tell Gerry I'll be with her in just a minute or two."

SHE WOULD NOT CRY. She had no choice. She had patients waiting and she couldn't have red, swollen eyes. Gerry, surely, would know something was wrong. Then she would ask why Callie was upset. How could she reveal to her friend that Zach Gibson was deliberately trying to sabotage her career?

What else could it be, after all? Why else wouldn't he have informed her of Eno's prognosis? Otherwise, why wouldn't he have officially handed over the older couple's care to her that Friday morning at the duplex and not blindsided her this way?

She had certainly been mistaken in her judgment—and admiration—of the man.

Had he been plotting this betrayal the night he kissed her? Did he think so little of her?

She didn't have long to nurse her indignation and try to ignore the ache in the region of her heart. She should have figured he wouldn't let her alone. He didn't even bother to knock, just opened the door and walked in.

"Callie, we need to talk."

She stood at the window with her back to him. It was a warm, humid day with the threat of thunderstorms predicted for late evening and throughout the night. The windows were shut and the air-conditioning turned on, so she couldn't feel the humid breeze that stirred the tops of the trees or hear the katydids chirping in the tall grass. "I ought to make you call me Dr. Layman," she said. She was ashamed of the pettiness of the demand the moment it left her lips, but she was too upset to apologize immediately. She crossed her arms under her breasts and continued to stare out at the grass in the meadow that was bright with stalks of goldenrod and purple wild aster. It was the middle of August now, and allergy season was in full swing.

"As you wish. We need to talk, Dr. Layman," he said.

She whirled away from the window. "Was that some kind of test?" she asked, hoping the anger would keep her tears at bay. "Did you want to observe how I'd react to that kind of traumatic situation—learning a man I consider my second grandfather is dying without a hint of warning?"

"I didn't realize you were that close to him."

"Well, I am. I love them both."

"It was a slipup on my part. I apologize, sincerely. You're not the only one who's an outsider. I haven't spent my whole life in this town. I'm doing the best I can to figure all the interconnections out."

"Someone should have told me he was ill."

"Eno doesn't want it all over town that he's dying. He's a proud man. I couldn't go against his wishes."

"Still—"

"I would have thought your father would tell you."

"I... He's never said a word." She fell silent a moment, considering. "I'm not sure he knows."

"I meant to bring up Eno's case that Friday, but it slipped my mind. Eno wasn't even supposed to be in here today. His regular appointment isn't scheduled until the first of next week."

"It's my fault," Bonnie cut in.

Zach and Callie had been standing an arm's length apart, glaring at each other. Now they swiveled their heads as though they were two puppets controlled by the same pair of hands. Bonnie stood in the open doorway, her dark eyes bleak, her expression filled with remorse. "Miriam called this morning to ask if there was an opening this afternoon. They want to get away for a couple of days. Go visit their daughter in Rogers City. She said Eno wanted to cancel his appointment altogether, but that made Miriam nervous, so he agreed to come in today if we could work him in." She held out her hand. "I'm sorry. Zach, you didn't have an opening and they said they would be happy to see Dr. Layman. Leola was busy on the other line. I just penciled him in," the nurse said apologetically. She used the formal title Callie had demanded of Zach, a measure of the nurse's distress. "I had no idea you were unaware of

Eno's diagnosis, Dr. Layman. I…I thought you must know, your family being so close to the Amstutzes and all."

Bonnie was only repeating the same point Zach had made. J.R. would have warned her if he himself had known. "It's okay, Bonnie. It's just a shock finding out this way, that's all."

"I'm sorry, Zach," Bonnie said. "I should have come to one of you right away. It's just been so busy with the high-school physicals all scheduled this week. I was proud of myself for being able to squeeze Eno in."

"It's fine, Bonnie. We're bound to have some miscommunication now and then."

Callie nodded her agreement to Zach's remark. After all, Bonnie was only following office procedures, doing her best to accommodate patients in a timely manner. "He's right. No harm done."

"You're sure?" Bonnie's still sounded as if she expected to be fired on the spot even after two decades of exemplary service.

"I'm sure."

"It won't happen again, Dr. Layman."

"I prefer Dr. Callie," she said with a smile. The peace offering was accepted. "I put

Gerry Seamann and the baby in exam room two."

"I'll be there as quickly as I can."

Bonnie closed the door and left her alone with her PA once more.

"I owe you an apology," Callie said through stiff lips.

"For the 'call me Dr. Layman' crack?" he asked. He had relaxed slightly but it was obvious he was still angry.

"For accusing you of trying to make me look bad. That was unforgiveable."

"Yes," he said. "It was."

"You're not going to make this easy, are you?" She took a couple of steps closer but kept the corner of her desk between them. She rested one hand on the surface, shoved the other into the pocket of her lab coat. "This is exactly why I didn't want to practice in White Pine Lake."

"Dying is a part of life."

"Yes, but when you care for someone, you don't always make the best decisions. You open yourself up to an inevitable failure."

"You might not. But then again you probably will. How would you counsel Eno if he wasn't a family friend?"

"Is this a test?"

"It's a question, that's all. Are you afraid to answer it?"

"I would tell him he should continue treatments only as long as he feels they are worth it. If and when he is ready to let go we…I…will do everything in my power to make sure he's comfortable."

"Which is exactly the conversation I had with him three months ago. Eno has had a good, long life. He's not ready to stop treatments just yet, but when the time comes, he will be at peace. You passed the test."

She sighed. "Did I? I should have been prepared for something like this. I've known these people all my life. It was bound to happen sooner or later." The shock of believing she'd been betrayed by Zach had faded, but the strength of her reaction left her vulnerable and off balance.

"It's real. It's life. It happens no matter what we do, no matter how well prepared we are." He lifted his hand as though he might touch her cheek, then stopped himself and curled his fingers around the bell of the stethoscope hanging from his neck, as she'd seen him do so often. But she wished he had finished the movement, longed to feel his comforting touch. "I hope your practice is a long and successful one, but I also hope you never become distanced enough from the rest of humanity to deny your own pain."

Burning out, just going through the motions, treating only the symptoms and not the whole person—it was a fate suffered by too many physicians. They both knew it was a real risk in their chosen specialty and needed to be watched for and guarded against.

Callie took a deep breath, willing herself back to calm. "I truly am sorry for what I said. I know you wouldn't do anything so underhanded and unprofessional. It seems I'm always apologizing." This time *she* was the one who had to restrain herself from reaching out to touch him, to connect as she apologized. It worried her, this sudden urge to be so close. She had been steeling herself from it ever since the night he'd kissed her, but her defenses were rapidly weakening.

"Apology accepted." Their eyes caught and held. She might have misjudged his motives toward her a few minutes ago, but physically she was beginning to be able to read him much better. He wanted to touch her, too, and was working to control himself. They were playing with fire, had been for days. It was why she had spent so many hours away from the tiny duplex—to remove herself from temptation.

"I'd better go," she said, though she didn't move. He was just on the other side of her desk, blocking her path to the door. "Gerry and the baby are waiting for me."

He moved out of her way, but he didn't free her gaze . "You'll handle the cases like Eno's just fine if you stay on in White Pine Lake. No one ever said it would be easy or that you'd be able to cure everyone, but it's worth it, what we do."

"I know."

"Don't ever let yourself forget it." He turned on his heel and left.

CHAPTER TEN

THE STORMS that had threatened all afternoon came in the night. Callie had been dozing off and on but the thunder and lightning finally became too heavy to ignore. She glanced at the bedside clock, a battery-operated travel clock she'd had for years. White Pine Lake suffered a lot of power interruptions for all kinds of reasons, from squirrels and birds in the wires, to falling tree branches and high winds. Some of them lasted for only a few seconds, others for several hours, but all of them played havoc with digital clocks. She hated waking to a set of blinking numerals that bore no relation to the actual hour of the day or night.

She squinted at the luminous dial. Not quite 3:00 a.m. She sat up. No use trying to sleep. Even with the door to her tiny bedroom closed, the storm couldn't be shut out. She got out of bed and put on her robe, though she couldn't find her slippers. The wooden floor was cool on her bare feet as she stood up and went to the kitchen sink for a glass of water. She was awake. She might as well stay up and watch the light show. Years ago, if Gerry or another of her girlfriends had been sleeping over, they might have snuck up into the widow's walk, or if she was alone in her room, she would have wrapped herself in a blanket and climbed onto her narrow window seat to watch the dark clouds and sheets of wind and rain move in off the lake. She wondered if Becca might do the same thing tonight.

If it didn't stop raining soon, tomorrow's expedition to pick market vegetables from Karen's garden with the twins wouldn't be pleasant. The project had been conceived when she had run into Ginger and her children at Kilroy's Ice Cream Parlor a block down the street from the White Pine. Visiting the ice-cream parlor had been one more attempt to spend as much time as possible away from the cabin, away from Zach. It had been another very long week. They had sat on the elevated deck of the former general store that still retained much of its rustic charm, from high tin ceilings to whitewashed bead-board paneling and wide-planked polished wood floors. From the deck they could look out over the lake, where the storm clouds had been beginning to pile up over the dunes. Becca and Brandon had had double-scoop cones, Brandon's bubblegum flavored and bright blue, Becca's chocolate, filled with peanuts and caramel, with the not-so-appetizing name of "Moose Tracks." Callie ordered a single dip of her favorite, black walnut in a dish, while Ginger settled for a glass of fresh lemonade.

"The baby's taking up all the space in her stomach," Brandon said, running his tongue around the top of the cone to catch the drips. "It's like a little alien, sucking up all the food she eats so it can grow big enough to split her stomach and get out." He raised the arm not holding his cone and waved it over his head while making a terrible grimace.

"Brandon, careful of your cone," Ginger said, sipping lemonade. She looked tired but not as strained and anxious as she had the day Callie and Zach had spoken with her at the clinic. Callie suspected her father had insisted Ginger keep to the reduced work schedule and increased rest breaks Zach had

prescribed for her. She would also be seeing the obstetrician in Petoskey early the
next week. Ginger was close to her due date
now and very big. Her blood pressure had
remained within normal levels, though—
information Ginger had offered to Callie
herself, and Callie was cautiously optimistic that her stepmother could carry the baby
to term and deliver him or her safely without further complications.

"Brandon, stop being gross," Becca said
disgustedly. "That's not how babies are
born." Callie held her breath, wondering
just how involved the subject was going to
get. For the moment they were alone on the
deck, but it was Friday evening and business
would be picking up soon as tourists and locals both came to enjoy an after-dinner treat.

Was Ginger the kind of mother who informed her children in vivid detail of all
kinds of biological processes they might
not be emotionally equipped to deal with at
eleven? Or was she the kind that would cling
to the storybook fantasies of finding babies
under cabbage leaves or delivered by a giant
stork in a top hat, until one day she would

discover in dismay they had already figured out much of it for themselves?

"Sometimes it *does* feel the way Brandon described it when the baby is moving around a lot," she admitted, laughing a little as she regarded her son with a mixture of exasperation and affection. "But that is not how babies grow or how they're born."

"The baby gets nourishment from Mom's blood. I told you that, dummy. There's a cord attached to her stomach and the baby's. When the baby comes out, they cut it," Becca said with all the authority of her fifteen minutes' seniority.

"And that's how you get a belly button." Brandon smirked. "I watched the same video you did in health class." Callie relaxed a little. The White Pine school system was fairly conservative in its curriculum. Reproductive lectures for fifth graders were pretty low-key.

"If you want we can discuss it later," Ginger said, appearing unalarmed by the prospect, "but not now when Callie is trying to eat her ice cream."

Ginger was a good mother. Her little brother

or sister would be well loved and well taken care of by both his or her parents.

"Thank you," Callie said faintly.

"I don't want to talk about it at all. It's gross," Becca said. "I don't want to have anything to do with it." She gave her mother a defiant stare and then bent her head to her cone.

Ginger closed her eyes for a moment as if gathering her patience. Blissfully unaware of the tension between his twin and their mother, Brandon kept right on talking. "I wouldn't mind a baby brother who was an alien," he mumbled around the edge of his ice-cream cone. "It would be better than another sister."

Becca stuck out her tongue but didn't dignify the remark with a response.

A family of tourists three generations strong came out the door of the ice-cream parlor just then, their hands full of treats, and made their way out to the deck. They arranged themselves at a table behind where Callie and the others were sitting, and the smallest of the trio of children promptly dropped his ice cream onto the floor and began to wail. By the time the ice-cream cone had been replaced and the commotion behind them had died down, the subject of where babies came from had blessedly been forgotten.

A long, low roll of thunder came from far out on the lake. "Not much chance of a sunset tonight. The clouds are thickening up too quickly." Callie followed her step-mother's gaze. Off in the distance, huge cumulus clouds towered over the dunes, their whipped-cream tops and dark underbellies reflected in the glassy surface of the lake. The sun had already disappeared into the mass, and only stray orange-red rays broke out here and there to gild one of the big thunderheads with coppery highlights.

"If it rains enough I won't have to water the flowers tomorrow," Callie said, taking a last bite of her ice cream.

"We've missed you this week."

"Fall sports physicals," Callie said. "We've been busy."

"It's hard to believe school starts in less than two weeks. The kids are coming with me to Petoskey to shop for school clothes and shoes. It is impossible to keep them in shoes."

"Brandon ruins his by dragging his feet as he rides his bike down the hill. I keep telling him not to do it but he won't listen," Becca scolded. "I'm just outgrowing mine." She regarded her feet with a scowl as if willing them to stay small.

"Sorry, honey. You come from a long line of women with big feet," Ginger sympathized.

"Ugh. Don't talk about school." Brandon shoved the last inch of his ice-cream cone into his mouth and chewed noisily. "I'm still hungry."

"You can't possibly be. You had two hamburgers, French fries and a salad not two hours ago."

"I'm still hungry." He folded his arms over his chest.

"Brandon," Ginger said warningly. He uncrossed his arms. "You can have some carrot sticks when we get home but no more ice cream."

"I'm not hungry for carrots," he muttered under his breath, "unless I can dip them in ranch dressing."

Ginger rolled her eyes and sighed. Callie repressed a smile. She was enjoying herself with Ginger and the twins; something she wouldn't have believed possible a month earlier.

"Hey, there's Karen," Brandon said, pointing to the street below the elevated deck.

Sure enough her mother was wheeling her vintage Schwinn Corvette with its oversize whitewall tires and big wire basket to a stop in front of the ice-cream parlor. Karen owned a Volkswagen Beetle but she seldom drove it during the summer months, preferring the bike. Karen disappeared from view for a moment while she parked her bike and then mounted the steps to where they were sitting. "Hello, everyone," she said. She was wearing heavy shoes, denim capris and a loose white peasant shirt with the sleeves rolled to below her elbows. She looked cool despite what must have been a warm ride in from the farm.

The temperature had reached into the eighties during the afternoon and the humidity was high enough to make it uncomfortable to sit outside. A floppy straw hat, which served to protect Karen's long, braided hair from road dust, was tied under her chin with a loosely woven rainbow-striped scarf. She took off the hat as she walked toward them, dangling it and the scarf from her fingertips.

"What brings you to town this late in the day?" Callie asked.

"Actually, I'm trying to find someone to help me harvest my tomatoes and cucumbers," she said, leaning against the waist-high railing that protected patrons from the eight-foot drop to the sidewalk. "I have a stand reserved at the farmer's market for this coming Sunday, as well as keeping my little stand at the end of my lane supplied. I can usually count on the farmer next door sending one of his sons over to help, but they're busy haying and he can't spare any of them."

"I'm not busy Saturday," Callie offered, she hoped not too grudgingly. "I'll come help you."

"I'll do it," Brandon said eagerly, raising his hand. "I'm saving up for the new edition of 'Zombie Wars' for my PlayStation. It's gonna be awesome. It's coming out real soon."

"I'll come, too," Becca said, surprisingly. "I'd like to see the goats again. I'll help pick tomatoes and maybe we can do some more carding if you have any fiber ready."

Karen looked slightly taken aback, then shrugged. "Why not? But only if it's okay with your mother."

"Are you guys sure?" Ginger cautioned. "It isn't as easy as it sounds. You have to know which vegetables are ripe enough to pick and be careful not to bruise them."

"We had never bused tables, either, but now Mac says I'm one of the best she's ever worked with," Brandon boasted.

"It will be hot if you don't start early in the morning. And you both like to sleep in on Saturday."

"Yes, the earlier we start the better," Karen agreed. "And you should wear old clothes. It might be muddy."

"I'll get up without you having to keep calling me," Brandon promised his mother. "Is it okay?"

Ginger seemed conflicted, as if her agreeing to the twins spending time with J.R.'s ex might be getting a little out of control. Callie felt a pang of guilt. She had set this in motion when she'd taken the children out to the farm in the first place. Once more she was reminded that good intentions had all kinds of unforeseen consequences. Introducing

Karen into the weaving of her new family was producing a very complicated pattern.

Callie gave her stepmother a slightly apologetic glance. "Is it okay with you, Ginger? I'd be glad to take them." Visions of a quiet Saturday spent sleeping in and maybe driving into the park to hike one of the dune trails was replaced with visions of washing garden dirt off bushels of tomatoes and cukes before hauling them into town in her Jeep. But it would also guarantee she wouldn't have to keep looking over her shoulder to avoid being alone with Zach at the cottage all the next day.

"If Callie's going to be there, I guess it will be okay." Ginger said, giving in with grace. Callie smiled her thanks and Ginger smiled back. Then she looked sternly from one child to another. "You have agreed to do this job for Callie's mom. That means you will do it, understand? You have both given your word. It is important to keep it. You are not to start whining and complaining if it isn't as much fun as you both imagine it's going to be."

"We'll do it," Brandon said. "Won't we, Becca?"

"We always finish our jobs at the White Pine. We'll do a good job for Karen, too."

"All right, then." Ginger smiled, although it didn't quite reach her eyes. "Karen, I guess you have yourself a pair of vegetable pickers."

Karen leaned forward and shook hands with both children. "It's settled, then. Don't worry about feeding them breakfast," she said to Ginger. "I'll make oatmeal and blueberry muffins." Brandon had wrinkled up his nose at the mention of oatmeal but brightened again when the words *blueberry muffins* were added. "I'd better be getting home. It's going to be dark earlier than usual tonight because of the clouds. Goodbye," she said and started down the steps of the deck… just as J.R. started up them.

Beside Callie, Ginger tensed. Becca was gathering up their garbage to drop it in the trash receptacle disguised as a rain barrel and Brandon was hanging over the railing, having spied something of interest in the massed hostas hiding the foundation. They didn't notice the quick look of distress that crossed their mother's expressive features as she watched J.R. and Karen exchange stilted greetings. But Callie did. Again a spurt of anxiety assailed Callie. Was she doing the right thing attempting to build bridges between her two families?

Karen continued down the steps to her bicycle, while J.R. came toward them with long strides, waving a greeting through the parlor's big plateglass windows to people he recognized inside. He wasn't smiling and there was a furrow between his eyebrows, but when he spoke his tone was jovial. "Hey, I wondered where everyone had gotten to."

"I told Mac we were coming here for ice cream," Ginger responded. "We met Callie at the counter and she joined us."

J.R. gave Callie a quick smile. "Hey, sweetheart. I've missed you around the White Pine this week."

"Swamped at the office," she said, returning his smile and experiencing a surge of nostalgia for the childhood nickname he seldom used anymore. If the new baby was a girl, would he call her *sweetheart,* too? Callie hoped so, and hoped she wouldn't be jealous when he did. She cupped her chin in her palm and thought how childish and silly that would sound if she said it aloud, but she suspected there would be a tiny pang the first time it happened anyway.

J.R. put his hand on Ginger's shoulder. "Mac passed on your message. It's quieter than usual in the taproom, so I decided to take a break and stretch my legs. I can't be gone long enough for ice cream, but I thought I'd walk home with you."

"I'd like that," Ginger said, smiling up into his eyes. "Ready, kids?" She rose heavily to her feet. J.R. put his hand under her elbow and helped her stand.

"I'm going to bed early so I can be really rested to pick tomatoes at Karen's tomorrow," Brandon said.

"Yeah, I bet you will." Becca rolled her eyes.

"Walk. Don't run," Ginger said automatically. Only she wasn't watching her son, but J.R. Brandon didn't run but he did power walk, arms pumping, across the deck and down the steps. Becca followed in a more dignified manner.

"Is it okay if we walk ahead?" she asked. "I want to get started on the new *Crystal World* book. It came from Amazon today and I can't wait to read it." Crystal World was a planet inhabited by gentle fairylike humans. They had formed a reluctant partnership with a warrior clan and their intelligent dragon allies to battle alien invaders who wished to take over their beautiful, unspoiled world. Becca had told Callie and Karen all about the books the day they carded wool and watched Karen spin it into yarn. One of the heroes of the series was a warrior prince, naturally—the very one in the poster in Becca's bedroom Callie had noticed resembled Zach to a startling degree.

"Becca, remind your brother to watch for traffic," Ginger cautioned. "You know how tourists are, gawking at the lake and the shops and not watching out for kids walking."

"We'll be careful." She didn't start running until she hit the last step and in fifty feet had caught up with her brother.

"What's this about going out to Karen's farm?" J.R said in a low voice. The deck was filling up. Customers were waiting in a line that now stretched outside the shop. Callie, Ginger and J.R. would have to walk single file to exit the deck.

"She hired the kids to pick garden vegetables tomorrow," Ginger explained. "I told them they could go. It will be a learning experience for them. They should understand that food just doesn't get off-loaded from a truck or dropped onto the grocery shelves already wrapped in plastic and ready to eat."

"But we agreed they shouldn't spend a lot of time at Karen's farm." J.R. grimaced. "I'm sorry, Callie."

She had stood up when Ginger had. "It's all right, Dad. I know it's awkward. But the kids really did enjoy themselves."

"It's helping them bond with Callie," Ginger said more firmly than Callie had ever heard her speak to her husband. "That's why I've agreed to it. It's my decision—"

"They're your kids," he finished for her. His face set.

Callie could see the remark hurt but Ginger didn't relent. She raised her chin a tiny bit. "That's not what I was going to say, J.R. I realize you are just trying to protect them from getting hurt and I love you for it. But you are right. They are my kids." Their eyes held for a long moment before J.R. nodded.

"I don't want them to be disappointed by Karen's self-centeredness like Callie was."

J.R. was fiercely loyal and protective of those he loved and cherished. He would lay down his life for any and all of them.

"I know, J.R.," Ginger said softly. Callie saw the tension slowly drain away from her body. "You want what's best for them. But she is Callie's mother. She is an important part of Callie's life *and* our lives, whether we're happy about it or not. I want to give her the benefit of the doubt, at least this once."

"Okay," he said with a hint of a smile, "as long as *I* don't have to deal with her." Callie stifled a sigh. Those big Norman Rockwell painting-type family Thanksgivings she'd always dreamed about were probably not going to happen with her extended family anytime soon.

"The twins will be ready at seven for you to pick them up," Ginger assured Callie.

Callie raised her hand in a small gesture of regret. "Dad, I'm sorry. None of this is Ginger's fault. I set this all in motion. She's just trying to get along with all of us."

"I understand that. I'm sorry I let it get to me. I guess I'm not objective when it comes to your mom even after all these years. I remember all the ways she disappointed you as a kid. I don't want her doing the same thing to the twins."

"That was a long time ago." She wanted to reassure him her mother's self-centeredness hadn't hurt her, but it had and they both knew it. "She's changed."

"Has she? I'm not so sure," he said, but more in sorrow than in anger.

And now, after all of that, she and the twins might not even go to Karen's. Callie put down her empty glass and wandered into the main room of the cabin to stare out the window at the storm. It was raining so hard the lights of the marina, only a quarter of a mile away, weren't visible, but she was looking more inward than outward anyway. It had been a rough day, a whole series of rough days since her confrontation with Zach. She'd been pulled in so many directions these past few weeks.

Intellectually she understood as well as anyone that life was a complicated business, but that didn't make it any easier when it involved people close to her heart. But as Zach had said, sometimes she couldn't make everything right, heal every condition and bring people together, no matter how hard she tried. The most difficult part was to keep from feeling as though she had failed them all. Especially Zach.

She crossed her arms beneath her breasts and shivered in the chill darkness. She might as well go back to bed. Nothing was going to get solved tonight. Tomorrow would come soon enough.

But she stayed where she was. The storm demanded her attention. Lightning flickered almost continuously across a sky as black as spilled ink. Thunder rumbled in long timpani rolls that never seemed to end. The wind lashed waves onto the narrow sand beach, their white crests slightly luminous in the darkness. Zach's small boat bucked at its anchor but the ropes holding it were strong and appeared to be riding out the storm. She couldn't make out the raft farther out on the lake where she and the twins had watched the meteor shower only a week before, but it had survived many storms over the years and would probably be okay. Rain drove against the windows. She should feel cozy and safe, watching from her snug sanctuary as the rain pinged on the steel roof and splattered against the windows—but she didn't.

She felt alone and a little sad with a steadily increasing sense of foreboding far out of proportion to her worries about her family; she couldn't shake it, but neither could she identify its cause.

Almost on the thought, the screen door on Zach's side of the duplex slammed open, banging against the stone wall with the force of a gunshot. Startled, Callie put a hand to her throat. What had happened? Had the door become unlatched somehow, caught by the storm's wind? She waited a moment, staring hard into the darkness beyond her window, working to get her pulse and heartbeat under control. Surely Zach couldn't have slept through a noise like that. The door continued to bang against the lightweight wooden frame as it was battered against the building again and again by the gusting wind. She knew he was home. His truck was parked beside her Jeep behind the cottage. Should she find her rain jacket and check on him? At least close the swinging door? How could Zach not hear it and come to investigate the source of the noise?

Her anxiety level ratcheted up. Something must be wrong. No one, no matter how sound a sleeper they were, could remain unaware of such a racket. More lightning shimmered across the sky, striking somewhere out on the lake, throwing everything outside her window into vivid relief. That was when she noticed him. Zach was on his knees with his hands curled around the porch railing, head lifted to the cold rain.

"Zach?" Raincoat forgotten, Callie was outside in an instant, hanging on to her own screen door with both hands as the wind tried to take it also. She slammed it shut and held on to the wildly swaying rocking chair to catch her balance.

Zach remained where he was as the rain poured off the eaves and blew onto the porch in silvery sheets. He was wearing only a T-shirt and sweats and he was already soaked to the skin by the deluge. She dropped to her knees beside him. "Zach, what's wrong? Did you hurt yourself?" The rain hit her like a million stinging needles of ice, making her breath catch in her throat. In a matter of moments she was as wet as he was, her thin robe and nightgown clinging to her, her hair plastered against her throat and neck. She reached out and laid her hand on his arm.

The muscles and tendons beneath her touch were rock hard with tension. He was shaking. She raised her voice and put all the authority she could muster into a repetition of his name. "Zach, answer me."

"I'm fine. Nothing but a bad dream. Go inside."

His voice was hoarse, grating, devoid of any warmth, like the rain-soaked night. Whatever had driven him out into this storm was more than just a bad dream.

"Not without you."

He shook his head. Raindrops flew from his hair and chin. "Here," he gasped. "I'm going to stay here a little longer. You leave, Dr. Layman. Now!" He was good at giving orders, but Callie was not to be put off.

"No." She sat on her heels. Did he believe she would leave him here in this condition, exposed to the elements, in real danger of suffering hypothermia or worse?

"Stubborn woman." He dropped his head. His voice was gentler now, weary as though he didn't have the strength to keep arguing with her.

"So I've been told." Her teeth were chattering. She couldn't help it. The temperature had dropped twenty degrees since sunset. The wind and rain made it seem even colder. The screen door still swung on its hinges, banging itself to pieces against the stone wall of the building, but she ignored it.

She couldn't begin to guess what kind of nightmare—or memories—tormented him. But she wanted to, so she could take his pain away.

The realization brought her up short. She was already way too attached to this man, a coworker, a colleague, a man scarcely more than a stranger.

But he was also a human being in pain and she was a healer first. She tugged on his arm. "Zach, come inside." He didn't budge. She swallowed a sob of frustration. If he refused to obey her, she wouldn't be able to move him. Should she call J.R.? Rudy Koslowski? No. He wouldn't thank her for letting anyone else see him like this. "Zach, please." The plea seemed to reach the dark place where he had gone. He raised his head and stared directly at her. For a moment there was no recognition in his eyes, only torment. The fitful light produced by the almost constant play of lightning between the clouds allowed her to witness his anguish, and it was almost too painful to bear.

She cupped his face with her hands. "You can't stay out here in this awful weather."

He bowed his head a moment, struggling to get a grip on himself. He raised his head and nodded. "All right." He put his hands beneath her elbows and pulled her up with him, as though she weighed no more than a child. He pushed a strand of wet hair behind her ear. His hands were shaking, his teeth chattered and his eyes were hollowed out, as haunted as his gaze. "You get inside, too. Get out of those wet things. Get warm and dry. Now. Go." He waved a hand toward her side of the cottage.

She shook her head. "Good advice, but you're not getting rid of me that easily, Doc." She wouldn't leave him. "Come, let's go inside."

He hesitated a moment longer, gathering his composure. Callie saw the effort it took and was awed by his determination to fight his demons to a standstill.

"You win," he said, grabbing the wildly swinging screen door. With one strong jerk he wrenched it off its loosened hinges and wedged it against the wall. Now only the creaking of the heavy pine rocking chairs competed with the sounds of the storm.

He reached out and ran his hand over the splintered door frame. "I'll fix it tomorrow." Callie nodded and took his hand.

CHAPTER ELEVEN

"I'M FINE NOW," he said for at least the third time. "Go to bed and try and get some sleep."

"No," Callie replied, just as patiently and stubbornly as she had twice before. "Not until you do." She flushed slightly but held his eyes stare for stare. She was wearing one of his old sweatshirts, an equally old pair of sweatpants and thick cotton socks she could barely keep on her feet. Her hair was wrapped in a towel around her head.

The sweatshirt was heavy enough to preserve her modesty but he tried to keep his eyes above shoulder level anyway, and mostly succeeded.

She had refused to leave him alone even to change out of her wet nightgown and robe. "Why do that?" she'd asked with irrefutable logic. "As long as it's raining and blowing so hard, I'd just get wet again on the way back." He'd still been too disoriented by the panic attack to argue with her. Besides, she'd been shivering as violently as he'd been, and they'd both hovered on the brink of hypothermia. She'd turned on a table lamp by the couch, watched from the door of his bedroom while he hunted out dry clothes for the both of them, then insisted he get in the shower first.

"You're the patient. I'm the doctor," she said, pointing to the bathroom door. "Go."

When he came out of the bathroom ten minutes later, she was changed and searching through his cupboards for plates and cups. Hot milk simmered on the stove and a box of instant-cocoa mix stood beside it. "You're supposed to get in the shower, too," he reminded her.

"I'm fine," she said. "I wasn't out there as long as you were. I'm still a little chilly, but warming up fast." She smiled at him from the shadows of the tiny kitchen, where only the range light provided illumination, but she didn't quite meet his gaze head-on. "I'm making toast and cocoa. It's what my dad did for me when I was little and couldn't sleep."

He hooked his foot around the leg of one of the slightly rickety wooden stools that fronted the narrow breakfast bar separating the kitchen from the rest of the main room, turned his back on the storm and sat down. He envied her those childhood memories. He was sure someone in one of the foster homes he'd been in had made him toast and cocoa, but for the life of him he couldn't remember which one.

"You don't have to do this."

"Of course, but I want some, too." She poured the milk into mugs, stirred the cocoa and added just a little cold milk from the carton to lower the temperature a bit.

"Cocoa's great, but I'll pass on the toast." He said it a little too gruffly, but he didn't want to be reminded of the past. He didn't want to think at all right now, but his brain refused to shut down.

She ignored his tone, just as she would ignore a patient's sharpness when it was caused by fear and anxiety. "Okay, we'll skip the toast. You don't have any little marshmallows, so this will have to do." She slid the mugs onto the counter and then came around the half wall to perch on the stool he'd pulled out for her.

"It's good," he said, taking a swallow. "Thanks."

She watched him over the rim of her mug. He held out his hand. Her brows furrowed. "What?"

"Want to check my pulse?"

She blushed slightly and shook her head. "Sorry, I'll stop watching every move you make. Habit, that's all."

"My pulse is back to normal and so am I. I'm fine, Doctor," he said, managing a grin. "Emergency's over. You can dial down to concerned-neighbor mode." He *was* okay. His nerves were still thrumming, but it was more because she was sitting here beside him so close their knees almost touched than residue from the panic attack.

"PTSD?" she asked without preamble, probably anticipating if she'd asked him to talk about what had just happened he would just change the subject.

He shifted slightly on the stool so he didn't have to meet her still-watchful hazel eyes. He braced his elbows on the counter and held the mug between his hands, absorbing the warmth and the homey smell of chocolate. He never made the sugary stuff for himself. He didn't even know why he'd bought it, except it seemed like something he should keep in his cupboard, the same as salt and flour.

He chose his words with care. "It's pretty much part of the job description after two tours attached to a Marine unit in Afghanistan."

"You've never shown any symptoms or the slightest sign you had a problem."

"Thanks," he said. "I've worked very hard to get to that point."

"Can you talk about it? About what happened over there?"

"No." It was too abrupt, but he couldn't help himself.

She winced slightly but didn't falter. "I understand why you've never confided in me. The only thing I know about PTSD is what I've learned in books. I've never dealt with it in the real world."

He swung his head around. "Stop putting yourself down."

She lifted her eyes to his. "I wasn't. It's the truth," she said simply. "I'm a good doctor, but I'm a green one. Facts are facts. So, please, help me understand a little more. If not for your sake, then for the next soldier or sailor or Marine I have as a patient."

He didn't have an answer for that one. She was learning quickly how to get around his defenses. "If you won't talk to me as a physician, will you talk to me as a friend?" She had her hands clutched around her cocoa mug. She was almost as tense as he was, but he realized she wouldn't be denied.

"I'm fine, Callie," he said, softly this time. "Really, I am."

"You frightened me. You were in a place so far away and so terrible I was scared you might never find your way home."

He leaned his elbows on the counter, both hands wrapped around his mug. "I was dreaming. I still have nightmares, but not as often. The storm must have set it off. Loud, sustained noises can be a trigger. I thought I had it under control. Most of the time, I do."

"I know a little of what happened to you over there in Afghanistan," she said, staring down at her own mug. "That night at the White Pine after the barbecue, you and Ron Seamann were at the bar getting drinks and Rudy and Gerry were dancing to the jukebox, remember?" He nodded. "Jen Koslowski and I were alone at the table. She confided to me how Rudy lost his leg. Jen was a little drunk and she was so proud that Rudy could dance again, when for years he wouldn't even try. She told me how close he came to dying. How you saved his life. Is that what your dreams are about? Rudy and the other men you needed to save?"

He wanted to get up and run out of the room. In the past he might have, but he *was* better now; he should be able to talk about it. So he made himself continue.

"I never remember much about my dreams," he said, deciding she wouldn't give up until he explained at least some of it, and he owed her that much. "High anxiety mostly. My guys are hurt. I can't get to them 'cause I'm not ready. My gear's not packed. My instruments are missing, all kinds of things go wrong."

"Or is it you can't get to them because you've been injured yourself?"

He shrugged. "You'd make a good shrink. I'm always slow and clumsy but I honestly don't remember—" He shook his head. "Usually I wake myself up, but tonight I was out the door before I got myself together. The rain helped."

She laughed a little, softly, with sympathy underlying the tinkling sound. "Rushing headlong into a monsoon will shock anyone into cold, hard reality."

"Yeah, but that's not what I mean." He'd never told anyone this, but he had no worry she would betray his confidence. "It's the rain. Storms spook me these days, but it's the rain I crave."

"I don't understand."

He set his empty mug on the counter, stood up and walked to the window. After a couple of seconds, she did the same. She stood beside him looking out into the night, not touching but almost. "I grew up in the desert in California. None of the families I was placed with were well-to-do. A couple were downright poor. We didn't have big swimming pools or spa rooms. It hardly ever rained. We were always worried about wildfires in the dry season. Then when I was about the twins' age, one of my better-off foster families took us to the ocean for a vacation. I'd never seen anything like it. I never even dreamed so much water existed. I couldn't get enough of the smell and the sounds and the movement. That's when I decided to join the navy."

"But how did you end up here in White

Pine Lake? We're a long way from the ocean."

"From salt water, maybe. As the crow flies we're less than a mile from one of the largest inland seas in the world," he said.

He was just enough taller so that she had to tip her head slightly to look at him. He liked that. She probably didn't.

The storm had moved off inland, the lightning reduced to mere flickers, the thunder a low, soft growl at the edge of his hearing. But still the rain came down. He watched it with both hands resting on the windowsill. "You might not believe this, but I spent eight years in the navy and never had sea duty. I did my medical training in Texas. After that, I was in Afghanistan attached to a Marine combat unit. There might be beautiful places in that part of the world. I never saw any of them. To me it was all heat and cold and dust and dirt everywhere I looked. I swore to myself that if I ever got home I'd never be out of sight of water again. I didn't have anything or anybody to tie me to California and the places I was raised. Rudy thought White Pine Lake was the greatest place on earth. So I came home with him on leave once. I was standing right over there—" he gestured toward the reappearing marina light "—suddenly I realized I was over three hundred miles from Great Lakes in Chicago where I did my basic training, and it was still the same water. I decided that was ocean enough for me."

"'Water, water everywhere,'" she quoted.

"And rain and snow in winter, and it's all fresh and clean and clear. And there are no sharks." He grinned.

"I've seen the T-shirt. Lake Michigan— Unsalted and Shark Free," she said, smiling also. The smile became a yawn. She covered her mouth with her hand. "Sorry."

"No, I'm the one who's sorry. I probably scared you half to death and ruined your sleep." He caught her hand and held it with his own.

She went very still but didn't attempt to break free. After a moment she laid her other hand on top of his. "Don't be sorry. And for the record, I was already awake."

He used the opening she gave him to change the subject from his problems to hers. "Are you still worrying about Eno's condition?"

She shook her head, her expression hard to read in the low light. "No, I'm sad but I'm getting a perspective on it. You're right. There are some things I can't fix. I just have to endure."

"Then it's your family that's concerning you."

She sighed. "As usual."

"Want to talk about it?"

She narrowed her eyes slightly. "We are done talking about you. Am I right?"

He nodded. She inclined her head. "So be it." She didn't say she would be there for him again if he needed her, but she would. If he could keep himself from doing what he longed to do—taking her in his arms and asking her to stay in White Pine Lake with him always—the step forward they had taken tonight might not come with the usual two steps back. "I'm guilty of trying to blend my families again," she said with a smile that wavered a little at the edges. The vulnerability in her smile made the urge to hold her even stronger.

"What are you up to now, Dr. Callie?" The rain was beginning to slacken. In a few more minutes, he would have no excuse to keep her with him. He lifted her hands and held them close to his chest. She bowed her head a moment, and he held his breath that she might move into his arms of her own free will. But she stayed where she was, so close but still so far away.

"My mother has hired the twins to help her pick market vegetables tomorrow—" She stared out the window where, indeed, the sky was beginning to lighten along the edges. "I guess I mean this morning, in just a couple of hours. We were having ice cream at Kilroy's when my mother showed up. I offered to bring them out to the farm, and Ginger went along with the plan, though I don't think she really wanted to. She only did it because I asked her to. Then my dad joined us, and, well, I figured out why Ginger had been so reluctant. He's not happy with the idea, or with me."

"I never pictured J.R. as a vindictive man."

She smiled. "He's not, but he is a very protective man, and he has never quite forgiven my mother for deserting me. For deserting both of us."

"Have you?"

"Yes, for the most part." She hesitated.

"Not completely. Maybe I never will. But now I've caused more tension between Ginger and my father, and that's exactly the opposite of what I wanted to do. Suddenly that cruise-ship job is looking better and better."

"You sound like you're giving up."

"It's way past three o'clock in the morning. No one's very optimistic at this hour."

"I can't argue with you there."

She blew out a breath and it came close to a sigh. "I want us all to be comfortable with each other." She seemed to hear the uncertainty in her own words. "That's a lot to ask, isn't it?"

"I'm not much of an expert on family dynamics, blended or otherwise."

"But you are certainly skilled at getting your patients to open up to you. Listen to me, rattling on to you like one of those women who don't have proper boundaries." She attempted a smile, but it faded away like the sound of the rain on the roof. "Am I wrong to attempt so much?" she asked softly.

"If anyone can, it's the stubborn and laser-focused Dr. Layman. But not if you're sailing the seven seas in a floating hotel."

She tilted her head slightly and studied

him through her lashes. Long, straight lashes that could veil the emotion in her hazel eyes. "Are you telling me I should stay if I'm offered the position?"

"I'm not telling you to do anything, I'm only stating the obvious. You can't blend a family long-distance." He paused. "Would you consider it?"

"The committee hasn't asked me. But yes, I would consider it. Especially after today."

"Why today?"

"Us."

"Us?" His heart rate kicked up a notch.

"We made it through everything that happened tonight, and we're still on speaking terms," she said with a little smile. "That is real progress."

"Yes," he said. "I guess it is. Thank you for everything you did for me tonight."

He leaned down and kissed her before she could object. For a moment she held still, then very quickly she returned his kiss before pulling away.

"Zach, I don't—"

"Yeah, it's not a great idea. But hey, it's the middle of the night. Great ideas are few and far between."

"You say the strangest things." She shook her head, not quite smiling, not quite frowning. "I have to go. I don't want anyone to see me leaving your side of the cottage."

He wanted to point out no one was likely to be out spying on them at 4:00 a.m. in this kind of weather, but he kept his mouth shut. He dropped her hands and put some distance between them, anxious not to undo any of the progress they'd made. "Try to get some rest. There's still a couple of hours until daylight."

"I intend to do just that. My things." She looked around for the plastic grocery bag he'd given her to hold her wet nightgown and robe. He leaned over the old leather sofa he slept on most nights and handed the bag to her.

She waved her free hand down her side. "I'll return your clothes as soon as I get them washed."

"Don't bother. Just leave them on the porch. I do laundry most Saturdays."

She flushed, opened her mouth to protest, then relented. "Okay, I'll leave them on the rocker. Try to get some sleep yourself," she said.

"Sounds like a plan." A moment later he heard her door open and then close very quietly. He stood staring out at the still-dripping eaves. The birds were beginning to stir. Dawn would be coming soon but he wouldn't be awake to welcome it. The horror of his midnight dreams had receded. When he closed his eyes, he might dream again. But it would not be of blood and heat and death— it would be of her.

CALLIE'S MOTHER CALLED just after six, sounding tired and distracted. "Callie, I'm going to have to cancel our plans for today."

"What's happened?" she asked, frowning down at the cup of coffee she'd just poured, unable to stop herself from recalling her dad's words about Karen's habit of disappointing people. She was suddenly suspicious.

"A tree came down in the storm last night. One of the big old cedars."

"That's a shame," Callie said, meaning it. "Any damage?"

"It missed the house, but it's across the driveway. Armand Zimmer and his sons— the ones who farm the fields behind the house—are coming to cut it into firewood and clear up the mess. So I'll be too busy to pick the vegetables. The cukes will be okay for a couple of days, but I don't think my tomatoes will hold until next week. I'll have to give up my spot at the farmer's market and just put them all out at the stand and hope for the best," she rattled on nervously. "The problem is I'm not comfortable having the children here with chain saws and axes—"

"That's okay, I get it."

"Thanks, sweetie. I knew you'd understand." She sounded relieved. "I don't have your dad's private number anymore, and frankly, I'd really rather not speak to him if I don't have to, so could you explain this all to them?"

So much for Callie's daydreams of everyone getting along. "Sure, I'll just stop by the White Pine and explain what's happened on my way out to the farm."

"I'd appreciate you doing that for me, but you don't have to come out here. I'm used to managing on my own."

"Well, you're not managing on your own today. I'll help stack firewood instead of picking tomatoes. I don't suppose you got around to making those blueberry muffins?" she asked a little wistfully.

Karen laughed, sounding relieved she'd have Callie to help. "No, I didn't. The power was out for almost three hours here and I just wasn't up to making them in the wood-stove." One of Karen's more successful on-line videos was of her baking bread in her antique woodstove. She made it look easy on the internet videos, but it wasn't. Callie had tried it herself when she was home at Christmas and much preferred the convenience of a good mixer with a bread-hook attachment and a reliable electric oven.

"I'll grab a couple of Mac's cinnamon rolls when I stop to explain the situation to Ginger and the kids. How does that sound?"

"Make it a dozen rolls, then I'll be able to give Armand and the boys a plate to take home. Armand's wife is away in North Dakota caring for her father, so they're all batching it."

"A dozen it is." Callie looked at the half banana she'd planned for an early breakfast and reached into the cupboard for a box of cereal to add to it. It was going to be an even busier day than she'd anticipated.

Before leaving the cottage, she laid Zach's clothes on his rocking chair. She studied the broken screen door and considered just how much strength it took to wrestle even a light-weight door off its hinges, as he had done last night. She paused, listening for sounds of movement from inside, but could hear nothing. She hesitated a moment longer, wondering if she should check on him. Her dad kept a spare key above the roof edg-ing, but she decided against using it. Zach had been fine when she'd left him only two hours ago. He was probably sleeping, dead to the world, and she didn't want to disturb his rest. She wished she could stay until he awakened, but she had promised Karen she would come as soon as she could. She hoped his dreams this morning were pleasant ones.

ZACH WOKE FROM a light doze, sensing more than hearing that Callie was nearby. He was lying on the couch, where he'd spent the re-mainder of the night in a dreamless sleep. He held his breath and stayed very still, hop-ing she would tap on the door and call his name, but after a moment he heard the sound of her footsteps going down the steps and onto the gravel path that skirted both sides of the cottage. Another minute passed and her Jeep coughed and sputtered to life, and then he heard her drive away. Off to the White Pine, as she'd planned. Maybe that meant Karen hadn't backed out on the twins. He hoped not.

He sat up and ran his hands through his hair. He rested his elbows on his knees and stared down at the floor. He felt as if he'd been run over by a truck, but the aftereffects of the panic attack were already fading away. In the early weeks and months after his return from Afghanistan, he'd been almost paralyzed with anxiety and depression, not able to function for hours and sometimes days if it was a really bad episode. Last night should have been the same, but it hadn't been.

Because Callie had been there for him.

He recognized that truth at the very core of his being. He wanted her with him now.

He stood up and opened the door. The splintered door frame was going to take a couple hours of work to repair. It would give him something to do today. But he'd have to wait until the hardware store opened to start the project. He might as well go fishing for a couple hours. His clothes were lying neatly folded, socks on top, on the seat of the pine rocking chair, exactly as she'd promised. He picked them up and brought them inside, picturing her as she'd been last night, wet hair wrapped in a towel, the sleeves of his faded old sweatshirt folded over her strong but narrow hands and wrists, pant legs dragging, the socks he'd given her so big she could scarcely keep them on her feet. A corner of his mouth kicked up in a grin. A little girl in her big brother's castoffs. The smile faded away.

She wasn't a little girl and he wasn't her big brother. She had dragged him kicking and screaming out of his nightmare and then, when he had broken his own word and kissed her, she had kissed him back. And just like their first kiss, it had moved him in a way no other kiss had ever done, with tenderness and hope and love.

The realization he was teetering on the brink of falling in love with his boss brought him up short. It was love, wasn't it? Not some gratitude for saving his sanity last night kind of thing?

No, he knew himself better than that. He'd

never felt quite this way before. Callie Layman was the most stubborn woman he'd ever met, the most principled and the most intriguing. They had argued; they had made up. They had shared the good and the bad in the past twenty-four hours. They had kissed, and it had been one heck of a kiss. They had both wanted more. A lot more. Now all he had to do was prove to her that they were meant for a partnership that was both professional and personal. One that would last a lifetime.

CHAPTER TWELVE

CALLIE DIDN'T HAVE any trouble finding a
place to park at the White Pine so early in the
morning, and she wheeled into a spot right
in front. The restaurant opened at 6:30 a.m.,
but that was mostly for the early-rising coffee
drinkers. The breakfast crowd on Saturday
usually didn't start showing up until a little
later in the morning.

She walked up the steps, breathing deeply
of the clean, crisp air, letting it clear her head
of the last lingering cobwebs of fatigue from
the night before.

The storm had taken its toll on the petunias
in the flower beds lining the steps—their
heads were bowed, their petals muddied.
The hostas were slightly bedraggled, too,
with raindrops still clinging to their broad
green leaves. She noticed the plants were already done flowering, a sure sign fall was
just around the corner. Labor Day was less

than ten days away. Summer was coming to an end.

She walked into the lobby, cool and shadow filled, and glanced into the taproom. It was silent and deserted, clean-swept and tidy, the chairs tucked neatly under the tables, the bar stools lined with military precision along the bar. In another twelve hours, those same tables would be filled with laughing couples and groups of friends, watching the big-screen TV, listening to the jukebox, awaiting the arrival of the DJ for his monthly karaoke night. Maybe she would come down for an hour or so. Maybe Zach would be there, too? She shook off the pleasant fantasy. She already spent far too much time thinking about the man.

She headed into the dining room. The big room was filled with morning light and smelled of coffee and bacon and cinnamon rolls. There was only one table of tourists seated for breakfast, hikers, judging from their cargo pants and sturdy boots, fueling up before heading out for a day exploring the dunes' trails. At a second table against the back wall sat the regulars, a group of the town's businessmen and retirees who met to exchange gossip and weather reports before going about their days. Today the group contained a surprising number of the members of the Physician's Committee. Callie's breath caught in her throat. What were they doing here on a Saturday?

"Hey, Dr. Callie. Morning to you," Harvey Kilroy greeted her with a wave. "Saw you at the shop last night but I was too busy bringing out ice cream from the cooler to say hello."

"Glad that you're so busy."

"It's turned out to be a pretty good summer," he agreed.

"'Bout time," Bob Budde, the owner of the grocery store, grumbled. "Economy's been bad too long."

"Amen to that," Silas McGruder, the owner of the marina and bait and tackle, seconded.

His son-in-law, Owen Carson, who had taken over the business when the older man retired, asked, "How'd you weather the storm, Dr. Callie?"

Ezra Colliflower didn't speak but lifted his mug in greeting.

Callie managed to return Ezra's smile and answer Owen at the same time.

"Kept me awake—" she put her hand on the "in" side of the kitchen's swinging double doors "—but today's going to be lovely." All five men nodded in agreement with her assessment. "Have a great day, gentlemen." She included all of them in another smile and slipped into the kitchen. The smile remained. She was fitting in again, accepted as a doctor and one of the locals. It felt good.

"Hi, Callie, we're all ready to go," Brandon announced with a wave and a sleepy smile that was so sweet and innocent it gave her heart a little twist. He and his sister were dressed in what she suspected were last year's clothes, faded T's and jeans that were a little ragged and a couple of inches too short. Brandon was wearing the Detroit Tigers baseball cap that had been rejected along with the team jersey at Christmas, and his sister had her hair pulled back into a no-nonsense ponytail.

"Hi," Becca said and returned to her dish of fruit and toast and orange juice. She didn't look as sunny as Brandon, but Callie hadn't expected her to. Her stepsister wasn't as easygoing as her twin, still downright prickly on occasion, but not as openly hostile as she'd been just a month ago. Maybe she'd accomplished more than she gave herself credit for.

"Hi, yourselves." She had hoped she'd arrive before they got up, but they had been true to their word and were already dressed and ready for a day working in the garden. "Was that some storm last night or what?" Callie asked, giving herself a little breathing room before she had to break the news to the twins about the downed tree.

"Awesome," Brandon said around a mouthful of cereal.

"I would have slept through it, but Brandon was afraid and came into my room." Becca sniffed, dunking a half slice of toast in her glass of orange juice.

"Was not."

"Were, too."

"She's lying. We sat on the window seat and watched it. It was awesome," Brandon insisted, glaring at his sister.

Becca ignored him. She popped the toast into her mouth without letting any of the orange juice drip onto the table.

"I used to do that when it was my room,"

Callie said. "Sit on the window seat and watch the storms out over the lake."

"Cool," Becca responded noncommittally. Callie didn't say a word about talking with one's mouth full. She was a big sister, not a parent.

"Good morning," Mac called out as she emerged from the walk-in cooler at the rear of the kitchen with a plastic-wrapped baking sheet of cinnamon rolls. "What brings you out this early in the morning on your day off?"

"Morning, Mac. Are those cinnamon rolls spoken for?" Callie asked.

"They are. You'll have to wait for the next batch. These are going to the private dining room." She raised one eyebrow. "Special meeting of the Physician's Committee."

"Oh, dear," Callie said faintly. Becca's and Brandon's eyes were on her. "I guess I'll just have to come back into town later and pick up the rolls. Will you save me a dozen?"

Mac took pity on her and didn't say anything more about the meeting. "Consider it done. Heading out to your mom's?"

"We're going to pick veggies at Karen's," Brandon piped up.

Ginger and J.R. came down the stairs as Brandon spoke. Ginger paused at the bottom and put her hand out to steady herself against the wall and catch her breath. "Whew, we need to seriously consider putting in an elevator," she said. "Hi, Callie, some storm last night, wasn't it?"

"Hello, Ginger. It certainly was. Hi, Dad."

"Coffee," he croaked, giving her a grin.

Ginger rolled her eyes and gave her head a rueful shake. "I don't think J.R. would have any trouble joining a monastery where you have to take a vow of silence."

"At least in the morning." Callie giggled.

"I'm the strong, silent type."

Ginger laughed, too, went to the coffeemaker and took down a mug from the rack hanging off to one side. "Here you go," she said to her husband.

"Thanks." He took the steaming mug from her hand and held it for just a moment longer than necessary as they exchanged a private smile. It didn't appear to bother Ginger that her husband wasn't a talker, the way it had Karen. There were other ways for two people in love to communicate, Callie was coming to realize.

"They kept their promise, Callie," Ginger said, "even after the storm kept us up half the night." She made herself a cup of tea as she spoke. "I only had to call Brandon twice and he was out of bed. That's almost a record for him on a summer Saturday." She was wearing an oversize pink shirt and black shorts and sandals and looked rested despite the storm.

"But I'm afraid there's a problem." Callie explained about the downed tree. "It's just not going to work out for us to spend the day at the farm."

"We're not going? Why couldn't we help stack firewood or something?" Brandon demanded. "I have to earn some money."

"And I wanted to watch Karen spin, too," Becca said, although she didn't seem as angry as Callie had feared she might be. Perhaps she'd underestimated the twins' level of maturity.

Ginger's expression had tightened momentarily but it cleared as the reason for the change in plans became clear. "I agree, though, that eleven-year-olds and chain saws could be a volatile combination."

"I'm not a bit surprised to hear one of

those big old cedars came down," J.R. said with an exasperated shake of his head. "Did it miss the house?"

"Yes," Callie said cautiously. "It fell across the driveway. The Zimmers are coming to clear it up and haul it away."

"They'll do a good job." J.R. was leaning against the big stainless-steel prep table, where Mac's minions would soon be hard at work chopping vegetables and peeling potatoes, his precious coffee mug cradled between his hands. "Karen's such a back-to-the-earth type these days she doesn't want to take down the straggliest popple on the property, let alone one of those giants. Woman doesn't have a lick of sense about some things. All it takes is a hard rain and wind, or a heavy snowfall to bring them down."

Callie found she'd been holding her breath and let it out on a soundless sigh. It wasn't a flattering assessment of her mother, but at least neither Ginger nor her father appeared inclined to blame Karen for breaking her promise to the children. She had been worried for nothing.

"How am I going to earn money for my game?" Brandon demanded, cutting to the heart of the matter. "I'm not scheduled to work here until Tuesday and that's my last week before school starts. I still need twenty-five dollars."

"You can help me later today," J.R. said, pouring a second cup of coffee. "I've got a meeting in half an hour, but before that, I'm going up to the widow's walk to make sure nothing's leaking. And while I'm at it, I'm going to measure for a new railing for the stairs, and we'll probably need to replace a couple of floorboards, too." Everyone, including Mac, stared at him in surprise. He shrugged, not meeting Callie's gaze; he hadn't intended to mention the Physician's Committee meeting aloud. Once in a while she could read his mind as easily as he could read hers. "It would be fun to watch the Labor Day fireworks from up there this year, like we always used to."

They had discontinued the family ritual the year Karen had walked out on them and Callie had cried through the entire fireworks display. She realized much later that J.R. had used the storm damage that followed as an excuse to stop her from going up there, where he feared she went to brood about her mother's absence. It was another change from the old ways, and it was a good one. "That'd be great," Callie said and smiled.

"Come with us, Mom," Brandon coaxed, but Ginger demurred.

"Some other time," she said, patting her stomach. "Just getting up and down the stairs from the apartment is about all I can handle these days."

Becca's sandy eyebrows drew together in a scowl and she dropped her eyes to her food. Callie was reminded that Becca's unhappiness with Ginger's pregnancy was a sore spot that hadn't yet been healed.

"I second the motion," J.R. said, giving his wife's distended stomach an assessing glance.

Ginger smiled but her eyes strayed to her pouting daughter and the smile faded a little. "Be gone! All of you! I'll stay here and go over next week's menus with Mac. Unless you'd rather stay here and help us, Becca?" she asked hopefully.

Becca shook her head. "I want to see the view from up there."

"You guys go on up," J.R. said. "The key's where it's always been, Callie." He looked as if he wanted to comment on Becca's bad manners, but he caught Ginger's slight negative shake of her head and held his peace. "I'll get my tape measure and something to write on and be right behind you." He headed toward the storage area beneath the stairs where he kept his tools.

Five minutes later, panting a little from the climb, Callie and the children entered the third-floor attic. Nothing had changed, Callie noted. It never did. In years past a wall had been built to divide the attic roughly into thirds, situating the cupola and its skylight on the other side and leaving this portion with only the light from the small dormer windows. The roof was steeply pitched, the dividing wall running parallel to it, giving the room a very odd shape. Headroom was limited and the wall space was full of dark nooks and crannies—and spiderwebs.

"Eeek!" Becca squealed. "I hate spiders."

"Spiders are our friends. They eat bugs." Brandon scoffed at her squeamishness.

"I don't care." Becca put her hands on top of her head to protect her hair. "Give me your hat."

"No way." Brandon plunked his hand on

top of his own head in the event she should try to grab it.

"I'm not fond of them, either," Callie agreed, brushing aside a particularly big web—one thankfully devoid of prey. "But I have to admit they're fascinating creatures. Just not up close and personal."

"Exactly," Becca said emphatically.

Callie stood on tiptoe and slid her fingers over the door frame to the nail where the key to the cupola stairs had hung for years. On the other side, the glassed-in skylight would bathe the larger room in sunshine, and dust motes would dance in the still air like gold dust.

Behind Callie's back, Becca whispered to her brother. Callie couldn't quite catch what she said, although she could guess. "Too high for us to reach," Brandon whispered so loudly she had no trouble hearing him. "That's why we couldn't find it." There was the sound of a smack and a muffled "Ouch."

"Have you two been up here before?" Callie asked, keeping her smile to herself.

"Yeah," Brandon admitted, "but only this far. We could never find the key to the stairway."

"Well, now you know where the key is, but Dad will probably just find another place to hide it."

"There's nothing to do up here, anyway," Becca pointed out. "Just old Christmas decorations and stuff. I'd hoped there'd be all kinds of neat old things."

"It was one of the biggest disappointments of my childhood that there weren't any trunks of old clothes and furniture up here for my friends and me to play dress-up with," Callie confessed. "After all, the building's over a hundred years old."

"And most disappointing of all, it's not even haunted," J.R. said with a grin, coming up behind them so quietly they all jumped. He was carrying a toolbox in one hand and a crowbar in the other.

"I've always been glad of that," Callie said emphatically.

"Me, too." Becca shivered.

"Go ahead and unlock the door," her dad instructed. "But I'll go up first. I want to make sure the steps are solid. And don't lean on the handrail. It's in bad shape."

Callie inserted the key in the lock and opened the door. Sunlight spilled out of the opening just as she remembered. It was still early in the morning, the sun bright and climbing in the sky. But at night it was pitch-black in this part of the attic because there were no windows on this side of the building and no electricity. She stepped aside and J.R. walked through the opening, the kids on his heels, Callie bringing up the rear. The second attic room was the same odd shape as the front one but much larger because it contained the whole of the skylight area. Dust motes danced all around them, just as Callie remembered, only now they weren't magical. They made her want to sneeze. The stairway was to the right of the door. J.R. surveyed the steep ascent, then started up, testing each step before advancing to the next. He disappeared at the top and they could hear him walking around, tapping with the end of the crowbar, searching for weakened areas.

Brandon bounced up and down on his toes, eager to be allowed up. Becca stood quietly but her hands were clasped in front of her and Callie sensed her excitement. For a girl who was into woodland fairy princesses and dragon-bonded warriors, the cupola room would be magical, just as it had been for Callie at that age. She began to feel as excited for her stepsister as she was for herself. "Okay," J.R. called down after a minute, "come on up, kids, one at a time. And remember, watch the banister. It's loose."

"I'm first," Becca insisted. "I'm the oldest." She climbed carefully, following J.R.'s instructions to the letter. Brandon bounded after her, arms outstretched, hovering just above the handrails.

"Slow down, buddy," J.R. commanded, peering over the banister. Brandon obeyed, taking the last half-dozen steps nearly as sedately as his sister. Callie followed a few moments later, her heart pounding just a bit faster than the climb warranted. J.R. held out his hand to help her up the last couple of steps. "Look any different?"

"No," she said, smiling from ear to ear. "It's just as wonderful as it always was."

The twins were already taking in the view from the windows, kneeling on the narrow bench that edged the two long sides of the rectangular space, their faces pressed to the glass. "Don't lean too hard. We don't want you going through the glass and dropping into the petunias and frightening the tourists."

"Okay, Dad, we'll be careful," Brandon promised.

"I'll watch out for him."

Callie and J.R. moved a couple steps away to take in the view themselves. The sun was shining brightly through the surprisingly clean windows that rimmed the tiny room from just above waist level to the top of her head. The ceiling was sheathed in white pine, seeming as freshly cut as if it had been put up only a few days ago, not a hundred years before. From up here the lake revealed its commalike shape, the wide, rounded end ringed with cottages and the marina and the other familiar buildings of the town. The sun-spangled surface was dotted with boats and Jet Skis, and from this distance, the white and red and yellow boat sails seemed the same size as the white wings of gulls. Her eyes followed the shoreline as the lake tapered to a narrow point where it curved into the backside of the dunes, butting up against the national-park border. The parkland was still as wild and undeveloped as it had been when the voyageurs and Native

American tribes called this land home. Rising above the treetops were the golden sands of the Sleeping Bear Dunes, some of them over four hundred feet above water level. Beyond the dunes, the cobalt-blue band of Lake Michigan gradually blended into the brighter arc of blue August sky. "It's the most beautiful place on earth."

"Absolutely," J.R. agreed as she smiled over at him. "I'm glad you're home, sweetheart."

The twins were engrossed in watching the world go by below them, paying little attention to the two adults. Callie might not have another chance to talk to her father. She couldn't let the opportunity pass. "You said you had a meeting. It's the Physician's Committee, isn't it?"

"Yes," he said. "How did you know?"

"A quarter of them are downstairs already. Mac says they're going to offer me the position at the clinic. Is she right?"

"That woman is a one-man intelligence team. Yes," he said, "they are."

"Why haven't you said anything to me before?"

"I didn't want to influence your decision

one way or another. I wasn't certain you even wanted the position. You haven't talked to me about your plans for your future…well, not since Ginger came on the scene."

"It wasn't because of Ginger, Dad. I wasn't sure what I wanted to do, but for a while now I didn't believe it was coming home to White Pine Lake. I've been considering another offer."

His eyes narrowed. "What other offer? You've never given me even a hint something else is waiting out there for you." There was no censure in the remark but Callie felt a jab of guilt anyway.

"I'm sorry. I wasn't sure you'd be happy about it. It's with a cruise line. A two-year commitment. I'd almost never be home."

His expression tightened. "You're right. I don't like that idea, but the decision is yours. I won't beat around the bush—I want you here in White Pine Lake more than anything. I won't deny it. But I don't want you to regret staying here because you were pressured by me or anyone else. That's what I'm going to tell the committee. Then I'm leaving the meeting and coming up here to work with the twins, exactly as I promised them."

"I was hoping you'd make this easy for me, Dad," Callie said, but she was smiling. The distance she'd sensed growing between them the past couple of years seemed to melt away in this place that meant so much to both of them.

He shook his head. "I can't. You have to make this decision on your own."

"I'm a Layman," she said. "Looking out for White Pine Lake is in my blood, and I'm starting to believe I'm good at it. I'm still undecided about exactly what I want, but I'm willing to listen to what they have to offer."

He searched her face for a long moment, then nodded, satisfied by something he read in her eyes. What she saw in his was a promise to always be there for her. But she also saw that he now considered her an adult, an equal, capable of making her own life decisions. A smile began to lurk in the depths of his eyes. "If you do decide to stay, make sure those old skinflints downstairs make it worth your while."

"I will, Dad."

"I have to ask, Callie. Does Zach Gibson know you're considering staying on?"

"Yes," she said.

"You're sure you can work with him?"

"I believe so. I hope so. We're making progress." Once more J.R. looked deep into her eyes and she held her breath, hoping he wouldn't ask her anything more personal about Zach. She wasn't sure how she would answer.

"Okay," J.R. said, grinning. "I'll be here if you need advice on terms in the contract, but beyond that you're on your own."

"Thanks, Dad. I love you." She blinked hard to keep the tears at bay.

"Love you, too, sweetheart."

"Hey, Callie, come here. There's Zach loading up his boat to go fishing," Brandon called out, tapping the glass with his finger to draw her attention. "He's just now getting in the boat. It's cool what all you can see from up here." As quickly as Zach had snagged Brandon's attention, he lost it. "There's the clinic and the hardware store, and there's the school and our church and everything."

"And all the way across the lake, too."

Callie realized the entire conversation with her father had taken only a minute or so. So much had been said, so much communicated in so little time. It left her a little dizzy. She shook off the disorientation and went to kneel on the bench beside the twins.

"Where do they shoot the fireworks from on Labor Day?" Becca asked, but Callie scarcely registered her words or J.R.'s response. She couldn't seem to take her eyes from the small but easily recognizable figure setting out onto the lake in the silver rowboat. She wished she was going fishing with Zach instead of heading out to the farm. She wanted to share about her talk with J.R.

She wanted to tell him she had made up her mind about staying in White Pine Lake. Because she realized she had, somewhere in the past few days, or hours or minutes, decided to come home for good. Home to him.

It had taken all her will to leave Zach and return to her own side of the cottage. It had taken even more willpower to stay away this morning. Was this what it was like, falling in love? Not wanting to be separated from him for even a moment? For someone as risk averse as she was, it almost qualified as love at first sight. Her dad believed in it; he'd believed in love enough to trust his instincts a second time, even after the pain Karen had caused him. Did Callie have the same faith in her heart's choice? And how did Zach feel about her? He wasn't indifferent to her; those kisses and the connection between them last night were real enough. But she had never thought it wise to mix business and pleasure. And their working relationship was still rocky. Her life was taking a far different path than she had envisioned only a few weeks before. She just hoped she wouldn't end up with an unworkable partnership—and a broken heart.

CHAPTER THIRTEEN

THE DAY TURNED sultry and warm after the beautiful storm-washed morning. Where a few hours ago Callie had been able to see far beyond the lakeshore to the dunes, now a heavy haze blurred even the near shoreline. She wondered if it would storm again that night or only rain. If it stormed, would it bring on another episode of PTSD for Zach? She hoped not. She prayed not.

When she'd gotten to her mother's, Callie had welcomed the hard work of helping Karen and the two sturdy Zimmer boys clear the fallen cedar from the driveway, then haul and stack firewood. There had been no leisure to daydream. Through the morning, the air had been cool and clear, and the labor kept Callie's mind from dwelling on Zach and what had passed between them the night before.

But by the time they'd eaten a quick lunch, picked the tomatoes and cucumbers from the damp, sandy soil of the garden, washed and sorted the mounds of vegetables, and restocked the roadside stand at the end of the lane, it was just plain hot. After lunch, Karen sent the Zimmers home to their own farm with a quart of homemade salsa and tortilla chips and a half gallon of lemonade in lieu of cinnamon rolls. She offered Callie some, too, and Callie accepted with thanks. It would make a quick, light supper with a piece of fruit and her last chocolate cookie.

"I appreciate everything you did today," Karen had said with a quick hug as Callie was leaving. "It's so good to have you home."

Callie felt a little guilty not telling Karen then and there that she had decided to stay on in White Pine Lake, but she assuaged her conscience by reminding herself the Physician's Committee had not formally made the offer—but she didn't have to wait long.

Half an hour later, her phone chirped as she pulled into her parking space beside Zach's truck. It was J.R., informing her that she would receive a formal offer for a three-year contract as the White Pine Lake Community Health Center physician in charge on Monday.

She thanked her dad and walked around the side of the house in a slight daze. So much had happened today. She longed to tell Zach about the offer, but was reluctant at the same time. Had last night truly cemented their working relationship, if not their personal one, or was it just a lull in hostilities? She hoped he wasn't outside on the porch. She wasn't ready to face him quite yet. Her hair was coming out of the elastic she'd used to pull it back from her face. It had curled over her cheeks and the nape of her neck like it always did when the humidity was high. It made her look about two years older than Becca. Her fingernails were caked with garden muck even though she'd washed them twice beneath the ice-cold water of the farm pump. Her T-shirt was dirty and streaked with sticky pitch from the cedar and she probably smelled.

She peeked around the corner of the building. The porch was empty. If she hurried maybe she could get inside without him noticing her.

"Hey, you're home." It was Zach's voice but he was nowhere to be seen. She spun around, one foot on the bottom porch step, searching for him. "Here," he said. It never occurred to her to ignore the greeting and hurry on inside as she'd just planned on doing—not once she heard his voice. She hadn't spotted him before because he'd been in the lake, swimming. He hoisted himself halfway onto the dock and remained there, arms folded in front of him, the rest of his body floating free. "You look as if you've had quite a day," he said.

The sound of his voice drew her and after a moment's hesitation she didn't resist. "I have," she said, holding out her arms. There was no hiding how dirty and disheveled she was, so why try? "My mother has been working me like a slave. But that's not a bad thing. We get along better when we have a lot to do." One blond, winged eyebrow lifted a fraction of an inch as he watched her come toward him. Luckily her face was already red from the heat, because she could feel a blush spreading over her face and neck.

There was admiration in his eyes, too, and he made no attempt to hide it from her. "How about a swim in a cool, spring-fed lake to cool off?"

"Is that your prescription, Doc?" she asked.

"It is. And as it happens, there's one close at hand." He waved his arm out over the lake, quiet now in the still, hazy afternoon.

"What I need is a shower and clean clothes."

"A shower in stone-hard well water when the lake water is soft as silk?" He smiled, reaching down with one long arm and scooping up a handful, letting it dribble through his fingers like liquid silk.

"I need soap and shampoo," she said a little sharply, trying to keep her senses under control. But she realized she'd been moving the whole time he'd been talking. Instead of six feet from her door, she was halfway down the dock and still walking forward.

Admitting to herself she was falling in love with him was easy enough to do from the safety of the cupola room; when he was a mere arm's length away, she was wary enough to have second thoughts. She would just make sure he was okay before she went inside and tried to work through all the consequences of her decision in her mind. Yes, that was a good plan. She took two more steps and sank to her knees a few feet away from him.

"Water's great. Just the right temperature." His voice was low and seductive. She would love a swim. She would love to wash her hair in the soft, cool lake water. She would love to do those things with Zach by her side.

"I can't go swimming in my clothes."

"Why not?" he asked.

It was impossible.

Outrageous.

Not something a respected physician did with her PA.

At least, not in the middle of a Saturday afternoon. But under the stars on a night when there was no moon, she would love to swim with him.

She was determined not to reveal how much he'd shaken her. "I don't think so," she said forcefully, as though each word was a talisman of some sort to protect her from giving in to what she wanted most to do. Join him.

"Coward," he said very softly.

"I guess I am." She should feel in control of the conversation. After all, he was gazing up at her from what should have been a subservient position. But she didn't feel in control. He was much too close yet too far away.

He surged up out of the water and pivoted on his hands. Now he was close enough to reach out and touch, water dripping from every inch of his muscular, sun-bronzed body. The movement caught her off guard. Their eyes locked. Was he going to kiss her again? Here, where someone watching from a fishing boat or walking along the narrow sand beach might spy them? She hoped he wouldn't. She hoped he would. His eyes were dark, his expression unreadable. "Want to tell me what's got you so spooked?"

Not too long ago she would have put him off with a noncommittal response. Instead she said, "The committee met today. They made me an offer."

"Is it one you can't refuse?"

She managed a smile. "I haven't gotten the details. They want to meet with me on Monday."

"Don't let them run roughshod over you."

"That's exactly what my father counseled."

"He's a smart man. They'll bring up your family's record of service to the town and plead poverty and make you feel guilty for asking for a living wage."

She laughed, relaxing a little. Last night hadn't been a fluke. They had gotten past some invisible barrier, at least the biggest of the ones between them—trust. She trusted his judgment. She trusted his integrity. She could speak her mind and not fear betrayal. "I'll do my best. I always have the cruise-ship offer to hold over their heads."

"Exactly. Now, how about that swim?"

His change of subject unsettled her. She had hoped they could go on talking like this, but evidently he wasn't going to make the final call for her any more than her father had.

She shook her head. "Cold water does not get rid of cedar pitch." She spread her arms to show him the streaks of cedar resin on her skin.

"What were you doing? I thought you were picking vegetables."

She explained what had happened with the tree and the change of plan.

"You've got a couple of bad scratches there," he said. "Better let me put something on them after you shower."

She shivered at the mental image of his long, strong fingers stroking her skin. "Thanks," she said, "but I'm capable of doing that my-self."

"I didn't mean it that way, Callie," he said, his eyebrows drawing together in a slight frown.

"I know you didn't," she said, sighing. "I'm tired. It's been a long day."

"And last night was a long night."

"You are okay, aren't you?" She searched his face. He didn't seem as haunted and drawn as he had last night, but he did look like a man who was slightly exasperated with her. Oddly enough it didn't upset her as much as it would have twenty-four hours earlier. She enjoyed being able to knock him off balance once in a while, too.

"I'm right as rain, and to prove it I'll fix you supper."

"I'm too tired to eat. I'm having my mom's chips and salsa, then calling it a night." Suddenly she was exhausted. The adrenaline rush of learning her professional future was assured—if she wanted it—and being this close to Zach, dripping wet and handsome as the dickens, was just too much.

"Chips and salsa? No way, unless you're talking appetizers. I'm fixing bluegill fillets and grilled veggies with corn-bread muffins. And ice cream for dessert. I might even have a halfway decent bottle of wine we can open."

"I—"

"Come on, Callie. You have to eat. I have to eat. We might as well do it together."

Her willpower deserted her, as it did all too often lately where Zach Gibson was concerned. Oddly enough, so did her exhaustion. "It all sounds delicious. I accept your kind invitation," she said, inclining her head formally. But a strand of hair worked its way out of the elastic and flopped over her eye, spoiling the effect. He reached out and brushed it away, his touch as light as a dragonfly's wing. She shivered again but with pleasure. He snatched his hand back but didn't apologize.

"Dinner will be ready in half an hour. Or do you need longer?"

"That will be fine."

"ANOTHER GLASS of wine?" She had been staring for a couple of minutes at the small amount of pale gold liquid left in her glass as she twirled the stem between her fingers, obviously lost in thought. Zach hadn't interrupted her reverie, happy to be able to study her intriguing face without her noticing. But at his words, she looked up at him and blinked, and he had to brace himself against the full effect of those amazing, changeable hazel eyes. Greens and browns and flecks of gold, all swirling together like the leaves and needles of the popples, birches and tamaracks in autumn. He wondered how he could have ever considered her looks merely ordinary. *Striking* was the word he'd use to describe her now.

"No, thanks. One is enough tonight. I'm so tired I can barely keep my eyes open."

"I'll take that excuse as a result of your strenuous day and not because you're eager to call it a night and get me back to my own side of the cabin." They were eating at her little bistro table in front of the window, watching as the clouds grew low and dark and a light rain advanced in gray sheets across the ruffled surface of the lake. The rain had begun to fall, a whisper-light mist, just as he'd taken the foil-wrapped packets of grilled fresh vegetables and bluegill fillets off the heat.

He lifted the bottle. "Just a drop?" he coaxed.

"Just a drop," she agreed. He poured an ounce or two into the stemware he'd conned out of Mac when he'd dropped off a plastic bag of frozen golden morel mushrooms he'd found in an overgrown cow pasture one May afternoon, and sat the bottle down. "Everything was delicious, thank you. I'm glad my being late didn't spoil anything."

"That's the great thing about propane grills," he said, stretching his legs out in front of him. She had her legs crossed at the knee, swinging one foot. She was wearing strappy little sandals and the pale pink polish on her toes matched her fingernails. Her lips were a darker shade of pink and very, very kissable. "You never have to worry about the coals not being ready."

He had outdone himself in the culinary department tonight, he decided with a little mental chest-thumping. The fillets were flaky and moist, the veggies just right and the corn bread some of the best he'd ever made. He'd even scored a couple of points with the choice of ice cream—black walnut. He owed Mac for that tidbit of information.

"I was a couple minutes late because I got another phone call."

"Want to tell me about it?" He tightened his hand on the wine bottle instead of letting go. Who had she been talking to? A patient? A friend? Another man?

"It was my dad calling again. He's decided to attend the meeting Monday to lend moral support. He knows Ezra Colliflower has been a boogeyman in my life since I was a little girl."

"I'd be surprised if J.R. could stay away."

She smiled and his heart slammed against his chest wall. "That's not all he had to say. It seems my grandparents are on their way here from Arizona. They left this morning. They should be arriving sometime Tuesday afternoon."

"Didn't Eno say they weren't planning to visit for another couple of months?" He'd never met J.R. Senior and his wife, Evelyn.

Her hair, still damp and smelling of lavender shampoo, was pulled up in an untidy knot on top of her head, a more casual style than she allowed herself during office hours. As it dried, soft, curling tendrils had begun escaping all around the nape of her neck.

She looked relaxed and content, sexy and sweet all at once. A far cry from the up-tight, humorless woman who had arrived in the midst of the office flood a month before. "My grandmother says she never expected to be lucky enough to have another grandbaby, and she wants to be here when he or she is born. They're flying into Marquette and they'll stay with my grandmother's cousins. They have a place on the far side of the lake."

"You're glad they're coming, aren't you?"

"Yes," she said, her smile luminous.

"And by the time they get here, you'll be able to tell them you're home for good." He didn't quite make it a question but she responded as if he had.

"Yes," she said simply, her eyes fixed on his face. "I'll be here."

"Despite the rough couple of weeks we've had between us?"

"Despite that."

He fought to hide a rush of adrenaline. She was staying. "I'm glad to hear that." He didn't say any more, afraid he might yet scare her off. She went on talking about her grandparents.

"Although, if I'd taken the cruise-ship

offer, I could see my grandmother dragging my grandfather on a sailing trip. She generally gets what she wants that way."

"And you also won't have to keep worrying about how to explain to them about Eno's condition without breaking doctor-patient confidentiality."

Her smile faded and her eyes grew troubled. "Is it wrong of me to be relieved that the news will come from Eno and Miriam themselves? I've been so torn. It's been difficult not to confide in my dad these past days."

"No one wants to be the bearer of bad news, Callie. Having an M.D. behind your name doesn't inoculate you from that."

"It's going to be hard on all of them. They've been friends for so very many years."

"You'll be there for them. And your dad will, too."

She ran her finger around the rim of the wineglass. "Yes, I'll be here for them," she said, and for him, for them both, it was a reaffirmation of her decision to stay in White Pine Lake. There should be bells and whistles, confetti, balloons dropping. Instead they sat quietly and went on talking. "It seems strange, though, being the grown-up, the one who knows the secrets. I'm not sure I like it."

"It's never easy, that part of our work."

"No, it's not. But there's the baby coming. That will take their minds off Eno's illness."

"How do Ginger and your grandmother get along?"

"Well enough. My grandparents haven't been home much these past couple of years." Callie tapped her foot against the table leg, the only sign of agitation she let come to the surface. "With my mom, it's another story. She and Grandma are oil and water. But I don't want to go there tonight."

He longed to reach out and take her in his arms, gather her close and take her cares away. Callie was a healer, a fixer. Her family meant more to her than anything. He wished he could promise her that she'd be able to make everything all right, to make them into one big, happy blended family, as she wished. But he knew she probably wouldn't succeed. There were too many competing personalities, too many old hurts and new allegiances.

Finally she said, "Ginger can hold her own

with Grandma. It's funny, if you'd asked me that question a few weeks ago, I would have answered exactly the opposite, but not anymore. My stepmother's got a spine. I've been underestimating her, I'm sorry to say."

"Are you and Ginger becoming friends?"

"We're not quite there yet, but I hope we soon will be."

Her eyes slid toward the window. "It's almost dark. What time is it? I must have left my watch on the sink."

"It's going on ten."

"Goodness, it's getting late. I'm keeping you up."

He laughed; he couldn't help it. "Callie, it's Saturday night. I won't go to bed for a couple of hours."

She laughed, too. "Are you heading over to the White Pine for karaoke?"

"Not tonight."

"Thanks again for a wonderful dinner." She stood up and he recognized his cue to leave. It was still raining softly, and the twilight had deepened to true night. Lightning flickered on the horizon and thunder rumbled far out over the dunes. She scanned his face, gauging his mood. He met her scrutiny head-on as he rose from his chair.

"I'm fine, Callie," he said. "You don't have to worry about me, too."

She smiled a little tremulously. "Did I have my doctor face on?"

"Yes," he said.

"If it storms, it won't bother you tonight?"

"They almost never do anymore. Last night was the exception, not the rule. But you could come with me anyway."

She studied his face a moment longer. "You're teasing me again. Please don't. We should say good-night." If her eyes had been as sure as her voice, he would have followed her bidding, but they weren't.

He couldn't restrain himself any longer. He reached out and took her into his arms.

"I'm falling in love with you, Callie."

Her eyes widened with alarm. "No, don't say that."

"Why? I know what I want, and I want you. For now. For always."

She put her fingers to his lips. "Please, don't. We have so many things to work out between us. There's so much we have to learn yet about each other."

"I know what I need to."

"Zach, how can you be so sure? All we do is argue. How can we work on a personal relationship when we're still finding our way with our professional one?"

His lips twitched. "Making up will be one of the perks of our relationship. Tell me you love me, Callie. Because you do."

"I can't," she said, her eyes shimmering with tears she was too proud to let fall. "I'm not ready. I've already made one momentous decision today. That's my limit." She tried to smile. "It's not in my nature to be wild and spontaneous. I don't go cliff diving or bungee jumping or believe in love at first sight."

"I believe in love at first sight. And so does your dad. You're his daughter."

"I'm also uptight and straitlaced. You've pointed that out to me more than once."

He shook his head, making no attempt to hide his smile. "Deep down you're the opposite of straitlaced. You're filled with all kinds of spontaneity and even a tiny bit of mischief."

"I'm never spontaneous. I've been taught to keep my distance, to look at every possibility, to never take risks. You trust your

instincts. You act on them. I can't do that."
She took a deep breath. "Not yet."

"Aren't some things worth making a leap
of faith? Aren't we worth it?"

He lowered his head and kissed her long
and hungrily. At last she did what he wanted
her to do and melted against him. But her
hands were still caught between them, denying him that last sweet intimacy.

"Promise me you'll think about it, Callie.
About us."

"I promise." She reached up on tiptoe and
laid her mouth against his.

CHAPTER FOURTEEN

THE KISS WENT ON and on. Callie's heart beat in rhythm with Zach's. Stars began to sparkle behind her eyelids because she had forgotten to take a breath, and her ears were ringing like choir bells. Still, she leaned into the kiss and yielded to the strength and comfort of his body. All the barriers she'd erected to keep distance between the two of them, between Zach and her heart, all the arguments she'd just put forth suddenly seemed as insubstantial as mist on the lake. They could make this work. She could have it all. Zach and her career and a family, all here, in White Pine Lake, as she'd always dreamed. Zach lifted his head and she could breathe again. The stars winked out as she opened her eyes, but the ringing in her ears didn't stop. "Uh-oh," he said. "It's your phone."

"What?" She blinked and took a step away from his intoxicating nearness. The temperature hadn't changed but she felt chilled the moment she left his arms. She shivered. "I should answer it." She gathered her scattered wits. "I have to answer it."

Zach nodded, picked up her cell from the table and handed it to her. "Dr. Layman." She answered automatically before she registered the caller ID number.

"Callie." It was her mother's voice, breathless and filled with pain. "Oh, honey, I'm sorry to be calling so late."

"It's not late, Mom," she said calmly, though her heart had begun to beat hard again, and not because of the pleasure of being held in Zach's arms. "What's wrong?"

"I've done the stupidest thing. I've broken my wrist. At least, I think it's broken. It hurts so much."

"What happened?" Callie was already looking around for her purse and the keys to her Jeep. "Did you fall?" Had she been out in the barn this late at night? Or had she tripped in the house? Falling with the hands outstretched was the most common way to break a wrist.

"No. No, I didn't fall. When it started to rain, I went to shut the window in the dining room and the spring came out of the pin and the window dropped on my hand." The farmhouse had old-fashioned, heavy wooden double-hung windows that stayed open with metal pins that were spring-loaded and fit into small holes drilled into the frame. If the pins released unexpectedly and were not eased down, the window dropped with a great deal of force. "My wrist is swollen. I can't move my fingers and it hurts so badly." She sounded as if she might cry.

"Have you put ice on it?"

"I did but now I'm out of ice, too."

"I'll be there in ten minutes."

"I heard. FOOSH?" Zach asked, using the acronym for *fall on outstretched hand*. He was already moving to the door.

"No, the window dropped down on her wrist."

"Do you want me to come with you?"

"Yes," she said honestly, "but it might be faster in the long run if you meet us at the clinic instead."

He nodded. "All right. It's your call, Doctor. I'll have the X-ray machine ready when you get to the clinic."

She wondered if he felt as off balance and shaken by their just-concluded conversation and the kiss that had ended it as she did. If he did, he didn't show it. She hoped she didn't, either.

"Zach, about what just happened..."

"You're not off the hook, Callie. Sooner or later you're going to admit you love me, too, but I'm a patient guy. I can wait. Now we've got work to do." He waved her toward the door and reached into his pocket for his keys.

Callie led the way into the misty, rain-washed night. She waited impatiently for a break in the stream of cars and golf carts clogging Lake Street and wheeled the Jeep out onto the pavement. Zach did the same, but turned in the opposite direction toward the clinic. Once she was past the business district, traffic thinned out and the drive to the farm was uneventful, although the night was pitch-black and she was careful to watch for the telltale shine of deer eyes along the sides of the road. The security light on her mother's farm stand guided Callie into the lane that served as a driveway. She parked as close to the house as she could manage and hurried up the gravel walkway to the back porch. The ground was covered with cedar chips from the morning's tree cutting, and the smell of pine was heavy in the air. She let herself into the house and called her mother's name.

"Here I am." Karen was sitting at the kitchen table, pale and heavy-eyed from weeping. She held her arm high against her chest, her hand and wrist wrapped in an old, soft linen kitchen towel. "What a stupid, stupid thing to do. I tried to wait until morning to call you but it hurts so badly and I can't move my fingers anymore." She began to cry. "How will I ever take care of my animals with only one hand?"

"Shh, Mama," Callie soothed. "It will be all right. Let me take a look at it."

Compartment syndrome. The diagnosis leaped into Callie's mind. It was caused by crushing injuries to the long bones of the body, which increased pressure within the damaged muscles and cut off blood flow. Untreated it could result in the loss of the limb. One of the presenting symptoms was pain out of proportion to the injury. Maybe she should just bypass taking Karen to the clinic and head straight for the hospital? She wished she'd let Zach come along with her after all. He would decide if she was overreacting. She shook off the jolt of near panic. She could make this diagnosis as well as he could. "Mom, let me check your wrist," she repeated more firmly.

Karen moaned, cradling her arm. "It hurts, Callie."

"I know. I know." She held out her hands; reluctantly Karen lowered her injured arm to the table so that Callie could unwrap the towel and remove the plastic bag that had once held ice cubes but now was filled with tepid water. Karen's hand and wrist were badly swollen, a long bruise across her forearm already turning blue and purple, but the skin was not broken and the bones appeared to be in alignment. Gently, Callie lifted her mother's middle finger. Karen gasped and cried out loud.

"Don't. It hurts."

"If you're in too much pain, we can go straight to the emergency room." Callie kept her eyes downcast, not letting her mother see how shaken she was.

"No, I don't want that. It will take half the night to get there and it's already late." She started to cry again.

"Okay," Callie said calmly. "Let's just go

to the clinic and get an X-ray. Zach's already there waiting for us."

"Yes," Karen said, her expression lightening just a little. "Yes, that's better. I hate hospitals." She attempted a smile and Callie smiled back. Her mother had always suffered from what her grandmother Layman called "white-coat syndrome." Hospitals made her very nervous. It wasn't rational, Callie knew, but it was a common enough phobia.

"Zach's your practitioner, so we'll let him decide if you should go to the hospital, okay? Have you taken anything for the pain?"

"I made some willow-bark tea," Karen said. "It didn't help very much." Willow-bark tea contained a compound also found in aspirin and had been used as an anti-inflammatory and pain reliever for thousands of years. In Callie's medical opinion, it didn't work very well, but she wasn't about to have that argument with her mother right now.

"We'll get you something stronger when we get to town." Callie grabbed a sweater to throw over her mother's shoulders and gently got her into the Jeep. Fifteen minutes later, driving as carefully as she could to avoid potholes and rough pavement, she ushered Karen into the small room at the clinic that held the X-ray machine. Zach was waiting for them, looking incredibly handsome with his hunter-orange stethoscope around his neck, a stubble of dark blond beard shadowing his jaw and his hands in the pockets of his well-worn fatigues.

"You made good time," he said, catching Callie's eye for a heart-stopping second before transferring his full attention to her mother. "Have a seat on the stool," he said to Karen, who was still clutching her injured hand nervously to her chest, "and let me see what we've got here." He smiled reassuringly and dropped to one knee beside the stainless-steel table. He gently examined Karen's bruised and swollen hand, promising to be as gentle as possible. Callie slipped out of the little room to the medicine cabinet for pain medication and a muscle relaxer while Zach conducted his exam. She didn't remove the medication from the bottles but set them on a small table by the door with a plastic glass of water. Karen was Zach's patient; it would be up to him to administer the medication.

When Callie reentered the room, Zach glanced at the pill bottles and indicated his approval of her choice with a quick nod and a grin. It said more plainly than words that they were working as a team now. "Here's something to help with the pain."

Karen held out the palm of her good hand without an instant's hesitation, even though she was usually leery of taking medication from big pharmaceutical companies. "Thanks," she said and swallowed the pills with a few sips of water.

"We're going to step into the other room while I get the shots," Zach explained as Callie draped a lead-lined cape over her mother's shoulder and abdomen so that only her wrist and forearm would be exposed to the radiation. Then she followed Zach to the control panel behind a short dividing wall equipped with a large pane of glass so that they could see and communicate with their patient while not being exposed to the X-rays themselves.

When Zach was satisfied he had the right shots, Callie left the protected area and moved to stand beside her mother. Karen laid her head wearily against Callie's stomach as though she were now the child and Callie the parent. Callie stroked the back of her head where her hair was coiled into a heavy braid. She was wearing a caftanlike robe and leggings, and the hand-knitted sweater Callie had grabbed for her was soft against the palm of Callie's hand. "Mom, why don't you go lie down on the couch in the break room? You'll be more comfortable there."

"First let me put a brace on that wrist, Karen," Zach said, coming up beside them with a soft foam cast. "This will support your wrist and help relieve the pain."

"Thank you." Karen smiled up at him rather dreamily. The pain pill and muscle relaxer were beginning to take effect. "It's not throbbing quite so badly."

"Just what I wanted to hear." Zach moved her finger again very gently. She winced but didn't cry out in pain as she had before when Callie had done the test. A positive sign. Maybe she had been too pessimistic about the compartment syndrome. She hoped so. "Callie and I will take a look at your pictures and we'll decide where to go from there."

Callie led her mother down the short hall to the break room. The small room was adjacent to the rear entrance of the clinic, and it held a microwave, a coffeemaker and an old leather sofa that someone had donated at some point. Callie helped Karen lie down and found a couple of thin pillows—the disposable ones they used on the exam tables—and a much-washed cotton blanket from the linen cabinet in the hall storage closet. "How's that?" she asked, placing one pillow behind Karen's head and positioning the second on her abdomen to elevate her injured hand.

She laid her good arm over her eyes. "The room's spinning a bit. I'm feeling a little tipsy."

"It's just the meds. Relax and try to rest."

"Callie, how long will I have to wear a cast?"

"A few weeks, Mom."

"How will I take care of the goats? And The Girls?"

"We'll work something out. I'm sure the Zimmer boys will be able to give you a hand. And I'm here for you, too."

"You have enough on your plate without taking up sustainable-farm living. You never liked that life, anyway."

"That's true enough," Callie conceded with a grin. "But it doesn't mean I can't do it."

Karen gave a little sniff. "And my spinning and knitting? Oh, dear, what if it doesn't heal right and I can't do handwork anymore?"

Callie knelt beside the couch and patted her mother's shoulder. "Don't get ahead of yourself. If need be, Zach and I will consult with the orthopedists at the hospital. Your hand will be fine."

"Are you sure?"

"Positive."

"Very well, Dr. Layman," she said and sighed contentedly. "I like the sound of that. Dr. Layman. Have I told you that before? Have I told you how proud I am of you? My beautiful daughter, the doctor. Every mother's dream."

"Yes, you have told me, but *beautiful* is going a little overboard," Callie said, smiling at her slightly rambling compliment.

"It certainly is not," Karen insisted but her voice slurred a little on the last words. "You are lovely."

"That's the meds talking."

"That's your mother talking," Karen said firmly.

"I won't be a minute," Callie promised. She dimmed the lights as she left the room and hurried to the X-ray room. Zach had the pictures already clipped to the light board as well as on the flat-screen computer monitor in front of him. "How bad is it?" she asked, her eyes going to the larger image.

"Clean break," Zach said, indicating the thin, dark line across the ulna, the long bone of the forearm. "The bones are in alignment. The fracture should heal without any complications."

"Are you sure? I was afraid it might be compartment syndrome. She was in so much pain. She couldn't move her fingers."

"She's got a nasty bruise, but I don't think the damage is serious enough to produce compartment syndrome. It's usually a result of a far more traumatic injury in an acute form—car accidents, explosions, things of that nature." His tone suggested he had encountered such injuries in combat situations. She nodded, deferring to his greater experience. "She's never shown any indication of chronic compartment syndrome, has she? Swelling, numbness, transient paralysis."

Callie shook her head. "No, nothing like that."

"Then I think we're safe in ruling it out."

"Those windows are really heavy and Mom has a small frame for her weight." Callie voiced her last reservation.

"I've got a call in to the hospital. Someone will be on call in Orthopedics. The camera's up and running on the new system. We'll get a consult." All the while they'd been talking, Zach had been keying in his notes on Karen's injury and treatment. She watched his long, strong fingers at work and marveled at how gently he had held and manipulated her mother's injured hand. So many contrasts to this man. *Strength and gentleness. Dark and light.* Would she ever understand him well enough to anticipate his moods, read his emotions as some longtime partners, as married couples, sometimes seemed to be able to do? It was a tantalizing scenario.

The computer chimed an incoming call from the hospital's network. Zach closed out Karen's chart and keyed in the clinic's password. The screen went dark for a moment and then a tired but pleasant-faced man of middle age appeared on a split screen. The other side of the screen showed Karen's X-rays. "Zach, good to see you. What can I do for you?"

"Dr. Assad. I didn't expect you to be on call on a Saturday night." Zach's smile was wide and genuine. Ahmed al Assad was the head of the orthopedics department at the Petoskey hospital. Callie knew of him, but she'd never met the man in person.

"I got called in for an emergency this afternoon and haven't been able to get away again. We're swamped here tonight—a couple of ATV accidents and a senior who fell down her apartment steps and broke her hip. And it's not even midnight. Who is the lovely lady beside you?"

"Our new physician in charge. Dr. Callie Layman, may I present Dr. Ahmed al Assad."

Callie moved into range of the computer's small camera lens, just inches from Zach's face. She tried not to be aware of his warmth and the clean, masculine scent of him. He was so close, all she had to do was turn her head slightly and she could kiss his ear. "It's a pleasure to meet you, Doctor."

"The pleasure is mine, Dr. Layman. Rumor has it you are considering becoming a permanent member of our team." His accent was decidedly British, although Callie knew he was Canadian by birth.

"I'll be making my decision soon, Doctor." Dr. Assad was a member of the hospital board of directors. The Physician's Committee had to keep the governing body apprised of their plans and must have informed the board of their offer to her. She wondered how many other staff members had heard about the offer before she had. Several, at least, she supposed.

He pulled a pair of half-glasses from the pocket of his white coat and set them on his nose. "Want to give me the details on your patient, Zach?" He listened closely as Zach recited Karen's vital statistics and described her injury, nodding as he continued to study the images he was viewing. "Your diagnosis is spot-on, as usual," he said as Zach finished speaking. "Clean break, it appears to me. Could have been much worse if the window had caught her a few centimeters closer to the distal radius. There are as many treatment options for this kind of injury as there are physicians to treat them. I'm old-school, you know. Make sure the bones are in alignment, continue the meds as required, immobilize for four to six weeks and then some intensive physical therapy. Bring her in Monday. That will give us some time for the swelling to go down before we repeat the X-ray and cast it permanently. Unless you want to make the trip tonight? I am not going anywhere."

"I think it will be better for my mother to rest in her own bed tonight, Doctor," Callie said, ignoring the offhand manner of his pronouncements. It was a common enough injury, after all, and he was a highly trained surgeon; arrogance came with the territory.

"The patient is your mother?"

"Yes, Doctor."

"Callie's mother doesn't like hospitals," Zach said with a grin. He was as adept at dealing with high-strung surgeons as he was with nervous middle-aged women and small children.

Dr. Assad nodded. "Call my office first thing Monday morning, Dr. Layman, and we'll work her in after lunch," he promised, proffering a consult as a professional courtesy.

"Thank you."

"No thanks necessary, Doctor." Assad gave the screen a wolf's grin. "Anything else I can do for you, Zach?"

"That's all for tonight, Doc. Thanks for the second opinion."

"A pleasant night to you both."

"Good night." Callie smiled her farewell, but instead of ending the call, the surgeon leaned back in his chair and laced his hands behind his head.

"How much longer are you going to be in exile down there in White Pine Lake, Zach, especially now that they've got someone to take your place?" His tone was friendly but nonetheless carried an undercurrent of interest that wasn't lost on Callie.

"I've got a year and a half to go on my contract," Zach said, but he had suddenly gone very still and she could sense he didn't want to pursue the topic.

"Doesn't your contract include automatic opt-outs every six months? I'm positive Parsons told me something of the sort," Dr.

Assad probed, his grin disappearing completely. "Surely you aren't planning to be away from here for that long? Hasn't Parsons been in touch? He's going to be taking that position at the University of Michigan before the end of the year. Don't tell me you're going to pass up making the move with him?"

This time it was Callie who stiffened. Zach had told her nothing about the opt-out clauses. Nothing about an offer from Parsons, the hospital's hotshot neurosurgeon who was heading to Ann Arbor to set up a practice associated with the medical school's world-famous neurosurgical program. It would be a prestigious posting for Zach.

"Dr. Layman, help me out here," the orthopedist said genially. "Zach's on the fast track with Parsons. You've worked with him for what? Six weeks now?"

"A little less than that."

Assad waved his hand in dismissal of the technicality. "Surely you agree he's wasted setting broken wrists and conducting high-school physicals and scolding overweight seniors about their cholesterol numbers. If I had my way, I'd talk him into going to medical school. He's underutilized as a PA."

"Med school's not for me," Zach said, as if that simple statement settled the argument. But Callie was close enough to him to sense the sudden tension in the muscles of his neck and shoulders. Why hadn't he said anything about this offer? He'd never mentioned it, never hinted at it. Was that why he hadn't helped her make her own decision about staying on in White Pine Lake, because despite what he said about falling in love with her, he was going to leave her here and make a new life for himself three hundred miles away?

"We're lucky to have him in White Pine Lake," Callie said, realizing her dismay had worked its way into her vocal cords. "I would never stand in the way of advancing his medical career, though. If you'll excuse me, Doctor, I should check on my mother. It was nice meeting you, and thanks again for your assistance."

"Of course."

Callie straightened and started walking blindly to the doorway. Zach could leave the practice whenever he chose with barely enough notice for them to find a replacement, even a temporary one.

He'd kept it all from her even as he encouraged her to stake her claim on a life and a future in White Pine Lake. She'd let herself trust him almost to the point of admitting she was in love with him, too. And now this. It felt like betrayal. It was betrayal.

The sudden, sharp pain in her chest and the faint cracking sound that echoed through her mind was easily diagnosed. It was her heart shattering.

CHAPTER FIFTEEN

DR. ASSAD HAD BEEN RIGHT. It had been one heck of a night. How had he gotten himself into this predicament? Zach hadn't meant to keep secrets from Callie; he had just been waiting for the right opening, the right moment, to come clean about the job offer. He had never intended to take it or to leave White Pine Lake, but he owed Donnell Parsons a lot. The neurosurgeon had given him his chance at a normal life, stuck by him when the PTSD was at its worst. He wanted to talk to the man before he turned him down, offer his thanks and his regrets in person. But Callie wasn't aware of any of that. To her, the revelation came as a betrayal of their newly forged trust.

He stared out the rain-streaked window of his bedroom, then at his bedside clock. A battery-operated one he'd picked up in the dollar store when he got to White Pine Lake and found out the electricity wasn't all that reliable. It was a little after 1:00 a.m. It was going to be a long night.

He couldn't sleep, so he might as well get up and make himself a cup of coffee. His friends might have recommended a stiff drink, but he didn't drink on the nights he was on call as a first responder for the White Pine Lake EMS. He'd been taking weekend duty once or twice a month since he came to town. It kept his emergency skills up-to-date and eased a little of the pressure off the core group of EMTs and volunteer firemen who were responsible for their friends and neighbors.

Was Callie sleeping or was she lying awake, too? She had insisted on her mother coming home with her, since it had been raining hard when they left the clinic and she didn't want to make the drive out to the farm again that night. As they fitted Karen with a temporary air cast, the two women had argued back and forth about Karen staying with Callie—Callie gently and firmly, Karen objecting more for form's sake than anything else. Callie had won. Now Karen was sleeping at the duplex and he and Callie were back to square one with no chance of him explaining himself anytime soon.

"How the heck did it all go wrong so fast?" Man, now he was talking to himself. He rolled out of bed and pulled on sweats and a T-shirt and wandered out into the main room.

She hadn't ranted and railed at him. He had helped Karen into the Jeep and shut the door, and then Callie had just looked at him, raindrops glittering like diamonds in her hair. She'd folded an umbrella she had found in the lost-and-found basket—a kid's one, bright yellow with jungle animals all around the edge—and said, "You could have told me you were keeping secrets before you demanded I admit I'm in love with you."

"I kept it a secret from everyone because of how information flies around this town. And no, I'm not accusing you of not being able to keep a confidence, so don't even go there."

"I wouldn't, of course, but this just proves my point. I make my decision to stay. I find you might leave. We don't really know each other, our hopes and dreams. We are only beginning to trust. It's not enough, not yet."

He had shivered, and not just from the cold rain on his nape. It sounded so final the way she'd said it. She'd closed the silly little umbrella, handed it to him, got into the Jeep and drove away.

He rested his hands on the windowsill and stared out into the night. They had stood together, really together, in the same place just twenty-four hours earlier.

There was a storm somewhere out over Lake Michigan again, the same as last night. But tonight there was a difference; the lightning and thunder playing off in the distance caused him no anxiety whatsoever. His thoughts were all on how to redeem himself in Callie's eyes, not the brutality and horror of a faraway war.

The beeper he'd left on his bedside table went off. He waited, tensed, as the usual static and undulating tone that preceded an announcement from the emergency dispatcher played out. A few moments later her voice came through the speaker, calm and measured. "Thirty-eight-year-old female. Eight and a half months pregnant. Symptoms of possible stroke. Conscious and responding. Address—White Pine Lake Bar and Grill, 55 Lake Street, White Pine Lake. Please respond." Adrenaline shot into his system, banishing the last remnants of sleep.

Ginger Layman.

He snapped on the overhead light and found his shoes. Thirty seconds later he had his truck keys in his hand and was headed out the door. Callie's door opened and she stood silhouetted in the light. "Do you want to ride with me?" he asked. She didn't have an emergency scanner in her half of the cabin, but it didn't take a genius to figure out that J.R.'s second call would be to his daughter.

She shook her head. "No, go on, don't wait for me. I'll be right behind you. I just have to make sure Mom is okay." She was wearing the same clothes she'd had on earlier in the evening. It was obvious she hadn't had any better luck sleeping than he had.

Five minutes later he slid to a halt in front of the restaurant. Off in the distance he heard the siren of the mobile unit as it pulled out of the firehouse two streets over. The town's chief of police arrived, red and blue lights whirling. Two experienced EMTs, a married couple from a block away, slipped in behind his truck in a golf cart. Not bad response time for a group of volunteers in the middle of the night. He took the wet stone steps two at a time. J.R. met him at the front door. His expression was grim. "She's in the dining room," he said. "Hurry, Zach."

The ambulance unit pulled up, adding more red and blue lighting to the scene, overpowering the flashes in the sky. Lights came on in a couple of the cottages and motel rooms along the shoreline, but people stayed inside the buildings, watching from behind the curtains, avoiding the rain while satisfying their curiosity.

The bar at the White Pine closed at 1:00 a.m., so only the staff was still on hand inside. Rudy Koslowski emerged from the ambulance along with Owen Carson. Rudy was the best driver they had. He'd have them in Petoskey within forty-five minutes of closing the doors on their patient. For anyone else it would be an hour. Rudy handed off the big metal toolbox that held their supplies and equipment to Owen, who hurried up the steps. Rudy followed more slowly. Zach took the heavy box from Owen. Just as he walked through the door, Callie arrived and double-parked beside the police cruiser.

The dining room was filled with shadows and the lingering smells of good food. Only a single bank of lights above one group of tables near the kitchen door was lit. He was relieved to find Ginger seated at one of the tables and not stretched out on the floor. She was as pale as a ghost, her head resting on her outstretched arm, her right hand draped protectively across her distended belly. She was conscious and appeared alert. Zach knelt beside her and laid his hand on her arm. He put his differences with Callie out of his mind. He shut out all the extemporaneous conversations and movements around him, focusing solely on the woman in front of him. "Ginger, it's Zach Gibson. Can you talk to me?" He opened the big box and pulled on a pair of latex gloves as he studied her.

"Yes." She attempted to sit up straighter. "I have the most incredible headache," she gasped, resting her forehead on the palm of her hand. Zach pulled out a blood-pressure cuff and applied it to Ginger's arm. He wasn't aware that Callie had entered the dining room until she came over, pulled out a chair and sat down beside Ginger. She'd thrown a nondescript raincoat over the coral lace top, but she still smelled of lavender shampoo. From that point forward, a tiny portion of his consciousness remained aware of every breath she took and every move she made.

"Ginger, what happened? Dad said you got dizzy and fainted."

"I did get dizzy. I'm still dizzy, but I didn't faint," her stepmother insisted. "I bet it was my blood sugar. I didn't get a chance to eat anything because we were so busy this evening. Callie, will you go up to the kids? They're probably scared to death. I'm sure Becca is awake. How could she sleep with all the lights and the commotion right outside her window?"

"I will, Ginger. In just a few moments," Callie soothed.

Ginger's blood pressure was too high— dangerously high for a woman in her condition. Zach was relieved that she was coherent and so far had shown no signs of a stroke, but they needed to get her to the hospital as quickly as possible. He glanced up and caught Callie watching him, the worry in her eyes mirroring his own. From where she was sitting, she would have been able to get an approximation of Ginger's blood-pressure reading just by watching the way the needle on the dial reacted. "Can you move your arms and legs?" he asked, continuing his evaluation.

"Yes. It was just a dizzy spell."

"You fainted," J.R. said bluntly. "She scared the life out of me. I found her sitting here slumped over the table when I came out of the bar to lock the front door. When I spoke to her, she just mumbled. I couldn't understand a word she said. I called 9-1-1 immediately."

"I was just so dizzy it was hard to talk." Ginger defended herself, but her voice lacked the force to be convincing.

While J.R. was telling his story, Zach had checked Ginger's blood sugar. It was low, which could account for the dizziness and the confusion, but he wasn't willing to let it go at that. His gut was roiling, his instincts on high alert. Ginger had been exhibiting symptoms of preeclampsia for the past few weeks. With her blood pressure so high, she could go into convulsions at any moment. Callie feared that, too; he felt it. No matter what kind of turmoil their personal relationship was in at the moment, when it came to their patients, they were in sync. They were a team.

"Have you had any contractions?" Callie asked her stepmother.

Zach didn't have a fetal stethoscope, so he used the regular one to listen to the baby's vital signs. The heartbeat, while steady, was not as strong as it should be. He lifted Ginger's right hand and studied her fingers. The edema was worse than he had observed a few days ago.

"A few twinges now and then. I've been having them for a couple of days now. Everything's all right with the baby, isn't it, Zach?" she asked anxiously.

"You haven't said anything about having contractions," J.R. said. He had kept his distance while Zach performed his exam, but as Callie moved her chair to give him room, he dropped to the balls of his feet beside his wife.

"I didn't want to get everyone all excited and worried."

"Honey, I've been excited and worried

since the day you told me you were pregnant," J.R. said with uncharacteristic emotion.

"The fetal heartbeat is weak," Zach said carefully. "Has the baby been moving as much as usual today?"

Ginger lost even more color. Her face was ashen. She reached out and grasped J.R.'s hand with her own. "No. That's not a good sign, is it?"

"Let's err on the side of caution. I recommend, and I'm sure Callie agrees with me, that you go to the hospital."

"Do I have to? Can't we wait until morning?"

"No, Ginger. Zach and I are in complete agreement. It's not worth risking your health or the baby's waiting around here."

"We're going tonight. Now," J.R. said firmly.

"I can't just disappear. I want my children," Ginger said, stifling a sob. "Where are they?"

"I'll run up and check on them," Callie offered.

Ginger nodded. "Yes, please do." Her eyes widened with dismay. "It's so late. I'm sorry.

I didn't consider, we must have woken you from a sound sleep."

Callie laughed as she stood up. "Do I look that bad?" Her hand went automatically to her hair. Zach hid a grin. She was so successful at projecting that hard-boiled M.D. persona it always caught him by surprise when she did something as purely feminine as worrying about her hair. "I hadn't even gotten to bed yet, Ginger. Zach and I have been at the clinic. Mom broke her wrist. Zach had just finished setting it when Dad's call came in. It's like being back in medical school, pulling an all-night shift in the E.R." Except these people were her own. Zach realized her anxiety was as intense as anyone else's whose loved ones were endangered, but she didn't let it show.

"Karen did what?"

"She broke her wrist," Callie repeated patiently.

J.R. was reaching the end of his rope. "Is she all right? Is it a bad break?"

Callie smiled, attempting to put her father's mind at ease. Callie had been balancing between Karen and J.R. for years; she made it seem easy. But he suspected—no, he was certain—it took a toll. "She'll be fine. She's asleep at my place."

"Are you okay to leave her?" Ginger asked hesitantly.

"And what about the twins? Perhaps Mac can look after them?" J.R. said, searching for options.

"Don't be ridiculous. I'm their big sister," Callie responded with a catch in her voice. "They're staying with me. Mom will be fine at my place. The three of us will follow you to the hospital. Remember, Dad, I can't have any say in Ginger's treatment," she reminded him gently. "She's in the best of hands with Zach."

"We have all the confidence in the world in Zach. But I'd feel better having you there with us."

Callie smiled; the wonderful transforming smile she saved only for those closest to her. "I'll be there, Dad. After all, that's what family's for."

CHAPTER SIXTEEN

"YOU HAVE TO STAY here, J.R. Who's going to shut down the bar and lock up?" Ginger started to cry.

"Don't be ridiculous," J.R. said. "I'm going with you."

"We've got it covered, Mrs. Layman."

Callie swiveled her head in the direction of the speaker. She recognized one of the college kids who tended bar on the weekend. She hadn't noticed him standing just inside the dining room, she'd been so focused on Ginger—and Zach. "I'll lock up tonight, and Mac's already called in to tell you both she's got everything under control." Mac, like a number of other citizens of White Pine Lake, monitored the emergency police band on a scanner. "You're not supposed to worry about anything but yourself and the baby. Those are her exact words."

Good old Mac. Family wasn't always connected by blood. Sometimes they just happened into your life one day and stayed there until they were as much a part of you as if you swam out of the same gene pool.

"I want Becca and Brandon," Ginger whispered, tears threatening again as she realized the futility of any further argument. "I want to show them I'm all right."

"I'll go get them ready," Callie said. "The ambulance won't leave until you see them."

Zach took advantage of the opening Callie had just given him. He stood up, motioning to the other EMTs to bring in the gurney.

Ginger shook her head. "I'm not leaving on a stretcher."

"Consider it an adventure," J.R. said, helping her to rise from her chair. Zach took her other arm.

"Mom!" Brandon erupted out of the service door to the kitchen. His hair was standing on end. He was wearing Avenger pajamas and his face was streaked with tears. "Don't leave us here alone. What's wrong with you?"

Ginger sat down heavily on the gurney. She held out her arms. "Come here, baby. It's all right. I'm okay. I just had a dizzy spell, but Zach and Callie want me to go to the hospital to make sure the baby's okay. Where's your sister?"

"We've been listening behind the door. She ran upstairs. She's real upset. She says it's her fault you're sick! Because she's been mean to you about the baby." He flung himself into Ginger's arms. "Don't leave me."

"Callie?" Ginger's eyes were full of tears. "Please—"

Callie stepped forward, unhooking Brandon's arms from around his mother's neck and pulling him close to her side. He smelled of soap and fabric softener and little boy. "I'll get Becca and Brandon ready, Ginger. We won't be twenty minutes behind you, I promise."

"All right." Ginger let the EMTs swing her feet up onto the gurney. "Callie will take care of you."

"Shh, buddy, it's okay," Callie soothed him, drawing Brandon out of the room. "Come with me. Let's go find your sister."

"She woke me up. She said there were sirens and lights and they were headed this way. Then they stopped right out front! We couldn't find Mom or J.R. and I got scared. Becca's scared, too, but she won't say so."

He was talking a mile a minute, trying to look over his shoulder at his mother, but Callie kept him moving steadily forward. She stopped to grab a handful of paper napkins from a table dispenser and handed them to him. He blew his nose.

"Where is Becca now?"

"She's probably in her room. Or maybe she went up to the cupola?"

"It's pitch-black up there."

"We went to the hardware store one day on our bikes," Brandon said, forgetting his tears for a moment. "We bought flashlights—big ones— with the money we made busing tables."

Callie grinned down at him, trying to keep him from picking up on her own anxiety. "Dad forgot to move the key to a different spot, didn't he?" She suspected J.R. had left it deliberately to facilitate a few childish adventures now that the stairway and the floor were safe.

"Yeah," Brandon said sheepishly. "It's really neat up there."

"Did you sneak up to watch the storm last night?"

"No," Brandon admitted. "Becca wanted

to, since we were awake already, but then we figured, what if we get struck by lightning or something? Because of the copper roof and all. It would upset Mom."

"Yes, I imagine it would upset your mother." Callie nodded solemnly, swallowing a grin. "Smart reasoning."

"I wasn't afraid," he hurried to assure her, padding barefoot through the big, quiet kitchen, which was clean and scrubbed and waiting for Mac's arrival with the morning sun.

"Of course not. I believed you this morning, too."

"It seems like a long time ago. Did you get the tree all cut up?"

"Yes, we did. And then guess what? My mom had an accident and broke her wrist. She's at my place now resting because it was raining too hard to take her home." The stairway light was on and Brandon led the way to the family's quarters.

At her words, he stopped and swung around. "She did? That's too bad. Boy, what a night, huh?"

"Yeah." They walked through the darkened living room. "We'll check her room first," Callie decided. "If she's not there, you go get your flashlight and we'll go on up to the attic."

But Becca was there, to Callie's secret relief. She was just a small hunched figure in a frilly white nightgown silhouetted against the suddenly quiet darkness beyond the window. Ginger had styled her hair in a French braid that suited her aquiline features and gave her the look of one of the warrior maidens in her *Crystal World* novels. Callie went to sit beside her on the window seat. Becca scooted over a little so there was room for her brother on Callie's other side, but still kept a small distance between them.

"They're gone," she whispered, her arms wrapped around her knees, physically holding her emotions inside, as she did so often. "Mom and J.R. and Zach. They brought Mom out on a stretcher to the ambulance, and Zach got in with her, and J.R. got in the front with Mr. Koslowski and they drove away." Her voice broke on a sob. "Is Mom going to be all right?"

"Yes," Callie said. This was no time to dwell on the dangers of late-stage pregnancies in mature women. This was the time for her to be a comfort for these two frightened children, to be the big sister. The one who would make everything right. "And the baby will be okay, too. Zach will make sure of that." Even as she said the words aloud, she found herself believing them and, despite her heartache, believing in him.

"It's my fault if he's not," Becca sobbed. "I've been so mean to Mom. I didn't want her to get a new baby. I wanted it to be just the three of us, the same as it's always been."

Callie didn't attempt to take Becca into her arms, although she longed to cuddle the forlorn little figure. Her stepsister was such a bundle of contradictions, so prickly and easily offended, it would be better to let her make the first move. "I kinda felt the same way about you two," she confessed.

"Huh?" Becca looked up, her eyes wide, her cheeks tear streaked, searching Callie's face to ascertain if she was being truthful or just being a grown-up saying what she figured a kid wanted to hear. Callie met her skeptical gaze head-on.

"I thought you liked us," Brandon said, hurt.

Callie laughed, lightening the moment.

She gave him a quick hug and he snuggled closer to her side. "I do like you. I like you both all to pieces." She wasn't sure how they would react if she said she loved them, so she held back.

"We like you, too," Becca whispered.

"A whole lot," Brandon said. "Maybe we even love you."

Callie had to struggle to hold back the tears. "I love you, too."

"Really?"

"Really. The thing is, at first I didn't want to share my dad with your mom and you guys—and a new baby, too. It's been just me and my dad for a long, long time. Just like it's been you and your mom. I didn't want to share him."

"Your mom left you and went away for years and years. Mac told us," Becca said solemnly, scooting a bit closer to Callie's side.

"Yes, but now she's back and we're friends again." It was a simple explanation of a complex relationship, but she hoped it was the truth.

"Our dad died. He isn't going to come back," Brandon said. "I want to call someone Dad, and JR said I could. Is that okay with you?"

Callie pulled him close. "He's the best father in the world, if I do say so myself, and I'm absolutely certain he's happy you want to call him Dad."

"I want a grandma and grandpa." Becca dropped her head onto her knees. "We never get to see ours. They live far away and they never even call us on the phone or anything. Will your grandma and grandpa care if I call them that?"

"They won't mind a bit." Callie swallowed hard to keep a sob from escaping. Abandonment came in all kinds of forms, she realized, not just a mother who needed to take off and find herself.

"They *will* care if something happens to the baby. They'll hate me." She started sobbing in earnest. Callie reached out and wrapped her arm around Becca's thin, shaking shoulders.

"Stop blaming yourself," she said firmly but gently. "You can tell your mom you're sorry when you see her. Then you'll feel better. Why don't you both get dressed as quick as you can? I have a sneaking suspicion we're all going to get a little brother or sister before morning, and we don't want to miss our first chance to meet him…or her."

Callie was growing more and more anxious to be with Ginger and J.R.—and Zach. She might as well admit it. She was no longer a doctor first. She was a daughter and a sister and a woman who wanted to be near the man she had fallen in love with. She couldn't be objective anymore, at least not tonight. She could only worry and love, and pray for Ginger and the baby and for her own happy ever after.

"Everybody always says *he*. Only once in a while does Mom say *her*." Becca's solemn face transformed itself once more with the appearance of her lovely smile. "I've got a list of names. Mostly for girls. I want a sister."

"You have a sister," Brandon said, jumping up from the window seat ready to roll. "We have Callie."

Callie's heart melted, and she knew then and there these two children were no longer her stepsiblings; they were her brother and sister and always would be.

"Whichever it is, we don't get to choose,"

Callie reminded them both, struggling not to cry. "Now hurry! I want to check on my mom before we leave town."

"WELL, LOOK WHO we have here. Did they finally let you out of White Pine Lake for a few hours?"

Zach was standing at the nurses' station in the E.R., watching Ginger's monitor with a PA he'd worked with in the past. He looked up from the red and green undulating lines and pulsating numbers and greeted the heavyset woman in the long white lab coat. "Dr. Carmichael, how are you?"

She returned his greeting with a smile and an outstretched hand. "I'm fine. It's good to see you, too, Zach, though I wish it wasn't at two forty-five in the morning." She stifled a yawn behind one strong brown hand. Ophelia Carmichael was a Latina woman whose parents had come to northern Michigan many years earlier to work in the cherry orchards. They'd settled there and raised a family. She was married with grown children and must be somewhere in her late fifties. Zach had worked with her in the past and found her professional, intelligent and not a woman to suffer fools gladly. She examined Ginger's chart.

"Did she go toxic on us?" She toggled a screen on the electronic notepad she pulled out of her pocket, glancing through the notes Zach had made on the trip to the hospital, as well as the notes from the admitting physician and the nurses from Ginger's initial exam. While she was reading, the other PA excused himself to take a phone call, leaving Zach and the ob-gyn alone.

"She fainted or possibly had a mild seizure about two hours ago," Zach said. "Her blood pressure's still sky-high and the baby's showing signs of acute fetal distress. Here's the results of the ultrasound."

"Just shy of six pounds. That's a point in our favor. But these numbers worry me," she said, shaking her head. "Inducing's not an option. I don't want to put any more stress on the baby." Zach nodded his agreement. "Is there an O.R. open?"

"Got one on standby."

"Is she prepared for an emergency C-section?"

"She's been advised it's a possibility."

"And the husband? Is he with her?"

"Yes. And her stepdaughter will be here shortly also. She's Dr. Callie Layman, my new boss."

Dr. Carmichael's head came up. "I haven't met her yet, but her med-school records are impressive. How are you two getting along out there in the hinterlands?" She grinned to show she was kidding.

"We're doing great."

"What room do they have Mrs. Layman in?"

"Six," Zach said.

"Lead the way. Are you going to scrub in with me?"

It was an invitation he couldn't refuse, not only because Ginger was his patient but because he knew Callie would want him to be with her stepmother when she couldn't be.

"Thank you."

"Great. It will give you a taste of what you've been missing here."

"I'm happy where I am," he said.

"Sure you are." Her expression was a mixture of disbelief and pity. "Bring me up to speed on our patient." Zach was grateful for the change of subject.

"She's scared and she's worried for the

baby's safety. So is her husband, but he's not going to lose his cool, no matter what happens."

J.R.'s strength was one of the reasons he'd be the man Zach would pick to be his father, if Zach had been given such a choice. As it was, he'd be glad to settle with J.R. being his father-in-law...if he ever got the chance to make things right with Callie. "Mrs. Layman's also insisting on seeing her children before she goes into surgery."

The ob-gyn frowned. "We can't wait much longer for them to arrive."

"They're on their way with Callie—Dr. Layman. They should be here shortly." Dr. Carmichael lifted one eyebrow at the inadvertent use of Callie's given name but didn't remark on it further. "Has Mrs. Layman had her pre-op meds?"

"Yes. And the anesthesiologist has been in to check on her."

"Then I'll inform her we're ready to go as soon as the children get here." She headed for Ginger's cubicle, white coattails flying.

"Zach." Callie strode down the hall from the E.R. entrance, Becca and Brandon trailing behind. They all looked worried and wound up. Callie was still wearing the raincoat, but she'd added a royal-blue Michigan sweatshirt to ward off the chill of the wet night. The twins were wearing jeans and T-shirts and hoodies that were beaded with rain. So the weather hadn't let up. He'd almost forgotten about the storm. Funny, how outside considerations got away from you in the hospital. It wasn't like the clinic, where he could gaze out the window just about any time the mood struck him and see the sky and the lakeshore and the woods and meadowland stretching away into the distance. "I hoped I'd find you here," she said as she approached him.

He glanced at his watch. "It took you a bit longer than I expected."

She gave him a half smile. There were faint shadows under her eyes. It occurred to him that they were both going on forty-eight hours with very little sleep, operating now on willpower and adrenaline. "I brought my mother along with us. She was still in a lot of pain and I didn't want to leave her alone at the duplex. I figured we might as well take Dr. Assad up on his offer and have her wrist checked out. Mom's filling out the paperwork now. I'll catch up with her once the kids have seen Ginger. How is she doing?"

"She's being prepped for a C-section. Dr. Carmichael, the OB, doesn't want to take any chances."

Callie nodded. It was obvious she had a myriad of other questions but she wouldn't ask them in front of the twins. "Can the kids have a few minutes with her?"

"Certainly," said Dr. Carmichael as she came out from behind the curtain of Ginger's cubicle. Heads swiveled in her direction. "C'mon in, kids," she said, beckoning them forward. "Your mom and dad are waiting."

"You heard her say it. Our *dad*," Brandon whispered as he grinned up at Callie. Becca smiled, too. She reached out and took Callie's hand. Brandon grabbed the other one. Both youngsters were holding back a little, apprehensive, letting Callie lead the way. *The big sister.*

Zach was glad that at least one aspect of Callie's family building was going the way she wanted it to.

Zach didn't follow them down the hall, conscious once more of being the outsider, as he had so often been in his life. But then Callie beckoned him with her eyes. She waited as he hesitated, then smiled as he fell into step behind them. The ache in his chest lessened slightly. Maybe she would forgive him. Maybe there was still a chance for him to win her back.

Zach halted just inside the curtain and remained there, one shoulder propped against the wall. The small, harshly lit space was crowded with five people squeezed in among portable monitors and IV poles. But the twins barely seemed to notice. They had eyes for no one or nothing but their mother. Ginger held out her arms and both children moved to her side, Becca laying her head on her mother's shoulder, sobbing quietly, Brandon patting Ginger's cheek. Callie moved to J.R.'s side and he put his arm around her shoulder and she slipped her arm around his waist. "Thanks for coming so quickly, sweetie."

"I wouldn't be anywhere else," she said. She laid her cheek against his shoulder for a moment.

"I'm sorry, Mama," Becca choked out. "I'm sorry I've been so mean all summer. I promise I will be nice to you from now on. I'll be perfect and keep my room clean and help with anything you ask me to. I'll even change the baby's diapers," she finished in a rush.

Ginger laughed and wrapped her arms around her daughter's thin shoulders. "Oh, honey, don't cry. Thank you for wanting to do all that for me, but you don't have to make anything up to me. I understand. We should have talked about this sooner. I know it's always been just us, but I promise you I have enough love in my heart for you, your brother *and* a new baby. As a matter of fact, for all of you." Her eyes met J.R.'s, the last words spoken for him alone.

"And for Callie, too?" Brandon asked, tears running down his cheeks again. Callie found a box of tissues on the counter running along one wall of the cubicle. She held them out to Brandon and he blew his nose with a honk that would have made a decent goose call.

Ginger smiled. "For Callie, too, if she wants it."

"Yes," Callie said. "I do."

Zach watched from his place just beyond

the family circle as one more piece of Callie's family puzzle fell into place. The Laymans were fusing themselves into a blended family right before his eyes.

And he had never felt more alone in his life.

CHAPTER SEVENTEEN

"THANK YOU FOR bringing the twins to me," Ginger said to Callie. Then she lay back against the hard pillow of the bed and closed her eyes, as if she no longer had to fight the tranquilizing effect of her pre-op meds.

Callie took a quick assessment of the readings on the screens above and beside the high bed, both the one that monitored Ginger's vital signs and the one that monitored the baby's. Ginger's blood pressure had come down to within normal limits, and the baby's heartbeat was strong and steady. They had got to her in time. Under Dr. Carmichael's and Zach's expert care, Ginger's baby would be born safely.

Callie turned to share her relief with Zach only to find he was gone, the curtains swaying slightly where he had just been standing. Her disappointment was so acute it bordered on real pain.

The curtain was swept aside again and for

a split second she hoped he had returned, tall and reassuring, in control and in charge even in the set of worn blue-gray scrubs and a surgical cap he'd found somewhere. Only, it wasn't Zach but a tired, harried-looking surgical tech carrying a clipboard. She stopped dead in her tracks at the sight of all of them standing around Ginger's bed. J.R. was still wearing his White Pine polo shirt with a bar towel stuck in the back pocket of his khakis, just as it had been when he left the restaurant. He had a day-old beard and for the first time Callie thought he looked every one of his forty-nine and three-quarter years. The twins were tearstained and clinging to their mother's hand. For her part, Callie was sure she looked every bit like a woman who had been awake and on her feet for most of the past two days. The tech's distracted expression was replaced with a sympathetic smile. "I'm here to take Mrs. Layman upstairs," she said. "You can wait in the family waiting room on the third floor. There are couches and a couple of vending machines, and the nurses' station's just a few steps away."

"Thanks," Callie said automatically. "Take

care of her, Dad," she said, rising on tiptoe to give J.R. a quick peck on the cheek.

"Say a prayer," he whispered back, "for both of them, for all three of us."

"You'll both be fine." She gave Ginger's hand a quick squeeze. "Zach will make sure of that."

"Yes, he will." Ginger's smile was serene. They would be fine from now on because she and her stepmother would always have one thing in common—they both understood the importance of family. It meant as much to Ginger as it did to her. Her stepmother had proved that by entrusting her children to Callie's care, and in a smaller way by letting Karen be a part of their lives.

"Okay, kids, let's move out. We need to go check on my mom before we go upstairs."

"Your mother's with you?" J.R. asked.

Callie paused on her way out of the cubicle. "I forgot to tell you. She's here for a CT scan on her wrist. How's that for multitasking? Don't worry, Dad. I've got it under control."

"I'm sure you do." He gave her a thumbs-up. There would always be a residual bond between Karen and J.R. because of her, but Ginger and the baby were J.R.'s future. Karen was the past. Callie could accept that now. It wasn't a failure on her part; it was the way it should be.

"March, you two," she said with mock sternness. "We're in the way." Becca opened her mouth to object and Brandon started sniffling but they obeyed and followed Callie out to the main waiting room of the E.R. Karen was sitting in a wheelchair waiting for them.

"Have you had your CT scan already?"

"Yes, I'm all finished with it. They wheeled me right in. They said Dr. Assad would be down to talk to us about the results before too much longer."

"Then we should wait here until he comes."

The weariness Callie had been struggling to keep at bay pushed at the edges of her consciousness. She fought it using a visualization trick she'd learned in her early days of medical school. The technique worked well most of the time, but it had its limits. For a moment the fatigue got the best of her. How, she wondered, on top of everything else, would she get them all safely back home? She was so tired she could barely stay on her feet, let alone undertake an hour's drive back to White Pine Lake.

Becca went to Karen and patted her hand. "After you talk to the doctor, do you want to come upstairs and wait with us to get our new baby?"

A momentary spasm of pain flashed across her mother's face. Sometimes even Karen Freebeing must wonder if the price of her freedom and her vaunted self-sufficiency had been worth the cost. "Is that all right with you, Callie?"

Callie pretended not to notice Karen's moment of regret. She was certain her mother hadn't intended to show it. "We'll all be more comfortable upstairs."

She'd hoped to find Zach in the E.R., but she was disappointed. The empty feeling in the middle of Callie's stomach intensified. She needed to talk to him, just for a moment, to tell him that despite what had transpired between them earlier, she had every confidence in his skill and ability. That she was certain he would bring Ginger's baby, her brother or sister, into the world safely. But it seemed she wouldn't get the chance.

She peered down the long hallway. Painted

stripes of different colors decorated the walls, serving as guidelines to direct visitors to the various hospital departments. The blue surgery line stretched off into the distance toward a wall where it made a sharp left turn. While she watched, a man in a white coat came out of a room with Medical Imaging above the door. Dr. Assad appeared older and more tired than he had on the computer screen just a few hours earlier. The E.R. was quiet at the moment, but it was the quiet of the eye of a hurricane—or a lull in a thunderstorm.

"Dr. Layman. It is a pleasure to meet you in person so soon, but I'm sorry it's because you have another medical emergency in your family. I hope the outcome is favorable for both of them." Callie was surprised Assad knew about Ginger. Her surprise must have shown on her face. "Your mother told me about your stepmother's complicated pregnancy as she was having her CT scan," he explained.

Of course, how silly of her. She really was getting too tired to function well.

Before Callie could make a polite reply, the intercom system came to life. A woman spoke, her voice calm but with an underlying layer of suppressed alarm. "Code Yellow. All available personnel to E.R. Repeat. Code Yellow. All available personnel to E.R." Code Yellow referred to a mass casualty event. It was a situation every hospital trained their staff for and hoped never to experience.

"A bad accident," Assad revealed, answering Callie's unspoken question. "Three cars full of teenagers out far too late. The first one braked for a deer and caused a chain reaction."

"How terrible. Can I be of help?" The offer was automatic.

"I appreciate the offer but we have extra personnel on the way, and your place is with your family," he reminded her. "I've reviewed your mother's CT scan. The break was clean. It should heal well. If you want me to cast it on Monday, I will, but you and Zach can do it just as well and save her yet another trip to the city. If you have any further questions, do not hesitate to give me a call."

"Thank you, Doctor. We can manage from here."

"Certainly. Now I must go." He gave her hand one more quick shake and hurried away.

The E.R. was filling with nurses, medical techs and doctors in wrinkled white coats. She wondered if one of them was Donnell Parsons, the neurosurgeon whose offer to join him in a high-profile practice in Ann Arbor might take Zach away from White Pine Lake, away from her. She heard the wail of sirens in the distance. Part of her longed to stay and offer her services, but she was an outsider here, out of her element, and she might do more harm than good. She was not meant to be a hospitalist, a doctor who operated only in an institutional setting. Deep down she had always understood that about herself. She was meant for family practice, for taking care of the everyday aches and pains, the long-term health and well-being of all the people of her hometown, from the very young to the very old. She had made her choice. But what of Zach? Was the White Pine Lake clinic where he wanted to be, what he wanted to be doing? She wouldn't stand in his way, but if he wanted to leave, she wouldn't go with him. There was no future for the two of them as partners, or as lovers, if that was his choice. It was simply the way it had to be.

She was exactly where she'd vowed never to be, in danger of a broken heart and a broken partnership. But now she could count on her family to help her get through the misery of it all.

She moved behind Karen's wheelchair and started pushing her mother toward the elevators that would take them to the birthing unit on the third floor. "Are you all right, Callie?" Karen asked, twisting her neck to peer over her shoulder.

"Yes, fine," she said, even though she was anything but. "C'mon, kids. Follow me."

IT WAS ALMOST DAWN, Zach realized as he stepped out of the operating room, catching a glimpse of gray-blue sky through one of the long, narrow windows that faced out over the lake. The adrenaline rush of helping bring a new life into the world had so far kept his fatigue at bay, but he could feel it prowling at the edges of his consciousness. He ignored it. He was good at that; he'd had a lot of practice. He focused on his current objective: finding Callie to tell her everything had gone well.

As he'd left the room, J.R. had been holding their newborn son for Ginger's inspection, sharing those first moments of bonding for the three of them before Ginger was transferred to the recovery room. The baby was small, an ounce or two less than six pounds, but his score on the Apgar scale was high and his lungs were well developed—always a concern in a premature birth. He and Ginger would stay in the hospital for several days so that their conditions could be closely monitored, but as of now it appeared there would be no need to transfer him to Ann Arbor or even Traverse City for more specialized care.

J.R. had asked Zach to tell Callie and the kids the good news so he could stay with Ginger as long as possible. Zach appreciated the gesture. He wanted to be there to watch Callie's face when she learned she had a baby brother. He wanted to watch the twins' faces, too, he realized. Brandon would be triumphant. Becca more reserved, but thrilled all the same. He would go with them to the nursery, where they could admire their little brother briefly, cleaned and warm and wearing a tiny hand-sewn blue cap on his head of dark hair. Then the baby would be taken to Ginger in the recovery room for his first feeding. And later they would all be together in Ginger's room, and the picture taking and the oohing and aahing would begin in earnest.

Zach smiled to himself as he pulled off the paper cap and shoe coverings he'd worn in the sterile environment of the operating room. He was getting his second wind. He did love doing this, but not enough to give up what he had found in White Pine Lake. He had made his decision to stay in family medicine with less trepidation than Callie, but it was good to have it reinforced in his own mind.

Callie. The urgency he felt to be with her was stronger than ever. He had to make her understand why he'd kept the job offer from her. She'd just spent several hours interacting with all his old colleagues. He remembered her reaction, the dismay she'd tried so hard to hide when Assad had brought up the offer to go to Ann Arbor with Parsons. How many more chance mentions of the job offer had she been subjected to?

The music-box rendition of "Brahms's Lullaby" came across the loudspeakers. The hospital played the tune whenever a baby was born. Callie would hear it and know it was J.R. and Ginger's child that had arrived. She would soon be caught up in the excitement of greeting the new arrival. The nursery and birthing suites were on the third floor at the opposite end of the hospital. It was a hike, but he had made the trip a hundred times at least over the past couple of years. He headed for the stairway.

Suddenly he noticed the unusual amount of activity in the pre-op staging area for a Sunday morning.

Voices were hushed, the atmosphere was tense. Something was going on, something big. Announcements weren't broadcast into the operating rooms, so he hadn't heard anything, but whatever event had happened in the past hour, it was evident the whole surgical floor had gone on alert. He spotted Donnell Parsons coming off the elevator. Short, bull-necked and balding at thirty-seven, the man heading toward him looked more like a line-backer than a highly trained neurosurgeon.

But now Zach was convinced something was very wrong. Parsons never operated on Sunday unless it was an emergency. The neurosurgeon hadn't yet spotted him. All Zach had to do was turn and walk away.

He stayed where he was.

THE SOUND OF MUSIC-BOX CHIMES filled the waiting room. Callie turned away from the window. *"Brahms's Lullaby."* The baby was here. She had a brother or sister. She pressed her fingers to her lips.

Please, let them both be well and safe. She glanced at the overstuffed leather sofa a few feet away. The twins were asleep, one at either end, their heads pillowed on their arms. It could be quite a while before anyone came to escort them to Ginger and the new baby. She would let them sleep for a few minutes longer.

A man's figure came toward her from the direction of the elevators. She blinked the remnant of tears from her eyes, hoping for a moment it was Zach. But it wasn't. It was her father.

"Dad." She hurried forward. "How are they? Are they both okay? Is it a boy or a girl?"

He grinned, erasing some of the tension and fatigue from around his eyes and the corner of his mouth, taking ten years off his age. "They're both fine. It's a boy, Callie. I have a son."

"Oh, Daddy. A boy. Brandon will be thrilled!"

"He's twenty inches long, weighs five pounds and fourteen ounces, and he was born bellowing at the top of his lungs."

"That's wonderful. Strong lungs, just what we wanted."

"And all his fingers and toes...and—" His neck turned a dull shade of red.

"Important accessories?" Callie said, smiling.

"Yes." J.R. laughed, then suddenly became serious. "I would have been just as happy with a little girl. But a son..." He wrapped his arms around her and hugged her tight. "You will always be my beautiful baby girl," he whispered, his voice breaking slightly.

"I know, Dad." She hugged him. "When can we see him? I didn't wake the twins when they played the music in case there were complications." Her nerve endings were tingling as if her blood had suddenly turned to champagne, but beneath her delight was a tight knot of anxiety that wouldn't go away. Zach hadn't come with J.R. Where was he? What was keeping him from them, from her?

J.R. glanced at the couch where the twins were sleeping. "Where's your mother?" he asked, finally noticing Karen's absence.

"Rudy Koslowski offered her a ride home in the unit. She was exhausted. Rudy called me a few minutes ago. She's safe and sound back at my place. Zach and I will cast her wrist Monday morning."

"I'll help you make sure there's someone to do her farm chores for her."

"Thanks, Dad."

"There's not much your mother and I agree on anymore, but we do agree on how much we both love you. And she's been good for the twins. I see that, thanks to you. I'll do my best to be civil to her. I have a sneaking suspicion she's going to be around more often from now on."

Callie flushed. "Thanks, Dad. That's wonderful. Now, when can we meet the baby?"

"He's in the nursery. They're giving us a few minutes with him and then they'll take him to Ginger in the recovery room." Standard procedure and another sign that her little brother was strong and healthy and required no out-of-the-ordinary care.

"Let's wake the twins." They'd been talking barely above a whisper, but their voices had already done the job for her. Becca was sitting up, alert and a little apprehensive, and Brandon was all sleepy-eyed boy. But as soon as both of them saw J.R., they were wide-awake and the questions came tumbling out.

"Is the baby here? Is it a girl or a boy? Can we see it now? Can we see our mom?"

"Yes. Boy. Yes. And not quite yet. Your mom needs to rest a bit, but come with me and we'll meet your brother." J.R. held out his hands and the twins bounced off the couch.

"A boy!" Brandon did a fist pump in the air. "Did you hear, Callie? It's a boy. What are we going to name him, Dad?"

"I have no clue. We'll have to choose one soon, though."

"Callie, c'mon. Don't you want to see him, too?"

"More than anything." But something held her back a heartbeat as they started down the corridor toward the nursery window. The stairwell door opened. A tall man in blue-gray scrubs came toward her. Zach. Her heart contracted. "Dad, I'll be just a moment." J.R. halted at the sound of her voice, recognized Zach and nodded but kept on walking, pulled along by the twins' excitement.

Zach covered the distance between them in half a dozen strides and Callie didn't stand still, either. "I've only got a minute," he said. "And I'm keeping you from the baby."

"I can wait one more minute," she said and smiled. He looked tired but energized. In his element. The knot of anxiety tightened into real fear and rose into her throat, making it hard to breathe.

"I'm going back downstairs to assist Dr. Parsons with an emergency surgery, but I had to talk to you first."

"One of the teenage accident victims?"

"You heard the code called."

"And Dr. Assad updated me on what happened."

"There's one boy that is the most seriously injured. It's a skull fracture and spinal injury. We have to get him stabilized so the air ambulance can get him downstate."

"It's lucky you were here."

"It's the weekend. They're short-staffed and I owe Don Parsons a lot, Callie. He took a chance on me when the PTSD was so bad I didn't know if I'd ever be able to work again. I owe this hospital a lot, too. Hiring me, they took as big a chance as Parsons did."

"I do understand, Zach." But she was still afraid he would choose this opportunity over her and White Pine Lake.

"There were eleven kids in those three cars. I don't have a choice."

"I understand that, too," she said. "I wouldn't expect any less of you."

"I want to talk, Callie. To work it all out, but right now there just isn't time."

Her heart was beating fast and hard against her rib cage. She didn't want to play it safe anymore. She had to know where they stood. No more holding back, no more fear of saying or doing the wrong thing. "Do we have a future beyond your six-months option? I may not act on my instincts as quickly as you do, but when I make up my mind, I don't change it easily. I'm staying in White Pine Lake, Zach. For now, for always." It would break her heart to let him go, but she would.

"I'm not going anywhere, either. I tried to convince you of that tonight at the clinic but you couldn't quite trust me enough to believe me."

"But there's so much more here for you. Dr. Assad said you should consider medical school. He's right. Will a small-town family practice be enough for you five years from now? Ten? The cholesterol checks? The sports physicals? The premenopausal ladies with boundary issues?" She tried to smile, to keep her voice from breaking, but it wouldn't obey her.

"The more important question is, will it be enough for you?" He took both her hands in his warm, strong ones. The waiting room was deserted at the moment but they both knew they could be interrupted at any second.

"Yes."

"That's all I need to know. I doubt it will be all that staid and boring a practice for either of us. This has been one heck of a weekend and it's only Sunday morning. But I'll manage somehow. I'm still an EMT, remember. The middle-of-the-night calls will keep me sharp," he said with a smile.

She loved his smile. She loved him. She opened her mouth to say so but he beat her to it.

"I love you, Callie. I want you in my life every day in practice, in partnership, in love." He scrubbed his hand down his face. The stubble on his chin was a darker gold than his hair. "This isn't the way I wanted to do this. I wanted to have candlelight and roses and champagne on ice when I asked you to marry me."

"Marry you?" She fought to get her emotions under control.

"You will marry me?" It was half question, half demand. He was so close she could feel the heat of his body radiating out to her but still they didn't touch.

She opened her mouth to say yes but he put his fingers to her lips, still smiling, his blue eyes shining with love, reflecting the emotion in her own. "Hold that thought," he said, "till we find a moment alone."

EPILOGUE

"I DIDN'T THINK I would have to wait a week to do this," Zach said as he slipped the diamond engagement ring onto her finger. "Will you marry me, Callie Layman, for better or worse?"

"For better or worse and for always because I love you with all my heart," she said.

"That's what I wanted to hear." He lowered his head and kissed her, long and slow. "I've missed you."

"I've missed you, too," she admitted when the kiss ended. "How can two people work together every day and never have a minute alone for themselves?" She laid her head against his chest and let herself be lost in the pleasure of listening to the strong, steady beat of his heart.

It was Sunday again. The clinic had been a beehive of activity all week. Early season flu shots and the well-baby clinic they held the last Wednesday of each month had kept them all hopping. When she did have a free moment, Leola and Bonnie would pop into her office demanding the details of Karen's broken wrist, the baby's unexpected arrival and the terrible accident where Zach's skill in the operating room had helped save lives. By Thursday Callie could report that all the injured teens were out of danger, even the boy with the most serious injuries, although he was facing a long and difficult recovery.

On Monday, Callie had met with the Physician's Committee and signed a three-year contract to become the clinic's physician in charge. Ezra Colliflower had fussed and fumed at the amount of money the other members were willing to offer but Callie had held firm, insisting she wouldn't accept less than she was due, and eventually he gave in. On Friday, Zach had met with Dr. Parsons to formally decline his offer of a partnership. Then he'd extended his commitment to the White Pine Lake Family Health Center for the same three years. They were stuck with each other, J.R. had said with a grin when she'd told him.

The calendar had turned over to September without Callie even noticing. Tomorrow was Labor Day, the unofficial end of summer. There was already a bit of color in the leaves here and there along the roadway as she drove back and forth to the farm. Sunset came earlier and there was mist on the lake in the mornings. Fall was just around the corner and winter not too far away.

She knew Zack was becoming frustrated at their unavoidable separation—so was she. She had spent her nights at the White Pine with the twins so that J.R. didn't have to make the long drive from the Petoskey hospital, or with her mother, who still required help on the farm, although the Zimmer boys were caring for the goats and The Girls, for which Callie was grateful.

Ginger and the baby, Jack Richard Layman III, now known as Trey, had come home from the hospital on Thursday when his weight reached six pounds. His naming had been quite the family conclave the evening before their discharge. Callie and the twins had been present, as well as her grandparents. J.R. Senior and Evelyn had arrived on Tuesday as promised and made the trip to Petoskey before they even unpacked their bags. Between Evelyn's infatuation with the new baby and J.R. Senior's insistence on spending as much time as possible with Miriam and Eno, who seemed to have gained in strength and vigor since his oldest friend had returned to town, Callie figured they wouldn't be going back to Arizona anytime soon.

The twins had picked out their favorite names and were vocal in promoting their choices. Brandon had wanted his brother named for his favorite Green Bay Packers quarterback. Becca had lobbied for the name of the hero of her beloved *Crystal World* books. J.R. and his father had both been adamant they would veto Jack Richard the Third if he was going to be saddled with the nickname Little Jack, or if either of them got tagged with Old J.R.—or, worse, her grandfather had grumbled, "Really Old J.R." Ginger and Evelyn were just as adamant the tradition must be carried on. Callie, when asked to mediate, had thrown up her hands, laughing, and refused to be drawn into the fray, only suggesting that they could draw a name out of a hat. A suggestion that was met with little enthusiasm and pronounced a last resort.

It was Becca who had come up with a solution. They could call him Trey. "It means *three*," she said, coloring as six pairs of eyes had swiveled in her direction. "It's a game they play in the *Crystal World* books. That's where I learned the word. I looked it up."

"Why, Becca, honey, that's a great idea. I like it. I like it a lot," Ginger said, beaming as she looked down at the sleeping dark-haired baby in her arms. "Trey Layman. What do you think, J.R.?"

"Jack Richard Layman the Third, from this day forward to be known as Trey. All in favor say 'Aye!'"

The vote was unanimous. The baby, still sleeping peacefully, did not have a say in the matter.

Callie smiled, remembering the happy scene.

"You haven't fallen asleep on me, have you?" Zach asked, lifting her chin with the tip of one finger. "Most women who just got engaged wouldn't be falling asleep."

"Um, no. I was just thinking about everything that's happened this week. But since our relationship is going to be built on total honesty and complete trust, I'll admit I could use a nap."

"An early night? I could go for that myself," Zach said.

"On the other hand, it's so nice up here I kind of hate to leave just yet." The small cupola room had been transformed into a romantic little hideaway complete with a table and chairs, champagne on ice, candles and a vase of roses. "Did you know about all this?" she asked as Zach handed her a glass of wine. Her engagement ring caught a flicker of candlelight and flashed fire to rival the fireworks being shot off out over the lake. She seldom wore jewelry but the ring on her finger didn't feel alien at all; it felt just right. She would treasure Zach's ring, and the love and commitment it represented, for the rest of her life.

"I wish I could take credit for making this place so romantic, but it was Ginger and your grandmother who came up with the idea. They wouldn't let me in on the details. They only said that I was not to give you the ring before tonight." Zach took a swallow from his flute and made a face. "Too many bubbles."

"I think it's a lovely wine."

"Your dad's choice. I'm a beer man, re-member. Mac was the procurement offi-cer and your dad did the heavy lifting." Her mother, stepmother, grandmother and dear old Mac knew of their engagement, but they hadn't yet let anyone else in on the secret. Zach had insisted on asking her father for-mally for her hand. She should have thought it was an outdated, old-fashioned gesture, but she didn't. She had considered it roman-tic and respectful, and it seemed to have ce-mented some kind of bond between the two men, which pleased her very much.

"I'll have to think of something nice for him as a thank-you."

"Your grandmother also told me if I had never seen *To Catch a Thief* then I had bet-ter get a copy of it ASAP."

"*To Catch a Thief?* You mean the Grace Kelly, Cary Grant diamond-heist movie where she wears that incredible gold silk gown with the hoopskirt to a masquerade ball?"

"Leave it to a woman to remember the clothes. I think I was supposed to pick up on the scene on the balcony where they are kissing and the fireworks are going off in the background…" He put his hands on her shoulders and turned her to face out over the lake. "Like those." The Labor Day fireworks were just beginning. The first salvos sent showers of gold and silver sparks high into the black velvet night, an echoing boom following the blossom of fiery stars. If she looked down, she could see people watching from every vantage point along Lake Street, and the shoreline was dotted with campfires and lanterns in either direction. It had been a beautiful day and the weather had been perfect.

"Ooh," she said, laughing, "aah."

"Aah," he said, nuzzling her neck.

She turned in his arms, forgetting the fireworks. "I figured out the fireworks symbolism right away," he said, his lips brushing hers. "Want to fade out of frame together?"

It was tempting. But the family was all gathered on the porch, Ginger holding court with the new baby as friends and neighbors stopped by to offer their congratulations and ooh and aah over him, just like the fireworks. The consensus among people who remembered Callie when she was small was that he resembled her to a remarkable degree. That pleased her. "We should go back downstairs. They'll be wondering about us."

"I'm proposing," he said, all innocence. "It's taking longer than I expected."

He kissed the side of her neck and she began to have second thoughts about vetoing the fade to black he'd just suggested. She sighed. "I think I hear the patter of little feet coming up the steps."

Zach lifted his head, a slight frown between his eyebrows that she longed to kiss away. "That's not patter. Those are baby-elephant feet." Sure enough, half a minute later Becca and Brandon appeared at the top of the cupola stairs, flashlights in hand.

"What do the fireworks look like from up here?" Brandon demanded, squeezing by Callie to put his nose to the window. Becca followed more slowly, smiling at Callie and Zach, her eyes darting to Callie's finger to check if there was a ring. The smile widened when she saw there was.

"Wow," Brandon yelled. "That is awesome. But they're even better downstairs. And they're a lot louder, too!"

"Mr. and Mrs. Koslowski are here, and

Ron and Gerry, too," Becca informed them, "and Mac made chocolate cookies and Dad got ice cream." Callie raised her eyebrows slightly in surprise. It was the first time Becca had called J.R. Dad. Becca noticed her reaction. "I'm calling him Dad from now on because otherwise it will confuse Trey," she explained.

"Excellent reasoning," Callie said. She kept talking so that she didn't start to cry. "What kind of ice cream?"

"Black walnut for you. He said to tell you it's starting to melt, so you two had better come down if you want some."

"Of course I want some."

"Never get between a hungry woman and her favorite flavor of ice cream," Zach counseled Brandon.

"I'll remember that," he said. These days, if Zach said the moon was blue and made of cheese, Brandon would agree with him. "Let's all head downstairs to watch the grand finale from the porch."

"I'll blow out the candles," Becca offered.

"I'll shut the windows." Brandon and J.R. had used silicone spray to tame the uncooperative mechanisms. Now they opened and shut with relative ease.

"Dad and I are going fishing in the morning," Brandon prattled on. "Want to come with us?"

"Uh, I think I'm going to sleep in, buddy. I'll take a rain check," Zach said. He gave Callie's hand a quick squeeze.

"Okay. Hey! There are the guys. See 'em down there? Oh, cool, they have sparklers! Giant sparklers. They're as long as my arm! Come on, Becca. We're missing all the fun up here." They took off clamoring down the stairs, flashlights bobbing ahead of them in the darkness, blowing out candles and closing windows forgotten in their rush to join their sparkler-wielding friends.

"Definitely elephant feet," Zach said, taking Callie in his arms once more. "How many of them do you want, by the way?"

"Elephants?"

"Pattering little feet," he said, his eyes fixed on her face. She was suddenly breathless once more. They hadn't discussed children, but she knew he wanted a family and so did she. "I think eight sounds about right."

"Eight children!"

"Babies have two feet. Didn't they teach you that in medical school, Dr. Layman? Not eight babies, although I think I'd be up to the task if I needed to be. Four children. Two of each sex would be nice."

She considered it a moment. "You can guarantee two of each?" she asked, never doubting for a moment that he probably would produce two sons and two daughters if he put his mind to it.

"I'll do my best," he said, grinning wickedly.

She laughed. She couldn't help herself. "Why not? We'll just follow our instincts. Isn't that what you've been pestering me to do all along?" She smiled into his blue, blue eyes. It wouldn't be easy balancing a medical practice and raising a family, but she came from hardy stock, as her grandmother would remind her quickly enough. She had learned a lot about herself these past couple of months. She was up to the challenge. And she didn't have to do it alone. She had a partner. Zach would be a wonderful husband, a wonderful father. With his help and support, she would do fine. They would do fine. She was certain of it.

"Shall I bring the champagne?" he asked as he shut the windows. "Everything else will be okay until morning and daylight."

"Absolutely. It would be a sin to let it go to waste. We'll go down to the porch and show off my gorgeous ring and drink a toast to the future."

"A long and happy future," he said, saluting her with his glass.

"A long and happy future." She picked up one of the candles to light their way, then bent her head and blew out the rest. She straightened, offering Zach her hand. He laced his fingers with hers, his grip strong and sure.

"Let's go," he said. "The family's waiting."

* * * * *

REQUEST YOUR FREE BOOKS!
2 FREE WHOLESOME ROMANCE NOVELS
IN LARGER PRINT
PLUS 2
FREE
MYSTERY GIFTS

ReaderService.com

Manage your account online!
- Review your order history
- Manage your payments
- Update your address

---

*We've designed
the Harlequin® Reader Service
website just for you.*

Enjoy all the features!
- Reader excerpts from any series
- Respond to mailings and
  special monthly offers
- Discover new series available to you
- Browse the Bonus Bucks catalog
- Share your feedback

Visit us at:
ReaderService.com